THE SECRETS OF MOONSHINE

DENISE PARTON

One

The Arrival

The road all but disappeared, narrowing from a two-lane highway to nothing more than a roughly paved path winding around the massive granite walls of the formidable mountain range. If it tapered any further it would end, leaving me on a rocky ledge with no place to turn around. I fumbled with my phone fastened snugly in the car mount. The GPS stopped working a half hour ago leaving me with the final instruction, "proceed to the route." I thought I was on the route. Could I have inadvertently veered off course on that last sharp turn? It was possible, the night was black and with the drifting fog the headlights only gave a mere few feet of light. My mind had also strayed, drawing my attention elsewhere. A problem of late. No matter how hard I tried, I couldn't get Ryan out of my head. I wondered if he ever thought of me but doubted that he did now that he was with Gabriella. The idea of the two together caused my stomach to ache. As much as I hated to admit it, Bethany was right. I probably should talk about it instead of bottling up my feelings and trying to convince everyone I was okay when the truth was, I wasn't.

I shook my head, hoping to clear the painful images crowding into my mind and tried focusing on the road.

I looked in my rearview. Other than sporadic lightning in the distance, there was nothing but bitter blackness I glanced over at Bethany. She was resting on a pillow, propped against the window, and feigning sleep. Truth was, she was angry. This girl's trip was her brainchild, a way of getting me to open up and talk about my recent split with Ryan. Although it had been six weeks since he left me at the altar, I still wasn't ready to talk, even with my best friend. She'd been there for me, helped me cancel the wedding venue, the cake, the caterer and return my beautiful dress as well as gifts from the bridal shower she and Lil had thrown me. After all the traumatic duties were finished, I'd mentioned that I was thinking about taking a vacation to try and clear my head. She quickly took control and turned my little retreat into a girl's trip. I loved her deeply and knew she was only doing this because she cared but I needed her to understand that she couldn't fix what was troubling me. I needed solitude, to get away and process. I fancied laying on the beach and letting the roar of the sea and endless pina coladas drown out all the thoughts overrunning my head.

We had been on the road for several hours and every time she tried to talk about things, I continually changed the subject, refusing to discuss my personal pain. There were some things I wasn't ready to share with anyone right now, not even my closest friend. Beth should understand. Instead, she resorted to sulking, making it more about her than me, and in doing so, piled on guilt to an already painful situation. Her insatiable desire to always fix things was beginning to annoy me, so when I accused her of meddling, she withdrew and kept silent. It wasn't the best way to start a fun little trip. Let her pout. I usually wasn't easily agitated, but tonight something had me on edge. Maybe it was the lack of peaceful sleep over the past few weeks, or perhaps it was that every time I picked up a magazine, Ryan and Gabriella gloated at me from the front cover. Whatever the case, something crawled beneath my skin.

"Damn it's hot." I pushed the lever, rolling down the window hoping to get a cool night breeze. Instead, all I received for my effort was a wall of thick, stifling air. The night outside was still. Nothing stirred in the inky blackness, nothing I could see that is, but my spirit, sensed something. Lightning was brightening the sky more frequently now, making visible the misty mountains rising from the horizon, like iron gates forbidding entrance to anyone who dared continue through the rocky pass. An omen of sorts, agreeing the trip was a mistake and telling me to turn back. I shivered despite the heat and could not shake the premonition of impending doom. Why had I agreed to this?

I wiped my hand across the window, clearing away the fog, and peered out into the darkness. The road had tightened even more. With every curve I seemed to be driving further into a vacuum of nonexistence. No doubt about it, I was lost. A glowing orange light accompanied by a warning bell pierced the darkness, informing me that I was low on gas. "Shit." I mumbled under my breath. The needle on the thermostat was already creeping dangerously toward the red H. Could things get any worse? I glanced over my shoulder into the back seat. Lillian had given up on reading suffering from nausea once the road went curvy, and decided sleeping might relieve the queasiness she was feeling. I glanced back over at Bethany and decided to break the silence.

"Beth!"

She startled. "Damn it, Bronwyn, don't scare me like that. I was asleep." Beads of perspiration rolled down her forehead, wetting her hair and gluing it to her neck. "Why is it so hot?" She whimpered, pulling her hair into a quick ponytail before toying with the air conditioning controls. "I don't think this thing is working."

I pushed her hand away from adjusting the AC. "I turned it off. I think this steep mountain road may be a little too much for the engine." I pressed on the gas, pushing the car to the limit and then nodded my head toward the thermostat. "We're overheating and we're low on gas."

She wiped her side of the windshield with her sleeve and surveyed the emptiness lying before us. "It looks pretty desolate out there, not a great place to be stranded. Why didn't you stop for gas?"

"Because there isn't a place to stop. I would have turned around but where? I've never seen such a narrow road, especially one without a shoulder." I slowed my speed considerably, straining my eyes, looking for a place to change course but there were only solid rock walls or deep ravines, neither allowed a U-turn.

"So, where are we?" She asked.

"Hell if I know."

She grabbed my phone. "Why aren't you using maps?"

"I was. We went out of range. It stopped working some time ago."

Beth checked her phone as if she didn't believe me. "Are you going to keep climbing the mountain?" She voiced her disapproval while focusing on the deep ravines, running along both sides of the winding road.

"That's all I can do for now." I clutched the wheel, my eyes toggling from the road to the thermostat. "I saw a sign a way back that said: 'Moonshine 8 miles', so I figured there must be something ahead."

"I'd gladly take a swig of it right now," she let out a nervous laugh while I steered along the curvy descent, down the other side of the incline. "Come to think of it, it's probably just some advertisement for a still. We are in the Appalachians, you know?"

"Even so," I half agreed, "it might be a place to turn around.

"That, or a good place to fill up, and I'm not referring to the gas tank," she chuckled until a loud clunking interrupted her lighthearted demeanor. I watched in horror as steam billowed from underneath the hood. The headlights dimmed and then flickered, before leaving us in darkness. My heart seized as I lost sight of the road.

"For God's sake, stop the car!" She screamed, clutching the dashboard, fearing an unavoidable plunge into the deep canyon.

"I'm trying, damn it!" I stomped on the brakes, pumping them in desperation. I braced myself, digging my nails deep into the steering wheel, as if the force of my grip could somehow help me stop our runaway car. But even if I did regain control, with no light to guide me, disaster was inevitable.

A fiery bolt of lightning ripped across the sky, exploding directly in front of us, engulfing the car in burning sulfur. The flash revealed a man standing in the middle of the dark road. I released a string of profanity as I gripped the wheel, turning it with all the strength I could muster. I was nearly standing on the brakes, struggling to avoid plowing straight into him. The sky lit up again, giving me another glimpse. To my horror, he remained unmoved by my runaway car speeding toward him. His hands were lifted high as if he were commanding me to stop. His saffron eyes penetrated through the windshield, invading my body with a sudden rush of heat. Then, in an instant, the light was gone, and darkness cloaked the highway once again.

Thunder applauded the performance, shaking the ground and rocking the car in an ear-splitting crash. The deafening sound left a hollow ringing in my ears, preventing me from hearing the gravel and debris racing into the wheel well, spraying the sides of our vehicle, as it skidded toward the deep ravine. I became detached, as if I were having an out of body experience while time switched into slow motion. Maybe this was the life passing before your eyes, theory some people encounter right before death. Except in this instance, the images blowing past me were of a life I never lived. Events I'd never witnessed, places I'd never visited and the faces of people I'd never met. Each scene played out like an unfamiliar movie across the screen of my mind.

I clenched the wheel; my arms trembling to regain control. Bethany's mouth contorted in a hellish scream as the wheel turned in the opposite direction, nearly snapping my wrist. The car jerked and skidded sideways spinning out of control. Bracing myself as best I could, I prepared for the inevitable when the car came to an abrupt stop. I quickly shifted into "Park." Bethany sat still, offering a prayer of gratitude, or calming her nerves, I couldn't tell.

"Do you think I hit him? "I glanced out the window in search of the man, but the road was dark.

"Hit who?" She rummaged through the glove box and retrieved a flashlight.

"The man in the middle of the road," I grabbed the light from her hand and shined it through the windshield.

"I didn't see a man," She took the light and shined it into the back seat to check on Lillian, jarred awake by the chaos.

"You okay sleeping beauty?"

"What the hell happened?" Lillian shielded her eyes from the bright beam. "Did you fall asleep?"

"No, I didn't fall asleep at the wheel, nor have I ever." I was quick to defend myself, "I just saved your lousy ass. A little respect would be nice."

"So, what happened?" She, too, swiped away the condensation. I collapsed against the back of the seat, defeated. "Car's not running."

"Are you sure it won't start at all?" Lillian was leaning over the front seat now.

I attempted to re-start, to prove the point. "Dead as a doornail."

"Did you try calling for assistance?"

"Haven't had cell reception for the past fifty miles."

Lillian checked her phone too and sighed. We should have arrived at the mountain resort hours ago. Where are we?

Bethany rummaged through the glove box again, this time pulling out a paper map and scanned it with her flashlight. "I'm looking for a town called Moonshine. Bronwyn saw a sign not too far back. Lillian craned her neck over the front seat to help us look but we came up empty. "Seeing that we are in the Appalachians, the sign could be advertising the location of a moonshiner's still." She suggested. "If that's so then there has to be someone who manages the store."

"It's midnight Lil, so I doubt it's opened." I purposely cast a pall over any hopefulness. Bethany glanced up from the map long enough to cast a sour look my way. It wasn't like me to be such a downer, but in truth I was annoyed and had every right to be. I tried getting out of this trip several times. "It's damn near midnight, and we were stuck out in the middle of nowhere." I sighed, loud enough for her to sense my agitation. "There's nothing we can do." I lifted my hands in defeat.

Lillian chewed her bottom lip, "Where are we anyway?"

"Lost."

"Not entirely," Bethany refused defeat. "You said you saw a sign, and whether a store is open or not, there should be a town ahead or something. Stores just don't exist by themselves. We could do some hiking."

Lillian continued to look out her window, distress etched across her face as she twirled her platinum curls around her finger the way she does when she's nervous. "I've read a lot of eerie legends and folklore about the Appalachians. There are things that dwell high in these woods, Things you would never want to encounter." She squinted her eyes straining to see past the bitter darkness while continuing to twist her hair and looking as if she might cry. "I'm not kidding," her eyes widened as if we weren't taking her seriously. "I listen to some interesting Podcasts and there have been many sightings of creatures like the Wampus Beast, the Wolf Man and Devil Dogs. Devil Dogs move fast and make horrific noises before they attack. There's also the Smoke Wolf. He's pure evil, kills for fun, and they say his howl can drive you insane. I think we should just lock the doors and stay put until morning. You never know what is out there. I just don't think we should chance it."

I usually delight in making fun of Lillian's superstitions. Getting a perverse pleasure in antagonizing her. However, tonight her angst had credibility. "I would tend to believe it. Except maybe not all forces are evil. Something kept us from plunging over the side of the mountain to our death. I wasn't in control." I shivered and ran my hands up and down my arms. "Believe me when I say it wasn't me who stopped the car."

Lillian continued her morbid warning. "You see! And why would our engine just quit for no reason? Like I said, strange things happen in these hills. A person could get themselves killed or disappear forever venturing out alone."

I looked out my window. The surrounding emptiness mimicked the hollowness I felt inside. To be honest, the void had been there for quite a while. My engagement to Ryan hadn't satisfied it. I knew that. It was just something to fill the space that always haunted me. Therefore, the breakup didn't devastate me. Maybe that is why I refused to discuss my feelings with Beth. I didn't understand them myself. How do you explain something you feel intensely but don't have the words to express? It would be like trying to describe colors to a blind person. It's quite impossible. A droplet of sweat dripped off my forehead and rolled down my neck reminding me of my discomfort and the need to escape the heat inside the car. There was no way I was spending the night in a cramped hot box. "Well, we can't just sit here. It's late. The highway is pretty much abandoned. No one is going to come to our rescue. We'll have to walk."

"Did you bring a gun Beth?" Lillian needed reassurance before venturing out into the forbidding darkness. Bethany was a crack shot and a big advocate on the right to bear arms but the one time when she should be packing, she wasn't. She gave a quiet "no."

Lillian fell back against the seat and groaned. Her usually pale face lost even more color at the thought of setting out on this daunting highway. I did harbor some guilt about my poor attitude. Bethany didn't plan the excursion solely for her own benefit. She did love me dearly and sincerely wanted me to enjoy myself.

"Actually, this is my fault. I am the one who got us lost. You two can wait here and I will go and look."

"Like hell!" Beth vetoed the idea. We stay together. I think we all could use some fresh air." The curvy road made me nauseous too Lil.' Plus, I would love to stretch my legs." I shot her a grateful smile. "Beth's right, there should be something up ahead. Those podcasts sensationalize stories to get an audience. Take them with a grain of salt. We'll be fine." I grabbed the flashlight, opened the door, and lit the path outside.

The thick, humid air wrapped around me like a damp blanket as we stepped from the car and into the night. Thunderclouds hung ominously in the night sky, obscuring any light the moon had to offer. Another flash of lightning ripped through the darkness. A slight shiver invaded. The road was empty and the man I saw earlier was nowhere in sight. Only ghostly trees moved in the breeze, standing vigil, barring entrance to the dense forest, bordering both sides of the forgotten highway.

A slight glow of moonlight escaped its vaporous entrapment as the wind picked up, scattering the hovering clouds. Thunder rumbled in the distance, giving a subtle warning not to leave the protection of the car. Despite the hot, muggy air, a cold chill made its way up my back and, in the eeriness, I wondered if we had made a wise decision.

Two

We walked down the center of the narrow road without fear of being run down by oncoming traffic, seeing we were the only ones traipsing down the forgotten highway. I realized I hadn't passed a single car the entire time I'd been driving. This confirmed my suspicion that I had indeed veered, off course. I kept to the road, remembering that the last time the GPS gave instructions, we were less than an hour away from the resort. It was a straight shot, save for a quick left turn at arrival. That was nearly two hours ago.

"So, tell me Bronwyn," Bethany tried not to show her frustration, "how long before you realized you went the wrong way?"

"I didn't go the wrong way." I defended myself. "I was on the main road, and everything was normal. We'd reached seven thousand feet elevation when the curves became intense. I took a sharp one that seemed to almost go into a complete circle. Once it straightened back out, every-thing looked different. The road narrowed and the shoulder disappeared. Even the sky changed. I swear the moon vanished, and then the wind picked up. Lightning struck in the distance, we lost cell reception, and the GPS stopped. Lillian shivered, "Sounds like we were transported into another dimension or something." The words no longer left her lips when a sudden gust blew from behind, warning us, the impending storm was creeping closer.

"That's pretty far-fetched." I dismissed her theory, but the memory of the man in the road continued to haunt me, forcing me to give some credibility to her unlikely premonition.

"You must have missed the turn to the resort and not realized it." Beth argued. "I don't think we were transported to another dimension."

"It's very possible," Lillian came to her own defense, taking my description as a plausible reality. "There are strange forces at work here." She snatched the flashlight and shook the dwindling light to prove her point. The beam had gradually changed from bright white to a fading yellow glow during the course of our short walk. "I swear I replaced these batteries before we left last night." She switched it off and on a few more times, shaking it violently, before it lost all light completely.

"Now you broke it." Bethany grabbed it and examined it herself.

"It's not me," Lillian's voice quivered. "I swear these are brand new batteries. Like I said before, there's a force here beyond our control."

Up until now, Lillian's extreme superstition had always been a source of entertainment, but not now. Tonight it annoyed me simply because I found myself unwillingly giving credibility to her delusions. I was too smart to get sucked up in the weirdness of the moment, and too courageous to retreat in fear. The night was dark and stormy, so what? I bet the path wouldn't be so intimidating in the daylight. "Let's keep moving," I suggested, not wanting to waste any more time and get caught in a downpour.

We shuffled along in the darkness depending on the sporadic lightning for guidance. The strikes were more frequent now, lighting the sky like midday, giving us a better sense of our surroundings. We huddled together, moving deeper down the narrow road while the trees lining both sides bent beneath the wind, bowing like peasants at our arrival.

"I think we better get the hell outta here," I yelled, competing with the wind. "This storm isn't waiting much longer and I sure as hell don't want to be standing out in the open when the lightning strikes move closer."

The rolling thunder applauded my assessment, another flash exploded across the sky, spotlighting a dark hooded figure skulking between the trees. My heart skipped as dread bent my knees weakening me. "Did you see that?" I grabbed Bethany's hand, choking on the words.

"See what?" Lillian squeaked out.

"A person, someone, I don't know."

"That's great!" Beth was hopeful. "Maybe, we've reached Moonshine, or someone's house or something."

"Maybe," I allowed her to keep hope despite my impending feeling of doom. The person looked more like the grim reaper, not a welcoming committee. But then again, the flash was swift and perhaps I mistook a man's rain slicker for macabre cloak and dagger attire.

"Hello!" Beth competed with the wind. "Anybody out there?" No one replied to her distress signal which didn't surprise me. A stalker wouldn't likely answer a greeting and give themselves away.

"Where'd you say you saw them?" She wasn't giving up on my discovery.

They were darting in and out between the trees, like they were following us."

"Oh," she quieted and then began scratching the back of her head. "Probably just a deer."

"No, it was a person. They're wearing a black hooded, rain slicker...or some kind of robe..." My voice faded off into the wind. Despite the darkness, I watched the color drain from their faces.

Lillian stepped in close and grabbed my arm. "Are you scared?" Her throat constricted, choking on anything else she might ask. If I were to admit to being a little concerned, she might fall apart. All the years of listening to podcasts and investigating paranormal mysteries, were coming back to haunt her. "Not scared... a little apprehensive...maybe."

On the heel of my words, the wind responded with vigorous energy. Nature howled a warning for us to turn back. We were trespassing in a forbidden land. A cool burst of air swept past, encircling us, like a band of phantom soldiers. My long dark curls danced across my face, impairing my vision even more.

"Onida," a faint whisper floated along with the wind, falling slightly upon my ear. Shivering, I pulled my untamed hair together, holding it down with my hand as I whirled around to see who called out.

"What are you doing?" Lillian asked, uneasiness still carved on her countenance.

"I heard something," I kept my eyes fixed on the dark road.

"Well, I didn't hear anything." Her nerves were on edge and the look on her face told me I'd better drop the subject before she fainted.

"Well, I did," I kept up my search, concerned someone would materialize from the darkness. After a few minutes I sighed and turned back. "You're right, maybe it's just the wind."

The breeze blew up again, scattering more leaves and debris onto the road. For a second time, I heard the summons. Stopping, I paused to listen, certain I heard a woman singing. Her mournful ballad called to me, from deep within the woods.

"What now?" Bethany's anxiety seemed to be joining up with Lillian's. "Why are you stopping?"

I tilted my head to the wind and spoke above it. "Can you hear that?" Fear plastered itself across Lillian's face. "Hear what?"

"Someone's singing."

Again, the girls paled. I glanced into the woods, sensing something menacing beyond the trees, a threatening evil, well hidden in this mountain forest. A deep longing beckoned, a yearning I could not comprehend, and I wondered what kind of force could empty me of fear and draw me inside. The summons was not asking me to embrace the malevolent, but rather to vanquish it. The woman's voice was empowering, giving me courage. I let go of Lillian's arm and moved toward the woods.

"Where are you going?" Bethany tried grabbing me, but I slipped past her reach. "Someone's in there."

"Are you crazy?" She joined me at the edge of the forest but would go no further. "There's nothing in there but a death trap!" I ran my fingers over the needles of a towering pine, releasing their scent, which was especially pungent in the night. I pushed past, ready to enter the dark threshold of the woods. Bethany grabbed my arm, catching it this time. "I can't let you go in there alone. It's suicide!"

"Come with me then." I beckoned. "I thought you brought us on a retreat so we could have some sort of adventure." Bethany swallowed and ran her hand through her hair. "I didn't want us to get killed in the process."

And then, as if God heard Beth's prayers, heavy rains began showering down, and drowning out the woman's call. My courage suddenly gave way to anxiousness, my peace shattered by sudden panic. Just as I decided to do an about-face and make the long run back to the car, lightning streaked across the sky, revealing an old-fashioned covered bridge on the road ahead. "Over there!" I pointed, then sprinted for shelter with the girls on my heels. We made it to the wooden structure just as hailstones began dropping, bouncing off the rooftop, and collecting on the road.

We collapsed in the center of the narrow highway; our clothes soaked and clinging to our skin. I wiped the water from my face and glanced around. The wooden roof sheltered us from the falling rain, and plummeting hailstones, but unfortunately it also blocked out any light, once again, leaving us in total darkness. A cold chill traced its bony finger up my spine, prompting me to scoot in closer to the girls. My body tensed, sensing a presence in the dark recesses. And then, I detected another invasion, one that overpowered the scent of falling rain. Taking a deep breath, I identified the smell of cigarettes, the smoky odor that clings to clothing, or in this case, the heavy hooded robe of our stalker. Fear swarmed around me, consuming the courage I experienced only minutes before. The cloaked man was on the bridge with us. My mind raced, competing with my heart as I tried to calm the anxiety skyrocketing inside while deciding what to do.

I hugged my knees while trying to stay calm, and keeping my shivering controlled. I listened for movement, but the rain and hail pounding on the roof was deafening, drowning out any would be shuffling on the bridge. Telling the girls what I knew would only be an effort in futility. They would ask a ton of questions which would result in me having to yell above the storm to be heard. No, I wouldn't do that. Again, my back stiffened, as I sensed a presence closing in. A small gust moved past, brushing a soft piece of fabric against my back. Someone was directly behind me! I sprung to my feet, ready to bolt out into the storm. "Let's go!"

"What? Now?" Bethany questioned, unmoving. "It's too dangerous. The lightning is striking too close."

"We have to go now!" I yelled, ready to leave them to fend for themselves.

"No!" Lillian pulled me back down to the ground, surprising me with how much strength she stored in those scrawny arms of hers. "It's too dangerous; we should wait till the storm passes."

"Someone is under here with us." I argued above the pounding rain. "We are being followed!"

"I don't see anyone." Lillian argued. Where in the hell did she suddenly get her courage? Only minutes ago, she was superstitious, afraid to venture out alone, now she was more afraid of the storm than anything the mountains had to offer. I was wasting precious time pleading with them, but, if I dashed out into the severe weather, they were sure to follow. My arms were wet, so it took no effort to free my hand from Lillian's grasp. I began to run when the headlights from an oncoming vehicle changed my plan. Waiting for the precise moment, I leaped in front of the truck, causing it to come to a skidding stop, barely missing me. It was the motivation the girls needed. Jumping to their feet, Bethany yanked me away. "Are you crazy?"

The headlights dispelled the darkness, giving the light, I needed to confirm my suspicions. I turned in time to catch sight of a cloak billowing in the wind as the shadowy figure jumped from the side railing, making their escape into the raging river below. The door swung open, bringing my attention back to the truck and the person stepping from the cab. My fear suddenly dissolved as I looked into the eyes of the most beautiful man I had ever seen. Pulling away from Bethany, I stepped into the glow of the headlights, oddly lured into this stranger's presence.

"Ke ...is..." he started to say something, but stopped, swallowed, and bit down hard, a muscle folding in his jaw. Steadying himself, he grabbed hold of the door. The same heat sensation I felt earlier, gathered in the soles of my feet, and permeated upward through my body. My throat tightened. My eyes locked helplessly on the man, and I had no strength to pull away. Somewhere, deep in the recesses of my soul, I'd witnessed this event before. A fleeting vision of me, standing with this stranger, in the falling rain, flashed across my mind like deja'vu . Perhaps I'd dreamt of it once. Whatever the reason, my heart ached for something I couldn't explain.

Bethany offered her hand, attempting to break the long, awkward stare between the man and me. "The name's Bethany Baker. Our car broke down a couple of miles from here. We're looking for some help."

The stranger shook Bethany's hand, yet never removed his eyes from me. "Name's Travis. Get in the truck."

℃ℂ

The cloaked figure soared through the air and landed on the trespasser lurking near the bridge. A quick slicing of his knife and his victim slumped to the ground. Their blood, mixed with the rain, washing the evidence of his kill away, on down the river, snaking alongside the abandoned highway. He cleaned his knife, wiping it against the fabric of his cloak. He lowered his hood, swept the hair from his eyes, and peered from behind the trees, focusing his attention on the bridge above him.

His men were moving through the forest on guard and ready to attack any that posed a threat. He'd given orders to watch the car, not knowing who was inside. The enemy disabled it, nearly sending it into the deep ravine. Had Barak not intervened, the travelers would have plunged to their death. Since the adversary's plan had been thwarted, they would certainly attack again. They would not rest until the one was dead, and since no one knew who it was, they would surely kill them all. Soon the forest would become a battleground. Tonight, the rivers would run with blood.

The girls were on foot, headed toward Moonshine. They were vulnerable since neither had a clue of the danger surrounding them. He recognized one of them. The thought of her caused his lips to pull upward in an impish grin. Even though it had been six hundred years, her arrival was proof the final battle had begun.

The cloaked man pulled the bodies off the ground and tossed them under the bridge, keeping them from view. He would dispose of them later tonight, but right now, he must get rid of the rest of them. Travis was here and it would be a catastrophe if any of them caught a glimpse of his face. None of them knew this was where he'd been hiding all these years, and it was his duty to keep it that way.

Three

Travis pulled his pickup alongside our car allowing us to retrieve our overnight bags before taking us to the local inn, which he said he owned. He offered lodging for the night, advising it was best to take shelter and deal with the car in the morning."

I left my pillow and blanket figuring there would be plenty at the inn and snatched the novel I'd been struggling to read. The book was a defense, a barrier to retreat behind, while being alone with my thoughts. People would be less likely drum up a conversation if I appeared to be engrossed in a book. I wasn't sure if it would deter Bethany, but still, I thought I'd give it a try. The novel was not proving to be that inspiring. Nevertheless, I placed it in my bag just in case sleep would not come again tonight.

The opening of the truck's door diverted my attention. Again, I was taken aback by this mystifying stranger as he approached to help with our bags.

Our eyes locked again. His, so dark they appeared almost black much like the inky sky above us. Yet instead of storm clouds, secrets whirled deep within. He held my gaze, robbing me of the strength to look away.

The intensity of his stare unnerved me, bringing on the peculiar heat sensation again, re-creating the inexplicable emotion I felt earlier. I pressed my lips together and looked away, wondering if the girls had noticed our encounter. No one seemed to pay any attention. They were busy grabbing their belongings. I glanced at Bethany. Surely, she had noticed since not much escaped her. However, she remained completely aloof.

"We need to move quickly while there's a lull." His shoulder length hair blew in his face, yet his eyes never left mine when he spoke. "More storms are headed this way. Believe me when I say, it's only going to get worse. The sky darkened as massive clouds continued to march across the moon, cloaking any light it had to offer. Thunder growled a long rumble like a waking monster, and I wondered if these mountains were nothing more than fossilized beasts rousing from millions of years of dormancy. The ground rolled beneath our feet, rattling my chest. The blinding darkness added to the anxiety of the situation. I held my overnight bag close as I made my way to the pickup. Travis stood by the uncovered bed, holding a tarp.

"It's what he uses to wrap his victim's bodies in before he buries them," Bethany offered. Lillian wasn't amused. "Stop it! Do not bring those dark thoughts to my mind. You know how it affects me!" Bethany gave me a sly grin. It always gave her immense pleasure to torment Lillian anyway she could. I returned the smile, despite the gnawing fear that her explanation might be right.

A few minutes and several sharp curves later, Travis pulled off the road and onto a narrow driveway, rolling to a stop in front of a three-story Victorian inn, tall and imposing against the lightning-streaked sky. Vines snaked up the exterior, as if something evil had claimed the hotel for itself, gobbling up the wall and any guest who dared to enter. The front door carved from heavy oak was etched with symbols, unreadable through a rain-soaked windshield. A few flickering candles in the windows were the only sign of life emanating from inside. I read the uneasiness on the faces of my friends. Lillian was surveying the inn as if it could be her final resting place. I thought about making a run for it, but where would I go? There was nothing for miles. I envisioned myself sprinting through the drenching rain, into the woods, only to meet my demise by encountering the hooded figure and disappearing off the face of the earth forever. A second bolt of lightning intercepted my thoughts, striking only thirty yards from the truck. The crackling sound of splitting wood, accompanied by the burning aroma of sulfur was enough incentive for us to bolt for the shelter.

The scarce glow of candlelight made it difficult to make an accurate assessment of the place. We appeared to be standing in an entrance hall of some sort which evidently doubled as a living room. It gave the impression of comfort, furnished with soft leather couches in addition to several overstuffed armchairs. The colors and fabrics were muted by the darkness. A mammoth stone fireplace covered an entire wall, and a sizable picture window without covering, gobbled up another. The floor was a well-polished hardwood, swathed by soft, throw rugs, which cut the chill off the bare floor. An elevated antique desk stood at the far side of the lobby matching a colossal banister that came to rest at the end of a spiraling wooden staircase.

"Welcome, weary travelers," a cheery voice rang out from behind the lofty desk. I stepped further inside the room to view the person who offered the greeting. The light of a small glowing lantern revealed a woman who appeared to be our age. Her loosely braided hair was swept to the side and rested gently over her shoulder. Her welcoming smile covered most of her face, revealing a missing tooth on the upper left. A noticeable scar traveled from the corner of her left eye halfway down her jawbone. Despite these flaws, I could see the beauty hidden deep within her face. She was quite lovely, nevertheless, an obvious accident had taken its toll on her.

"Sorry about the darkness. Our power was knocked out by the storm. Should have light tomorrow. Just step up and sign my register and I'll be getting you into your room." Lillian warily made her way to the front, her slender fingers curled tightly around the pen. She wrote her name as if she were signing her death certificate. She handed the pen to me. I scribbled my name across the line and took the key from the woman who flashed a perplexing smile and then quickly exchanged glances with Travis. Their knowing looks increased my discomfort. The strange bit of heat once again rushed through my body. Maybe it was a premonition of danger; after all, I'd heard stories of people who had a sixth sense enabling them to foretell impending doom. Such as people who bolted from a flight at the last minute, only to hear that the plane crashed moments after takeoff. I prided myself on my intuition and discerning abilities, but I had never experienced anything this strange before. Perhaps, it was because I'd never been in extreme danger until now. My heart raced as the rising heat reached around my neck.

"The name's Mavis." The woman said, interrupting my thoughts of doom. "Travis and I own the Inn. If you need anything, give us a holler!" I nodded and noticed the plaque embedded in the wood of the desk. "Sandalwood Inn. Travis Colton and Mavis Colton proprietors." Avoiding another awkward stare from Travis, I lowered my gaze and took to the winding staircase. Room number two was down the hall and to my left. I inserted the key and pushed open the door. The space was dark except for the glow of a flickering candle, burning on a nightstand, between two queen beds. An heirloom dresser and mirror also occupied the room, along with a desk and an overstuffed chair. There was an adjoining bathroom, complete with a quaint old-fashioned tub on legs. Clean towels and washcloths lay folded on the vanity top, along with a basket of sweet-smelling ointments and homemade soaps.

Lillian quickly changed out of her wet clothing before dashing for one of the beds and throwing her overly stressed body across the feather mattress. Bethany was quick to follow Lillian's lead. As much as I wanted to do the same, I decided on a bath first. The old-fashioned tub seemed rather inviting, and despite the heat and mugginess of the night, I shivered in my wet clothes. After lighting a candle and placing it on the small table near the tub, I filled the bath with warm water and added the sweet milky potions from the basket. Delightful scents of lavender and jasmine quickly permeated the room. I peeled off my soaked clothing, stepped into the inviting tub, and allowed my body to melt in the balmy water. Closing my eyes, I leaned my head against the soft foam pillow attached to the tub and released a breath I had held for much too long. Outside, the fierce winds and rain continued to wreak havoc, causing the inn to creak and the door to shake. Even though I was uncertain of my surroundings, I was content to finally have shelter. I sank deeper into the tub and found myself dozing off and on as the candle cast hypnotic images on the dark wall.

My sporadic dreams were nightmarish. I could see the stranger Travis standing behind sheets of falling rain. I longed to reach for him, to be where he was, yet he pushed me away. Then, without warning, the ground disappeared from underneath, and I felt myself falling, plummeting into darkness. The drop jolted me awake triggering a kick that splashed water over the side of the tub. Shivering, I climbed from the bath deciding it would be best to continue sleeping in the bed rather than a basin filled with water. Toweling off, I dressed and then tiptoed into the room, so as not to wake the girls. Lillian was sleeping soundly, spread across one of the beds, claiming the entirety of it for herself. Bethany had staked her claim on the left side of the other, furthest away from the door. After checking to see that it was indeed locked, I blew out the remaining candle and climbed into the soft comfort of the mattress. The rain had slacked off to a gentle patter and the winds diminished from a deafening roar to a steady whistle.

"You know what's weird?" Bethany whispered.

I flinched; surprised she was still awake. "Besides everything?"

"You saw Travis, the man that picked us up?"

"Uh huh," I wondered if she had experienced the same peculiar heat sensation that I had when he looked at her, or if she had noticed the long stare between us.

"Did you see his wife? I mean, how do those two go together at all? Is she lucky or what?"

I smiled in the darkness. "Beth, I think you've reached an all-time low in shallowness."

She sighed. "You were pretty quiet all day."

"Uh hum."

"When are you going to snap out of this funk? When do I get my partner in crime back? I miss you."

I remained silent. Although I agreed with her that I hadn't been myself lately. I had no answer as to when I would snap out of it, as she had so simply put it. I hopelessly tried to move forward and continue with life; however, it wasn't that easy, especially when I felt no energy or motivation to do so.

"I wish I could," I sighed. "Believe me, I wish I could. I don't know what's wrong with me. Everything's just blah. I feel lost inside."

"All this because of Ryan?"

"Good night, Beth." I refused to engage in any conversation about him. A final rumble of thunder sounded in the distance. The last bit of rain tapped gently on the window. My eyes grew heavy as I faded off to sleep.

Just outside the inn, a shadowy cloaked figure placed his knife inside the folds of his robe. Camouflaged by the massive fir trees, he stood vigil, watching the inn, and waiting.

Four

DAY ONE

The morning sun streamed through the picture window, piercing through the lace curtains and filled the room with light. It wasn't the gleaming rays of sunshine that stirred me to consciousness, but rather the delicious scents traveling from the kitchen, up the winding staircase, and directly into room number two.

I squinted from the brightness of the morning and raised my head from its cushioned cradle. Lillian's bed was empty, but Bethany still lay in the exact position as the night before. I was glad to see we were still alive, and that no one had crept into the room while we slept and bludgeoned us to death. Lillian was missing but I figured she was downstairs having breakfast since she was known to be an early riser. Besides, there was no sign of a struggle anywhere. Considering the uneasiness I felt right before bed, I was surprised at how soundly I'd slept. Yawning, I looked over at Bethany. "You awake?"

She stirred groggily. "My body's still asleep, but my nose woke up some time ago. Have you ever smelled anything so amazing?"

"Not since visiting my grandmother's house."

We both sat up and looked around the room. The morning light gave it a more inviting appearance. The room exuded warmth with pale yellow walls, trimmed with white crown molding and adorned with beautiful oil paintings. White lace curtains hung over a sizable picture window; their fabric complementing the snowy comforter covering the four-post beds. Everything about the room was friendly, cheerful, and inviting in the bright morning light. It was so different from last night.

Bethany was the first to climb from the feather mattress. She gave a loud yawn and then crossed over to the window.

"What do you say we follow our noses?"

"Sounds good." The smell of a hearty breakfast was the only thing strong enough to pry me from the comfort of the bed. I pulled a pair of cotton shorts and a tank out of my bag and headed for the bathroom.

Bethany pushed back the curtains as she opened the window. Lovely floral scents rushed into the room riding on the morning breeze. The new day unmasked a world of beauty outdoors as well.

"Wow, this is amazing!" She announced her discovery so that I could hear from the bathroom. "This is amazing," she repeated. "Bronwyn, come here! Quick!"

Still brushing my teeth, I appeared from the bathroom. "What?"

"Look." Bethany pulled back the curtains. Surrounding the inn, as far as my eyes could see, were the most exquisite gardens. Plants, flowers, and trees of every species bloomed in the fertile soil below. An ornate fountain stood in the center of the circle driveway, bubbling over with fresh water. Numerous flowering plants and crawling vines found their way up the fountain, all drinking from the water in its basin. To my far right, a river lazily trickled over droves of natural rock. Bees hummed and birds sang, very much at home in this blossoming paradise. Movement near the stream caught my attention. Travis busied himself, clearing away broken branches and debris that had fallen during the storm. The morning heat had resulted in him removing his shirt, revealing his perfectly sculpted body, much to Bethany's delight. She was right. His wide shoulders were sculpted with muscles, each rippling as he grabbed hold of the hefty branches and tossed them effortlessly into a pile of collected rubble. With a jerk of his head, he brushed his dark hair, now curling with perspiration, away from his forehead and continued his clearing.

"See what I mean about him and Mavis not going together? My God, he is in great shape! Look at those muscles, those washboard abs, those strong buttocks!"

"That's enough Beth! Male descriptions are my job, not yours." I walked away from the window for fear he might look up and lock eyes with me again. I returned to the bathroom to spit out the toothpaste and rinse when I noticed my hands were trembling. I splashed cold water on my neck, hoping to cool off the heat and stop the shaking before Bethany noticed and began asking questions. I took a deep, calming breath before coming back into the room. "Pull yourself away from the window, Beth. He's a married man, and more than likely has an inn full of kids."

"You're probably right." She sighed and backed away, allowing the curtain to fall slowly while she took in every glimpse she could possibly manage.

Mavis was busy pouring more batter into the waffle iron as she hummed a happy tune. A bowl of brown speckled eggs sat next to a sizzling cast iron skillet, along with a platter of diced potatoes waiting to be cooked. Fresh strawberries and various types of melons lay on a tray, peeled, and sliced. Glass pitchers of orange juice and iced water sat on the massive wooden table near an open kitchen window. The morning air wafted inside, swirling about the room with the aid of a large ceiling fan.

Mavis closed the waffle iron, grabbed a pot of freshly brewed coffee, and headed to the table to replenish the empty mugs; it was then I noticed she used a walking stick for assistance.

Bethany refilled her glass with orange juice, marveling that it was indeed the best juice she had ever tasted. She asked Mavis an onslaught of questions from what brand she was drinking, to why the eggs were spotted. She was delighted to learn everything was homegrown, from the orange juice in her glass to the cage-free eggs in the bowl. Mavis even claimed the two children, who had stormed into the kitchen with their own barrage of questions, were home grown as well.

Carla Jo, the eldest of the two, zeroed in on Lillian as she bit into her fluffy waffle. "You're from California! Do you know any famous actors?"

Mavis eyed her daughter as she stirred the cooking potatoes. The girl was only twelve and already boy crazy "Carla Jo, you know the rules about bothering the guests."

"You're beautiful!" Molly's small voice rang out as she stared in awe at Lillian. It was no wonder. Lillian resembled a Disney Princess, blonde hair, blue eyes, perfect nose, and full pink bow lips. She had a voice to match, and I often wondered why she didn't live in New York and pursue a career on Broadway instead of trying to make it big in Hollywood. Lillian smiled, pleased with Molly's adoration. "And so are you dear. Come sit here, next to me."

"Is it alright momma?" Molly asked, wide-eyed. Mavis smiled as she cracked another egg, sending the yolk into the sizzling hot skillet. "I reckon so dear but mind your manners."

Molly eagerly climbed up into her chair and took her seat beside her famous guest.

I sipped my coffee and stared out of the open window, ignoring the idle chatter at the table. I preferred the sound of birds chirping, the low honking of the geese out on the water and the slow gentle movement of the wooden wind chimes as they played their hollow tune. The cool morning breeze floated through the window, tenderly touching my face, while bringing in the many scents of the outdoor gardens. I wasn't certain, but thought I sensed a bit of inspiration...a feeling foreign of late. The sudden stimulation enticed me to venture outdoors, fall into the soft green grass, inhale all the scents, and lay there for hours and dream. I predicted my dreams in the gardens would be peaceful and untroubled, not like the nightmarish haunts that accompanied my nights. I hoped to get the chance to tour the inn's grounds before the car was ready for departure. It would be a shame to miss such an opportunity.

"Bronwyn!" Bethany nudged me hard in the ribs, bringing my attention from the outdoors and back into the busy room. Travis was in the kitchen, washing his hands in the sink. He had showered and donned a gray t-shirt that stretched tightly across his sculpted chest. Bethany shoved her hip into me with the intention of having me slide down the bench to make room for him. I suddenly found the food on my plate interesting.

"Thank you," Travis took the offered seat. Mavis hobbled over to the table and handed him a plate and then patted him lovingly on the back before limping to the stove. He poured himself a glass of water and then dished only fruit and eggs onto his plate.

"You know Ryan Reese?" Carla Jo screamed with delight.

The name took my attention away from my food and to the trivial banter. It was as if someone had tossed the pitcher of ice water right into my face.

"Ryan is my absolute favorite actor in the world!" Carla Jo gushed about her crush. "I've seen his movie so many times! Tell me everything you know about him!"

I searched the faces of my comrades, wondering who had betrayed my secrecy.

"Sorry, Bronwyn." Lillian offered an apology. "The kid wanted to know if any of us knew Ryan."

Carla Jo sat wide-eyed. "So, you really know him?"

I tried to hide a grimace. I wanted to say no. It wouldn't be a total lie because his actions of late made me feel as if I didn't. I sighed. "Sore subject, hon."

Mavis came to my rescue. "That's enough Carla Jo. Your breakfast is more than done. You got chores to do."

"Awe momma."

"You heard me. Now scoot!"

Carla Jo gave a pleading look at Travis, whose mouth melted into a sympathetic smile, "You heard your mother."

Carla Jo removed herself from the table, and with slumped shoulders, left the room.

"I'm sorry," I apologized to Mavis. "She didn't know—"

"Your car's been towed to Larry's Garage." Travis changed the subject between taking bites of his breakfast.

"And where might we find Larry's garage?" Bethany asked.

"In town."

"And where would the town be?"

"A mile down the highway. Just follow the road; it'll take you right to it."

Bethany tried one more time for a definite location. "Could I have a business address for the garage?"

"Don't need one. You'll see it when you get there."

There was no other choice than to follow his simplistic advice. As always, Lillian kept her very professional and agreeable disposition, thanking Travis for the information, and then announced she was going up to the room to shower. Mavis left to retrieve fresh laundered towels for her use.

The once crowded kitchen cleared instantly, leaving only the three of us at the table. Much to my dismay, Bethany, who thrived on chatting, quickly tried to drum up a conversation with Travis.

"So, Moonshine. I've never heard of this place. Have you lived here all your life?"

"Not sure, my life's not over yet." He responded.

"Fair." She laughed, enjoying her little chat.

She irritated me. Why did she feel the need to talk to him? Why couldn't she just leave things alone? I had purposely avoided looking at him the entire time he had been sitting at the table. He was finished with his meal and would more than likely leave if she shut up. The last thing I wanted was another suffocating gaze.

"You're just so far away from everything." She stated the obvious. "Where the hell is this place? I mean being off the grid is good for vacation but I'm not sure I would want to make a life like that." My frustration with Bethany turned into a quick reprimand. "Bethany, don't be rude."

"I'm not being rude." She defended her question. "I am just curious as to how someone could live so far away from society." She turned her attention back to Travis. "Have you ever considered that there might be a better, more fulfilling life for you someplace else? I mean. What if you're missing something being secluded up here."

Travis took the last bite of his fruit and finished off his water before answering her. He stood and took our plates to the sink. "Missing something?" he said, looking directly into my eyes, "Sometimes things have a way of finding you."

The heat sensation began again, from the soles of my feet, rising upward through the rest of my body. My head began to spin and as much as I wanted to bolt from the kitchen, I feared if I stood, I might fall. This wasn't the reaction of giddiness by being in the presence of a beautiful man. This sensation was something I'd never experienced before. It was a suffocating mixture of euphoria and chaos. Giving me a slight nod, he left the room.

"Now there's someone to write about," Bethany gushed. "If that man doesn't inspire torrid thoughts, then you're brain dead. You see what I mean about him and Mavis not going together?"

I'd had enough. "Be quiet, Beth! She might hear you!"

Beth pouted. "I want the old Bronwyn back. I miss her so much. I have no one to have fun with." She sighed melodramatically, "I guess I'll have to train Lillian." I smiled at the thought. Pampered Princess Lillian, her partner in crime? Bethany's threat was dismissed. "Tell you what," I suggested. "Why don't we venture into this metropolis of a town and see what we can find. We'll stop at Larry's Garage first." No matter our unfortunate circumstances, I thought it would be the experience of a lifetime to explore this mysterious and yet unseen town of Moonshine.

"Will you be fun?"

I smiled at my friend. "I'll be a blast."

We headed across the Inn's lawn. The scents from the garden filled our lungs while we followed the cobblestone path that wound its way through the property. I was amazed at the variety of plants and the flora covering every inch of the ground.

"Sandalwood Inn." Bethany enlightened us by reading aloud the words on the beautifully hand-painted sign near the property's edge. We came to a stop when we reached the narrow highway. It was unnecessary, for there was not a single car traveling this forgotten, winding road.

Five

I was only half listening to Bethany and Lillian's conversation as we headed to Moonshine. It was nearly one in the afternoon and the midday heat was taking its toll. However, the temperature wasn't the reason I was disengaged. It was the person following us, masking themselves behind the gargantuan trees that captured my attention. I figured it was the same person I'd seen last night, and whoever that may be, was hiding underneath the hood of the black robe, hot on our trail again. With every curve, I desperately hoped to see some hint of a town ahead, but just like last night, every turn proved more of the same endless highway.

I had no intention of alarming the girls by telling them about our stalker, certain that one word of impending danger would result in a wave of hysteria from Lillian and a barrage of questions from Bethany. My best defense was to be aware of the person without them knowing, so I continued walking silently, blocking out the conversation and lending my ear to the woods on my right. I cast a casual glance over my shoulder, and noticed the cloaked figure move in rhythm to our steps, like a lurking long shadow. My mind traveled back to the bridge and the billowing fabric as they jumped. A cold chill feathered up my spine.

"Bronwyn!" Bethany interrupted my thoughts, startling me, so that my response seemed somewhat biting. "What?"

Her expression soured. "You promised you'd be fun, but you haven't said a word since we left. Are you certain we're going in the right direction? We've been walking forever and there's no sign of a town anywhere."

I shrugged. "How should I know? I'm wondering if there is a town. I mean, think about it. We trusted a couple of strangers. And for the matter, why are there no other guests at the Inn? Do you realize, no one outside of Moonshine knows where we are right now? No one, not even us." Lillian paled despite the heat coloring her face. "We can't call our families because there is no cell reception, and the phones at the inn are supposedly out of order because of last night's storm. Travis said he had our car towed away to some garage we've never seen. They could have been removing evidence that we were ever here. We've all heard of people who just disappear, never to be seen or heard from again. I wonder if this is how it starts."

My words were taking their toll on Lillian, whose expressions of impending heatstroke changed to full fright. "Stop it!" She snapped. "I can't handle this right now."

Bethany grinned, thinking I was playing around just to frighten Lillian, so any warning of impending danger was dismissed. I decided to let it go for now. We continued walking without conversation while I was left to dwell on the direst circumstance that could possibly befall us. A rustling from the woods shattered our silence.

"What was that?" Lillian gasped. I decided that maybe now would be a good time to fill them in. "We're being followed."

"We are?" Lillian clutched her chest and spun about to see. "How do you know?"

"Don't make a scene, Lil," "I turned her back around and nudged her along. "Keep moving as if you're unaware." Lillian slowed again, craning her neck as she glanced over her shoulder. "I don't see anything."

"Just keep walking. Don't try to look." I kept my eyes fixed on the road ahead.

Lillian picked up her pace, turning our casual stroll into a brisk power walk. Bethany jabbed me in the side again, her grin stretching across her face. She thought I was kidding. I didn't correct her. There was no need to try and convince her otherwise. If we kept walking hopefully, we would reach the town soon and get out of these infernal woods.

"Could be Bigfoot, Wolf Man or one of those Devil Dogs." Bethany suggested, trying to evoke more fear. Lillian broke into a full-on run at the thought. "Slow down Lil," Bethany was laughing so heartily it slowed her pace. "Dang, I've never seen you move so fast! Don't get too far ahead. There's safety in numbers."

I glanced behind me to see the hooded figure move from between two trees. Just as I was about to suggest we make a run for it, the loud blast of a horn sounded behind us.

A familiar white pickup joined us. I breathed a slight sigh of relief when I saw Travis in the cab, and the two children standing in the back, waving wildly at us. The dark shadow retreated and disappeared deeper into the forest.

"Would you like a ride?" Travis asked through his open window.

"Oh God, yes!" Lillian responded, her relief overflowing. Travis stopped the truck in the middle of the road and climbed from the cab to lower the tailgate.

Carla Jo eyed me, her enthusiasm brimming over. "Get in and tell me all about Ryan!"

The last thing I wanted was a conversation with a twelve-year old about Ryan Reese. At this point, though, I would do anything for a ride. Bethany nudged me with her elbow. "I'll take care of this one. You sit up front."

"I owe you one," I whispered, climbing into the cab, and wondering why my anxiety continued to rise, even though I was safely in a vehicle and no longer vulnerable to the stalking figure in the woods. The thought of a few minutes alone with Travis frightened me almost as much as the cloaked predator. I decided to take the opportunity to investigate what I could, about the strange person lurking in the woods. I wasn't sure how much I could trust Travis, if at all. Diverting my eyes from his, I looked out the window. "Are you sure it's only a mile into town? It seems longer?"

"It's a country mile. If you stretch it out, it'd probably be three."

"That figures." I wished he had explained that simple fact before we had set out on foot. "What kind of creatures you got roaming around?"

"Just the usual, raccoons, deer, coyotes, wolves, and bears" he kept his eyes on the road. "Why? Did something spook you?"

I turned away from the window to look at him. Something had spooked me, and by his nonchalant answer, I had a sneaking suspicion he knew exactly what I was talking about. The premonition of danger began to overwhelm me all over again.

"You could say that. I thought I saw something following us..." He said nothing as he steered the truck around a few sharp curves.

"...It was kind of creepy..." I waited for a response, but to my dismay he offered none, so I tried once more. "It looked like a person wearing a black hooded robe..."

Again, he gave nothing away, not even in profile, nothing but silence from the driver's side of the cab.

"That doesn't surprise you?"

"Why should it? It was more than likely some kids gawking at the visitors from California. We don't have a lot of guests. Things like that are a big deal around here."

"And yet you own an inn." I challenged his statement. Another one he refused to comment on. "How could anyone know we're here?" I tried again. "We arrived late last night, and the phones are down."

"Word travels faster than you can dial a phone around here. Besides, I'd say that Convertible Mercedes, with California plates being towed into town might have announced your arrival."

I felt a bit silly. Maybe he didn't know. His explanation seemed so obvious. However, I knew what I'd encountered, first on the bridge last night, and now on the road in broad daylight. Gawking teenagers wouldn't have been out in a storm of such magnitude. Besides, it was hot. Why wear such a heavy hooded robe in the midday heat? I decided to leave the matter alone. Either Travis knew of the person in the woods, or he didn't.

Either way, I would play innocent, feeling it was my best defense. After all, we would probably be leaving soon. I turned back to the open window.

Within minutes, he rounded the final curve, unveiling the elusive town of Moonshine. Any fears or anxieties I may have experienced were dismissed promptly, as I gazed upon this storybook village. It was as if the heavy curtains on a stage swung open to reveal breathtaking scenery behind them. Hidden within the bosom of the mountains was the most charming little hamlet I'd ever seen. Quaint old-fashioned storefronts lined the main road. Each business was unique unto itself, untouched by corporate franchises and chains that littered most of the country. Cottages and cabins of assorted sizes dotted the rolling hillsides, each residence surrounded by beautiful gardens like that at the inn. Lush green grass blanketed the town for miles, interrupted occasionally by glistening brooks of clear water. The fragrant bouquet of pine, spruce, and balsam fir, along with assorted floral aromas, wafted through my open window. The man-made scents of fresh bread and sweet pastries drifted from the local bakery, accompanying nature's delicious smells.

The citizens of Moonshine were out, walking the streets. Travis drove much slower now as the happy residents waved, calling out his name. He nodded slightly each time, acknowledging the greetings. He pulled into Larry's Garage. Sure enough, my car was sitting out front. Adults and kids gathered around it, pointing, and talking, excitement glowing in their faces. Some people were taking pictures of the broken-down vehicle. I felt somewhat embarrassed; maybe Travis was right. Possibly, I'd let my imagination overwhelm all reasoning. I glanced his way, catching his eye and gave him a slight smile. "I guess you're right."

"It's alright. Storytellers are meant to have large imaginations."

Without warning the heat sensation began passing through my body once more. My heart raced, stealing my breath. How did he know I was a writer? I'd never told him. My mind whirled as I raced through the conversation at the breakfast table. No, it had never come up. How could he have known?

He opened my door and then the tailgate for the girls. "I'll be in town most of the day. Let me know if you want a ride back."

Leaving us with the offer, he climbed into his truck and drove away.

Larry's garage resembled an old-time service station. Soda and vending machines stood out front, offering refreshment to anyone with pocket change. A small garage housed several items awaiting repairs, along with my luxury car that Larry proudly displayed out front.

Larry surveyed the engine. His excitement went unnoticed by Bethany, who was hovering over him. Larry only half listened as he pulled and prodded at the complicated engine, offering only a grunt every now and then, just to keep her satisfied. A soft-spoken country fellow, Larry was the only mechanic in the small town. He kept busy repairing everything from toasters to lawn mowers. Much to his delight, a challenge worthy of his expertise had presented itself. He stood from his squatting position and slammed the hood.

"Can you fix it?" Bethany was hopeful.

Larry spit out his tobacco juice that had been pooling for some time. "I can fix it. It'll be a full day's work."

"That's great." She stared at the black gooey substance. "That shouldn't put us too far behind."

"Full day's work if I had the parts. I'm gonna have to order 'em. You're lookin' at eight to ten business days."

"Oh," was all a stunned Bethany could muster. "You're serious?"

Lillian, who had been resting on a shaded bench near the vending machine during Larry's diagnostics, suddenly jumped to her dainty feet. "That will not do! We have an extremely important vacation with non-refundable deposits on facials, massages, mud baths, dinners, you name it, we cannot afford to miss it!"

He shrugged. "Looks like you'll have to go without your car. Cause it ain't moving."

Bethany's brow furrowed. "Are you even sure you know what you're talking about? Have you ever worked on a European car? I for one would like a second opinion!"

Larry removed his rolled-up ball cap from his back pocket and placed it on his head as he headed inside. "Good luck with that, seeing I'm the only mechanic in town."

"Go ahead and order whatever you need." I smiled softly trying to smooth over Bethany's offensive behavior.

He thumbed through a parts catalog at his rustic desk that doubled as a workbench. There was no other way of looking at it; we would have to remain in Moonshine for at least a week.

Lillian sipped the cold drink she had purchased from the machine and sat the bottle down hard on the table. "I can't believe this. I can't believe we're stranded. How could this have happened?"

Finishing off my bottle of water, I placed it on the table in front of them and gave it a spin. The bottle whirled around a few times and finally came to a stop, pointing at Bethany.

"Could I have said it any better?" I laughed. "The guilty party has been identified by the all-knowing bottle."

Bethany scowled, grunted, and headed over to Larry's makeshift desk.

"I need to call a rental service and get a car for the week."

"Don't have rentals here," Larry said, never looking up from his catalog.

"You don't rent any vehicles of any kind?"

"Most people here don't use cars. We do just fine with bicycles and canoes but mainly we walk."

"What do you think, Beth?" I jeered. "Maybe we could load up a couple of canoes and paddle there? If we get a good current, maybe we could make our reservations by Friday."

Lillian gave me a disapproving look.

"I'm sorry," I apologized. "But in my defense, I didn't think this trip was a good idea in the first place. I had a strange feeling from the beginning."

"How far is the nearest town?" Bethany ignored my 'I told you so,' and tried another route.

"You're lookin' at a hundred miles and it's smaller than Moonshine."

Lillian groaned and let her perfect posture melt into a slump.

"I'll call and cancel," Bethany said softly.

"Phones are still down." Larry said, leaving his desk to tend to the items he had neglected all morning.

Lillian watched Larry feed change into the soda machine and retrieve his cola, popping off the cap and taking a swallow before heading into his garage. She watched him until he disappeared before turning her attention back to us and caught me giving her a curious grin. "What are you looking at?"

"I could ask you the same question when it comes to Travis." She lifted her chin in defense.

Rolling my eyes, I tossed the empty water bottle into the recycle bin. "I'm starved. Let's go find some food."

Six

We grabbed the only available table in the busy café and took a seat. A lone waitress scurried busily from one tabletop to the next. The moment she noticed us, she left the table she was serving and eagerly headed our way. Her bright red hair was piled high on her head in a sloppy bun, except for some pieces that escaped her scrunchie and fell into her face. She had used a brick red pencil to match her eyebrows with her hair. The line crooked and strayed from the natural brow line, as if she had applied her cosmetics hurriedly or in the dark. A green shimmer shadow painted both eyelids and bubblegum pink gloss covered her thin lips. She wore a badge, with her name handwritten on the front.

"Can I get you girls something to wet your whistle?" Nell asked cheerfully. Lillian squinted her eyes at Nell. "I... we don't have a whistle..."

Bethany leaned across the table and took the opportunity to enlighten Lillian on some of the culture she had learned in her short research of the Appalachians. "She's asking if you want something to drink. It's amazing really. There is an entire manner of speaking in these mountains that we've never heard." Realizing she did not need a whistle to place an order, Lillian happily requested strawberry lemonade. Bethany and I decided to try the sweet, iced tea. So, while Nell swiftly disappeared into the small café to retrieve the refreshing beverages, I took the opportunity to soak up the atmosphere.

Tables of many varied sizes were adorned with non-matching linen tablecloths; small vases with fresh cut flowers crowned the top of each. Strings of miniature white lights hung in the trellis overhead, offering a starry ambiance effect for the evening diners. A countertop table was fastened to the outside wall just below a large window from which customers could peer into the café's kitchen. Whenever the chef would retrieve fresh baked goods from the oven, Nell immediately placed them on the countertop to cool. Mouth-watering aromas drifted from the hot cuisine and directly onto the patio, increasing everyone's appetite. As I assessed the place, I noticed the diners pretending to be engaged in their own private conversations, even though all eyes were constantly upon our table. Lillian also picked up on this scenario right away. "I feel famous," she gushed. "Everyone's looking at us. I wonder if this is how celebrities feel." She had appeared on a few TV series and had small roles in films. She was still awaiting her big break. Lillian was beautiful but her acting was a bit melodramatic, which in my opinion kept her from getting the roles she really wanted.

"You are a celebrity—of sorts..."

"Thank you for the compliment, Bronwyn." She gave me an appreciative smile, but I'm not recognizable. Not yet anyway. People don't notice me; not like they do Ryan." The words had no more come out of her mouth than she covered her lips with her slender fingers. Her eyes widened. "I'm so sorry! I didn't mean to bring him up again."

"The celebrity lifestyle isn't for me," Bethany interrupted, trying to cover up Lilian's fopaux. Lillian rolled her eyes. "Now, I know you're lying. You make more Instagram reels than anyone I know." Bethany's face turned a bright shade of red as Nell returned to the table and placed the cold drinks in front of us. "Are you havin' lunch?" She laid the straws on the table. "We're serving tuna and cucumber sandwiches today with a side of strawberries and mango."

"Oh," Lillian said, realizing there were no other choices. The long walk had stirred our appetites, so we agreed on lunch. Nell scurried off to collect three tuna sandwiches, returning in record time, and placing the healthy food on the table.

"We need to discuss our present situation." Bethany waited while Nell refilled her empty tea glass before continuing. "Looks like it's going to take some time to get the car running again. Larry said he can fix it, but as we heard, he doesn't have the necessary parts in stock. He said it could take between eight to ten days. So, we're pretty much stranded."

"There goes our spiritual healing vacay" Lillian pouted. "What the hell are we going to do for ten days?"

"We're screwed," I said, pushing my plate away. "I for one have no desire to stay here for more than one night, let alone ten days! I want out of here. I find this place a little disturbing!"

"Bronwyn, lower your voice!" Lillian chided. "People are watching."

"I don't care!" I said louder than before.

"Well, you better!" She shot back. "They're going to be our neighbors for a while."

I decided now might be the best time to inform them of my suspicions. I lowered my voice for their benefit and leaned onto the table. "Something's not right about this place! I don't think we're safe here!"

"Why don't you feel safe?" Bethany's eyes widened in surprise. "Everyone I've met so far has been quite accommodating and friendly."

I leaned in closer and whispered. "It's a front. Someone was stalking us last night while we were looking for help, and then I saw them again, while we were walking here."

"So, you weren't fooling around?" Bethany turned to Lillian as if to validate my story. "Did you see someone following us?" Lillian shook her head. "I looked but I didn't see anyone." Bethany glanced back at me as if Lil's observation was the final word on the matter.

"Just because you didn't see anything, doesn't mean someone wasn't there. I know what I saw. Someone followed us all the way to the bridge, and someone was stalking us on the way into town a few minutes ago."

They exchanged knowing glances, clearly indicating they thought I'd lost my grasp on reality. I sighed, frustrated. "Call it premonition, whatever, I don't feel safe here. I believe we are being detained for some reason and I think we should do what we can to leave." Bethany broke the humiliating silence. "We're stuck here because the car couldn't take these mountain roads. And that my dear, is why the car stopped, not the work of a crazy serial killer, hiding on the side of a hidden highway."

"You always want me to divulge what I'm feeling, and when I do you try to tell me I'm wrong. Is it any wonder why I keep my opinions to myself?" I huffed a sigh and leaned back in my chair. So what if they didn't agree, I sensed something odd about the place, however picturesque it seemed. Lillian was right. The inhabitants of the town did seem friendly enough, like a large group of Southern people lost deep in the mountains, living in their own small world, seemingly untouched by the latest technologies and modern conveniences. Most of the people looked youthful, happy, healthy, and stress free. Still, despite their Norman Rockwell appearance, something wasn't right. My eyes fell on an unshaven man, sitting alone in the far corner. His long black hair partially veiled his face, and a pair of dark sunglasses completed the mask. He reclined in his chair, a leg thrown across the tabletop. A cigarette dangled from his lips. He, like everyone else, seemed to have his attention on us but with the dark glasses it was hard to tell for sure. He pulled the cigarette from his mouth and expelled a long line of smoke before flashing an impish grin my way. Terror gripped me, as another disturbing feeling manifested at the sight of his wicked smile. Could he be the person in the woods? My conviction grew stronger. Something sinister was at play here in Moonshine. I looked away, not wanting him to see the fear blossoming in my face and returned my attention to the table.

"I think," Bethany was taking control again, "we should look at the positive side of our situation. We can still have our retreat. We can be thankful that the car decided to give out within a few miles of a nice comfortable inn."

"The Bates Motel," I mumbled under my breath.

"With a nice family eager to take care of our needs," she ignored my sarcastic remark.   "We have every comfort right here. We could have had the misfortune of breaking down a hundred miles from Moonshine. Now that would have been a disaster! Since there is nothing we can do about our situation, my advice would be to make the most of it. We could use the time for self-improvement." She exchanged the word healing for self-improvement. God did the girl ever give up?

I decided to ignore her attempt to control the situation and look across the patio, curious to see if the roguish man was still looking our way. However, the table was empty and cleared as if he had never been there. I searched the courtyard and the sidewalk out front. There was no sign of him. Another shiver tickled my skin. I unwillingly turned my attention back to the table and Bethany's bombardment of ideas.

"Bronwyn you might get some inspiration that would help with your latest novel. Your recent excerpts have been kind of... off." Lillian immediately intervened before I could toss my glass of tea on Bethany.

"A few extra unplanned days could do us all a world of good. I for one could brush up on some of my audition sides and acting techniques."

"Is my book that bad?" I asked Beth, as my literary agent, not my friend. She always spoke the truth, never sugar coating anything when it came to my writing. She took a swallow of tea and wiped her mouth with a napkin. "Horrid? No. They have, however, been somewhat empty of the creativity I know exudes from you."

I sighed. I had produced stellar stories in times past, yet because of my recent heartbreak, my work lost some of its passion. Bethany didn't want to hurt me any further by bashing my latest manuscript. Lillian caught Bethany's eye and through her expression, encouraged her to speak the truth.

"No offense to you Bronwyn, I have refrained from discussing it because you have been hurting... but it's extremely hard to care for the characters when they are written one-dimensional, and are quite predictable. The first ten chapters are incredibly boring and a chore to read. You're just rambling. The publisher is rejecting this one unless you can fix it."

"Seriously?" I pushed myself away from the table. "You knew this and let me keep writing? I don't need your coddling. You could have told me. Thanks for wasting my time!"

"Bronwyn please," Bethany begged. "Don't take this personally. It's business. Sit down and let's plod through this."

"I don't want to plod through anything!" I bit back, "Besides I thought this trip was a vacation. I didn't realize it was writing workshop." I stomped across the patio, avoiding the stares of everyone as they watched me leave. Dodging their glares as best I could, I kept my eyes fixed ahead, as I left the café and ventured down the street.

∞

Bethany sighed, "Do you think I should go after her?"

"No, I think it's best if we just give her some time." Lillian popped a strawberry in her mouth. "She's been through a lot, and I know for a fact, she still hurts over Ryan. I know this is hard for you to understand, considering that you toss men away and get over them in six seconds flat."

"I do not!" Bethany snorted. "It takes at least ten.

"Bronwyn wasn't just planning a wedding." Lillian put things in perspective. "She was preparing for a marriage, a life with someone. This wasn't a high school crush."

Bethany pinched the corner off her sandwich and nibbled at the bread. "You're right. I'm just being selfish. I just miss her, ya know?"

Lillian nodded. "I do too. But it will take some time to get her back. She is suffering the progression of a shattered heart. There are three stages. Lillian felt the desire to share her expertise. "Stage one, extreme sadness, mingled with torrents of tears, and the consuming desire to convince the person who dumped you, that you can change and be who they want you to be. When those sincere efforts go unrewarded, stage two begins. This is the bitter and angry stage. The person who you once loved, you now hate. You burn all tokens of affection you treasured and held dear. You long for a casual encounter with the person just so you can act out your revenge and prove how intently you despise them. Soon, stage two gives way to stage three, the rebellious stage, which in my opinion, is the most dangerous of all. When a person rebels, they will do anything. They display desperate attempts for attention, go against all they have ever believed, justify an affair… the list goes on. It's a murky world then."

"Bronwyn's a smart girl." Bethany defended her best friend. "She's not desperate or dangerous. She has never been like everyone else. I think she'll be fine."

"Denying it doesn't make it any less true," Lillian was confident in her diagnosis. "As I see it, she's in the second stage, hate and bitterness. If we care for her, we can't let her get to stage three."

"Maybe." Beth admitted "but I think I know her better than anyone. I'm certain that time is all she needs and soon she will be her old self again, laughing, teasing, and ready for our next adventure. Who knows? Maybe she'll fall in love all over again."

"I hope you're right Beth," Lillian stirred her drink with the straw. "But right now, she seems like she might need a bit of intervention. All I'm saying is, since you are the closest to her, you need to look out for her. Sugar coating things won't help but neither will insults or forcing her to talk about things. Have patience with her and sometimes offer silence instead of advice so she can deal with her issues and get past them. We all love her and I for one will help you with this if you trust me. After all, I do have my degree in counseling, you know, even though I don't use it."

Bethany ran a finger through the condensation on her tea glass. Lillian could be right. She had noticed an unpleasant change in Bronwyn's personality, not to mention her latest bizarre suggestion that they were in some kind of danger.

The two finished lunch and decided to take a relaxing tour of Moonshine. Nell informed them of an enormous lake and scenic waterfalls. She recommended several nature trails that wound deep into the woods and mentioned stables where they could go horseback riding. She also informed them of the bakery and sweet shop, and an old-fashioned deli with a soda fountain that made the most amazing malts and shakes. She told them about the library and a small museum of Appalachian history.

With all these options, they decided to kill a few hours in town before heading back to the inn.

Seven

Canoe Rental. I read the sign posted in the window of the general store. It seemed to offer the perfect tranquil escape, just what I needed. It had been too long since I had experienced solitude. Bethany had been by my side ever since the breakup. Even now, at the inn, we were all three in the same room. I was in desperate need of some alone time, even if only for a couple of hours.

The tiny silver bells above the door jingled as I entered the store. The cool breeze from the much-overworked air conditioner pushed against my face. I hadn't noticed the intense heat and humidity of the day until now. I glanced around for a rental station. The market was quite large. A produce section filled with fresh fruit and vegetables took up over half of the store, reminding me of the farmers' markets I would frequent back home. A very small meat counter stood on the other side. The selections were quite limited, consisting only of fresh fish, caught in the local lake.

Carla Jo, accompanied by a couple of young girls, were ogling over the latest movie magazine. Not wanting the girls to see me. I chose an alternate aisle. I was in no mood to make small talk with Carla Jo, or anyone else. I'd already power-walked the entire way from the café to the market, while flashing forced smiles to all the people who offered me a greeting. I felt somewhat guilty for my rudeness; however, I justified my behavior today as self-preservation. It was not my intent to make new friendships right now. My stay here in Moonshine would be brief. What lifelong friendships could one possibly develop in ten short days?

After successfully eluding Carla Jo and her clan, I approached the bakery counter. A man wearing a white apron and a huge grin greeted me. He didn't offer me a hello, or how are you? His only greeting was an amusing antidote. I feigned a courteous laugh.

"I saw a sign that said you rent canoes?"

"Name's Gil." He gave me a toothy smile. "You sure picked a great day to go out on the lake. Tell you what," he tore a yellow ticket from a pad. "No charge today. This canoe ride is on the house as a welcome to Moonshine." My stone stature melted a bit. "That's not necessary, I can pay."

"I won't hear of it." His cheery voice rang out. "Save all your money for the festival." He pointed to a large sign hanging on the back wall. My eyes shifted to the beautifully painted banner.

Midsummer's Night's Cream
Moonshines Annual Ice Cream Festival
Saturday, August 16th

"Best ice cream in the whole world. All of it made right here by the amazing people of Moonshine. It's a magical night of dancing, games, and prizes. You and your friends will have the time of your lives." I took the yellow ticket from Gil.

"Thank you, I'm sure we will." I offered a half smile, realizing we would be in town for the event.

"You head on down to the lake hon," Gil said. "And I'll send Kevin on ahead to pull out a canoe for you." I placed the ticket in my back pocket and turned to leave when I nearly tripped over Carla Jo and her friends. All three were bouncing up and down, as if the whole floor were a trampoline.

"This is the lady who knows him!" Carla Jo squealed, clutching the magazine in her hand. Ryan's face was spread across the cover. I grabbed the headline.

"RYAN REESE... The Hero the World's been Waiting For!" I groaned. How stupid and naïve can people be? Did anyone realize he is not the hero he portrays in movies? Anyone could be a hero, if they quoted amazing lines that were written for them, had a stunt double to jump in and do all the dangerous work, and whose enemies were simply very nice people playing a role. Has the whole world gone mad?

"Tell us all about him, please!" one of the girls pleaded.

"Sorry to disappoint you, but he's a prick," I handed the magazine back to the devastated girls and left the store.

Just as Gil had said, I met Kevin, a shy young store clerk, who blushed the entire time he spoke with me. He'd already floated my canoe into the lake. He pointed out a small peninsula of trees jutting into the water, telling me to paddle that way and make the turn. "You'll be delighted with what you see." He promised.

He was right. The lake opened before me like a vast mirror reflecting the cloudless sky. Lofty trees and colossal mountains stood vigil, protecting this serene setting. Cedars, spruce, and fir trees of all kinds grew on the hillsides, releasing their sacred smell. Two bald eagles flew overhead, flapping their enormous wings before diving effortlessly and skimming just above the water. Both seized protesting, but defenseless fish and climbed back into the sky, disappearing across the hillside. I closed my eyes and took a deep breath, once again inhaling the invigorating aroma of the mountain and the warmth of the midday sun. I reveled in the quiet peacefulness of the place. There was no noise, save for the chatter of insects in the trees, an occasional splash from a jumping fish, and the chirping of birds. There was no traffic, no car alarms, no annoying cell phone ringtones, and no loud obnoxious conversations. I realized I'd not received a call in over twenty-four hours. I usually felt a strong irritation when I couldn't get a signal. Now, in this setting, I was quite thrilled that no one would be able to interrupt my solitude...not Bethany and her endless probing questions or Ryan and his annoying, blood thirsty attorneys. Positioning my paddle in the canoe, I laid back into the boat, enjoying the tranquility of this special place.

Eight

Falcon lowered his hood as he approached the hidden cabin. He removed the heavy cloak and flung it across the rocking chair on the front porch, raised his fist, and rapped softly on the door. It opened immediately. He took the last draw from his cigarette, crushing the butt underneath his bare foot before going inside. The others were already there. He didn't take a seat as they had. In fact, he hardly ever sat. It was his conviction to never allow himself to get too comfortable. Instead, he leaned against the wall and kept one eye focused outside the window.

"What do we know?" Mateo sat on the edge of his chair, waiting for a report. Travis nodded toward Falcon. "He searched their room while they were at breakfast. He can give you his report.

"The three of them live in California." Falcon took over, giving out pieces of information he gleaned while rummaging through their belongings. The blonde, Lillian, is an actress, the one named Bethany is a literary agent and the one using the name Bronwyn is an author...Seems like they were on their way to a mountain resort for a little vacation when they ended up here "Damn odd situation, if you ask me."

"She doesn't know?" Adam asked, breaking the hush in the room."

"It seems that way," Falcon shoved his hands in his pockets.

"And you have no idea where she has been all this time?" He asked another?

"No. It was my understanding that she was no longer with us." Travis swallowed.

"It doesn't add up." Mateo shook his head. "She would have had to be with him, all this time." A muscle arched in Travis' jaw as he gave a low snarl.

"No one knows where she's been, but it doesn't mean she was there." Falcon was quick to cut in.

Mateo huffed a laugh and shook his head. "Seems mighty suspicious."

"And you think she's trustworthy?" Jace Miles asked, curious as to what Travis thought.

Travis' lips formed a straight line as he eyed those in the meeting. "I have no reason to believe otherwise."

Collective sighs of unrest fell across the room. "But the prophecy states one will come, from Amadahy. Are we sure this is the fulfillment? Besides, there are three." Mateo wouldn't relent.

"What else could it be?" Falcon inched closer to the windowpane, keeping his focus outside. "The veil was torn last night. They breached the barrier. It wasn't an accident."

"No, it wasn't," Mateo agreed. "That's why there's a need for concern. There is only one power that could do that."

"Two powers." Travis snapped. "Two."

Mateo shook his head and looked at the council. The others were silent. No one spoke, each understood the severity of the situation. "Are you going to approach her?" He asked.

"No." Travis' answer carried ultimate authority. "The situation is much too delicate. Falcon and his men will continue to watch them. They are staying at the Inn, so Mavis and I have them under surveillance. Larry will keep delaying the repairs on the car until we know for sure. We've waited so long; a bit longer won't hurt."

"He's right," Falcon agreed. "Approaching her is not a good idea. It might set us way back, if not destroy everything. My men are investigating them. We should have more information soon. Our biggest concern is keeping Travis safe now that the door has been opened. The spies are infiltrating and more will come. Stay alert and be prepared to evacuate if necessary.

Nine

Moonshine proved to be a delightful experience for everyone. Lillian and Bethany had taken in the museum and learned some interesting trivia along with ancient Appalachian history. They checked out the local shopping, while looking for Bronwyn but couldn't find her in any of the quaint little boutiques. When Bethany suggested they check out one of the nature trails, Lillian quickly vetoed the idea. After remembering their walk into town, she had no desire to risk being mauled by wild animals.

Bethany found her way back to Larry's garage and spent the better part of the afternoon shadowing him to learn a few things about engines. Larry hadn't minded. He enjoyed the company, and Bethany was happy, having a chance to learn more about car repair from a ridiculously hot mechanic. Lillian found her way to the soda shop. She spent the afternoon in the air-conditioned store, treating herself to a thick creamy shake while reading a paperback novel she borrowed from the book rack.

It was now six o'clock and in keeping with Bethany's plan, Lillian met up with her at Larry's. Bethany advised that since they would be staying for a week, they should retrieve the rest of their luggage.

"So how are we getting all this to the inn?" Lillian asked, struggling with her suitcase as she pulled it behind her. "I'm quite certain I will not be able to roll this piece of luggage all the way back." Bethany agreed. It would be extremely difficult to drag their suitcases three miles down the narrow-crooked highway. Besides, they needed to bring Bronwyn's luggage to her as well. Remembering Travis' offer of a ride home, she suggested they look for him in town in the hope of hitching a ride back to the inn.

"All the bags are out except for Bronwyn's," Lillian announced, staring into the trunk at the remaining suitcase.

"I'm surprised we didn't run into her this afternoon." Bethany chewed her bottom lip as she pulled Bronwyn's luggage from the trunk. "It's a small place; I was sure we would see her somewhere." Lillian shrugged, "My guess is she walked back to the inn."

The wind began to pick up as Travis' truck rolled into Larry's garage. Carla Jo and Molly were sitting in the back, just as before.

"We need to get back to the Inn!" He barely put the truck in park before jumping from the vehicle. "There's another storm headed this way."

Bethany picked up the pace, dragging both bags as fast as she could. "Let's get moving Lil; I for one do not want to get pelted by rain and hail again tonight."

Scrambling, they began loading their luggage into the back of the truck. The wind began to increase as Travis slammed the tailgate shut. He glanced in the garage and then turned to the girls. "Where's Bronwyn?"

"Back at the inn, I hope." Bethany said.

"What do you mean, hope? You don't know?"

"She got upset at lunch and left the café. We haven't seen her since."

Travis let out a string of profanity as he slammed the door. Heavy raindrops began plopping on the windshield just as he pulled onto the road. The town had emptied out considerably, everyone taking cover from the impending storm. Bethany noticed him searching the streets, looking for Bronwyn as he drove. His deep concern aroused her curiosity and she wondered why he would search so intently for her. With the town now in their rear-view mirror, the truck picked up speed, racing toward

Sandalwood Inn. The dark trees lining the road swayed with the wind, giving everyone an ominous feeling of doom.

Ten

I sat up from my reclining position and stretched while releasing a fat yawn. My canoe was drifting lazily across the water. I wasn't sure how long I'd been asleep... or when I'd dozed off. The peaceful quietness of the lake, the warm sun on my body, and the gentle rocking of the canoe provided the hypnotic elements to induce me to sleep. It was exactly what I had needed, and I was thrilled that my nap had been peaceful, free of the dreams that had tormented me of late. Maybe instead of sleeping at the Inn I could camp out here, by the lake. It was an idea worth looking into. Retrieving the oar from the bottom of the vessel, I dipped it into the still, cool waters, and then gracefully and effortlessly guided the canoe to the dock. I should get back. Bethany and Lillian were probably wondering what happened to me.

A lone figure stood on the banks, waving to me, as I approached the shore. Shielding my eyes from the evening sun, I strained to see who had discovered my private escape. As I paddled closer to shore, a face came into focus...no, it couldn't be...no way...My heart leaped inside my chest, choking the voice from my throat. "Ryan?" What the hell was he doing in Moonshine?

I paddled closer, still not believing what I was seeing. No matter how much my mind wanted to deny what stood before me, my eyes didn't lie.

There he was, Ryan Reese, fixed on the shore, as if he had just walked off the cover of the magazine from the store. Right down to the silly grin plastered across his face. "Bronwyn!" he waved. I should have turned my boat around but instead I paddled close enough to the dock for him to grab the front and climb aboard. "Take me out on the water." His smile grew; so, without a thought, I paddled back onto the lake, all the while my mind was reeling with questions. "How did you find me?"

"You weren't answering my calls, so I did some investigating and found out where you were...and here I am." His arms stretched as wide as his grin.

The calmness of the afternoon suddenly shattered. Anxiety began rising within.

"You came all this way because of our script?" Anger seared within my voice.

"No babe." Still, he smiled. "I came because I heard about the baby."

I gasped. My mind searched for every possibility.

"How do you know about that? I never told anyone about the baby. Not Bethany, not even my mother."

He sat unmoved. The smile still plastered across his face. Feeling a bit of chill in the air, I noticed the sky growing dark. Fierce winds began to blow across the surface of the lake, making it difficult to maneuver the canoe.

"Ryan..." I struggled with my words, as well as with paddling.

"There is no baby. I lost it." His grin remained in place. "Good. I came to ask you to abort it, anyway."

I wanted to scream or at least whack him upside his head with my oar, but the swirling waters around the canoe sucked my attention. The wind accelerated, stirring up large waves that washed over the canoe's rails, pushing it further onto the lake. I struggled with making any headway as each wave tossed my oar back to the surface.

"Can you please help me?"

He shrugged. "You seem to be doing fine."

"No, I am not!" I yelled above the wind. "I could really use your help."

He shook his head. "You don't need me. You're the strongest woman I know. You'll survive this." With those final words, he dove into the swirling waters.

I gasped for air and sat up. Raindrops splashed on my face. I did a quick glance around the perimeter. No one was there. Ryan was gone, lost in the mist of sleep from which he came. So much for a peaceful rest. Still, I breathed a sigh of relief, grateful it was only a dream, but anger still gripped me. He'd once again invaded the peacefulness of my life, bringing immediate turmoil to my soul. I shivered at the thought of his manic smile.

The sky had grown unusually dark. That part of my nightmare was real. A chill fell in the air, triggering the wind to increase, bouncing the canoe about the water. I shivered at the sudden change of temperature. Only a few hours ago, the lake had been a peaceful paradise. The trees that before stood erect, pointing happily to the sapphire sky, now bent over, cowering in fear before the breath of the storm. The sky that had provided a playground for whippoorwills, warblers, larks, and water thrush was devoid of any chirruping. The vexed howl of the wind replaced their delightful songs. It seemed as if all nature cowered in fear of the arrival of some hideous creature. There was an overpowering feeling of doom, as if some foreboding secret, of which all of nature was aware, was being whispered across the expanse. I shivered uncontrollably from the iciness of the wind and the eeriness that penetrated my soul. My fear was deeper than being stuck out in the middle of a tumultuous lake in a thunderstorm. Rather it was a dark, menacing evil searching for me, ready to devour me. Thunder sounded in the distance, it was mocking menacing laughter, informing me I was done for, as smoky black clouds rolled violently across the sky.

I tried maneuvering the canoe to the dock. My muscles burned and my hands cramped from the tightness of my clutch. All efforts to slice the water ended in futility. The tumultuous waves continued to toss the oar to the surface, as if it were nothing more than a wooden spoon. Rain smacked the lake in a downpour. Heavy wind blew the torrential rain into my face making it impossible to see. My heart stampeded within my chest, an indication my circumstances were not good. Considering my situation, I guessed I was near the shore, yet with the increasing wind continuing to push my tiny canoe further into the lake, I was uncertain as to how close it was. I contemplated abandoning the boat altogether, and possibly swimming to shore. I was a decent swimmer and could perhaps move my body against the fierce waves, more easily than I could maneuver the canoe with a worthless paddle. However, as fatigued as I was, I feared running out of strength, and then having no place to rest. I decided it best to get as close to shore as possible, before taking the imminent plunge into the angry waters.

A streak of lightning zigzagged across the lake directly in front of me. My situation was growing dimmer by the second. I placed my arm across my forehead, shielding my eyes, to get a visual assessment of my distance from land.

My heart leaped with excitement. I was closer than I realized! Several trees were growing out of the water; many of their branches extended farther out over the lake. Tossing my oar aside, I reached out to grab a limb. My sudden movement, combined with the unevenness of the water and the overpowering waves, toppled my canoe, tossing me into the angry lake. The consuming water rushed over me, pushing me under the surface.

Disoriented, I emerged, trying to position myself toward the shore, while fighting the wind, waves and torrential downpour teaming up against me. I desperately needed a focal point. If only I could get a quick glimpse of the shoreline, I could swim there with all my might. I dared not waste my last bit of strength until I was certain of my bearings. Swimming in the wrong direction would cast me deeper into the lake, resulting in inevitable death. My legs burned beneath me. Exhaustion was setting in. I feared I couldn't tread the water much longer, yet certain if I stopped, I would surely be overtaken by the monstrous waves.

The sky was almost dark now; there was little light left. Dismal gray surrounded me on every side. I strained my eyes for one small glimpse of the shoreline. Just one glimmer of hope and I would exude every ounce of my strength to make it there.

Another bolt of lightning hit nearby. The flash provided just enough light to point my way to shore. My heart raced with excitement. With the last bit of strength, I forced my way, fighting against the powerful waters. Yet each wave that rose high above me pushed me back, keeping me from my destination.

I swam hard, determined that this would not be how my life would end! Thoughts of my friends and family receiving the dismal news of my death invaded my mind. I pondered how the news would affect Ryan and wondered if he would feel any remorse at all. More than likely, he would be delighted with my death, then he would be free to use the screenplay he was so desperately trying to steal from me. My simmering anger gave me an added bit of strength and new momentum. I tossed him from my mind. I would not allow him to be my last thought.

Another wave washed over me, filling my mouth with water. I coughed, strangled by the sudden rush of fluid. The rain's intensity increased, pouring over me along with the continual crashing waves. I was losing my last bit of strength at an alarming rate. Lowering my legs, I checked to see if I could touch the bottom. Nothing.

My heart ached. I wanted to cry. My strength was completely gone. My heart pounded so hard, marching from my chest directly into my throat, choking me, suffocating me. My heart pursed itself in desperate prayer as I prayed for help.

Feeling a small tap on my back, I whirled around. The canoe! Although it had capsized, it was amazingly still afloat! If I could manage to hang on to it, I might have a chance to drift to safety. Just as I reached for the canoe, an enormous wave pushed it toward me violently crashing into my head.

The sudden rush of pain devoured me. I gasped... all was growing dark and quiet. I felt my strength escape as my body went limp. With all my power ebbing away, I tried grabbing the canoe. My hand had no control to grip; it only slapped at the side of the boat before sliding down across the hull and into the water. All was dark, save for a bright piercing light that blinded my eyes, as the swirling waters took possession of my body.

There was no rain, no thunder, no howling wind, and no last thoughts, only a bright light followed by a quiet cold darkness.

Eleven

Mavis tossed dry, thirsty towels to the girls as they bolted for the door. "Dinner's in the kitchen when you're ready." Bethany caught the towel Mavis hurled her way and began to dry off.

"Is Bronwyn here?"

"Hadn't seen hide not hair of anyone all day."

Bethany dropped the towel from her face. "You mean she's not here?"

"Not unless she snuck in while I was out in the gardens. But I don't think so; with the kids gone, it's been quieter than a mouse around here."

Bethany did not wait for Mavis to finish before bolting up the staircase and into their room. It was the same as when they had left it earlier, except for Mavis' housekeeping. She pushed open the door to the adjoining bathroom. Empty!

"Bronwyn hasn't been back to the room," She announced halfway down the stairs.

"I don't think she's here, hon." Mavis said. "Like I told you, I hadn't seen hide nor hair of anyone all day."

Travis said nothing as he headed for the door. Bethany followed him. "If you're going after her, then I'm coming with you!"

"No, you'd do better staying put." Ordinarily she would insist on going but the authority in his voice caused her to back down and not argue.

"Take shelter if need be." Mavis' warning trailed him, as he left Bethany standing and headed out the door into the threatening storm.

He jumped into his truck and sped down the highway. He, if anyone, knew the dangers of this storm. It was angry, ready to take its vengeance. He also knew not taking immediate shelter was an invitation to death. However, the risk of staying put was too high. He had seen what the presence could do. He was powerless against the force. He could not stop it, but he would do all within his power to keep it from claiming another life; especially hers. The wind pushed hard against his truck, as if it sensed confrontation. He grasped the wheel; the chiseled muscles rippled beneath his taunt skin as he attempted to hold it on the road. The rain swept over his truck in sheets, blanketing his windshield, making it impossible for him to see even though the wipers were flicking back and forth at full speed. Straining his eyes, he looked through the blinding downpour. The sky was dark; the only light came from the forked light-ning that danced spitefully around his truck.

He turned for the lake, hating to think she might be on it during this incredible storm. Nevertheless, deep in the recesses of his soul he knew that was exactly where she was. He drove through town at full speed, before connecting to the secondary roads surrounding the water.

Storm clouds continued to boil, blocking out any light from the waning sun or rising moon. Reaching into the floorboard, he retrieved a powerful flood light and then lowered his window. The rain blew in, soaking him instantly. Holding the light, he scanned the lake. Nothing! He reduced his speed and continued his search, the beam of light, acting like a lighthouse tower on an angry sea, reflected off an object bouncing in the waters not far from shore. Leaning out his window, he aimed his light. It fell across the waters and landed on an abandoned, overturned canoe.

His heart sank. An overturned, drifting canoe was not good news. He practically jumped from his truck before placing it in park and ran down the bank to the lake, his feet slipping in the wet mud. Charging into the rushing waters, he made his way towards the bobbing canoe, all the while keeping his light aimed straight ahead.

His eyes caught sight of a hand, slowly sliding off the side of the boat, and disappearing into the dark lake. He hurled his light to shore and dove into the angry waters. Blindly, he searched but saw nothing. He dove further down and felt hair moving about his fingers. He wrapped his hand around the swirling tresses and yanked, pulling a body from its watery grave. With his other arm, he swiftly scooped her up and carried her to shore. He wasted no time searching for a pulse. Instead, he pulled her head back, and blew a few short puffs of air into her mouth. Her body jerked, as a geyser of water spewed from her lips.

Twelve

I lay on my side in the wet mud expelling lake water. The hard earth pressed against me was a welcome relief. How did I get here? Had I washed up on shore? I choked and threw up lake water mingled with what was left of the tuna and cucumber sandwiches. Rain continued to pound, flooding around me and I thought I might still drown even on dry land. I tried sitting up but all I could do was roll onto my back. Despite the blinding rain, I could see a form. My rescuer was kneeling in the mud, straddling me. Rain poured from his hair and off his jaw line onto my face. Relief flooded his dark eyes as I focused on him.

"We need to get out of here!" Travis yelled above the howling wind. "Can you make it to the truck?"

I looked over at the abandoned pickup, the headlights lighting the falling rain. With every second, the storm seemed to increase its intensity. Lightning flashed through the sky almost continuously now. Taking in a big breath of air, I gave him an affirmative nod.

He helped me to my feet, but my legs gave out almost instantly. With no time to waste, he scooped me up in his arms and ran up the slippery bank towards the truck. Kicking open the half-closed door, he threw me into the cab. The back tires spun in the wet ground, stirring up mud and debris, as he pulled back onto the road.

Summoning all the strength I could, I tried sliding my body over to give him enough room to drive but I couldn't budge any further than I was, so I leaned against his solid frame. In any other circumstance, I would never sit so close to a stranger, let alone a married man. But I had no strength to move. I was worn out and numb from the water that had long soaked through my clothes.

Lightning struck nearby, splitting a tree, and sending it into the road as if the strike had been intentional. Travis jerked the steering wheel barely dodging the falling trunk. I would've screamed if I had enough air in my lungs to do so. I'd never witnessed a storm of this magnitude. It was intense, yet for some strange reason, the fear I felt earlier was gone. Either I was too tired to panic, or perhaps, it was being in the company of this mysterious mountain man, who plucked my body from the swirling waters of death and was risking his own life to get me to safety.

He turned onto a narrow gravel road that disappeared behind a line of thick trees. It didn't seem as if we were headed back to the inn. But I couldn't tell for sure, being as disoriented as I was. The storm denied any visibility, and the headlights scarcely offered any guidance. Travis must have been driving off feel, off his knowledge of the terrain, which was quite impressive when he pulled into the driveway of a small rustic cabin. A warning siren blared, competing with exploding thunder as the pickup came to an abrupt stop. He grabbed my hand, dragging me from the cab as we dodged flying debris and bolted towards shelter.

He pushed open the door, the wind almost ripping it from its hinges. Wasting no time, he ran across the room, slung aside a heavy rug with his boot, and opened a trap door lying flat onto the floor. The opening gave way to a descending wooden staircase. Knowing my inability to maneuver the narrow stairs, he scooped me into his arms, and descended quickly. Reaching the bottom, he gently deposited me on a soft leather sofa, before climbing back up the stairs and securing the hatch. I sat in darkness until he turned on a small lamp, revealing a warm, cozy room.

The well-furnished basement seemed stocked for such an occasion. Other than the leather sofa I was soaking, there was an overstuffed armchair and a couple of end tables. Thick, warm rugs covered a wooden floor. A fireplace took over one wall and a small kitchenette the other. A bathroom lay at the far end of the basement. I shivered, wrapping my arms around myself to keep warm; as well as trying to stop my excessive trembling.

Travis noticed my shuddering. "I can build a fire."

"Thank you." My teeth chattered out the words. I wasn't sure if I was cold, or just traumatized.

Opening a large cedar chest, he removed some pieces of clothing, along with several soft, warm blankets. He handed me a T-shirt and a blanket and then pointed to the restroom. "You should get out of your wet clothes."

I took the offered items gratefully and disappeared into the restroom. Closing the door behind me, I flipped on the light and gasped at my reflection in the mirror. Blood poured from a gash above my right eye. My hair hung in wet tatters, and any makeup I had been wearing was gone. Mascara lingered around my eyes, creating a smoky sensuous look I usually wore only for a night out on the town. Combined with my pale face, the blood made me appear gothic and frightening.

My hands continued to tremble, slowing down my progress of peeling the wet, muddy clothes from my body. I took a quick shower, rinsing off the mud as best I could. I would have stayed longer, but I was waterlogged already, not to mention I was naked and alone with a stranger in a cabin basement far away from the girls. I toweled off and pulled the t-shirt over my head, careful not to stain the white fabric with the blood still oozing from my wound. The borrowed shirt was soft, with a comforting, musky smell of cedar and smoke. I placed my wet clothes over the shower railing to dry, wrapped the warm blanket around me and left the restroom.

Travis too had changed out of his wet clothes and removed the water from the sofa, giving me a dry place to rest. With a fluffy pillow and more blankets, he transformed the couch into a nice, warm bed. A small fire burned in the fireplace. He sat on the large, raised hearth with a small black leather case beside him.

The cabin creaked and moaned and even though we were several feet below the ground, I could still hear the storm raging outside.

He motioned for me to join him at the fireplace. On wobbling legs, I moved towards the large stone hearth and took a seat. He opened the leather case and removed gauze, various ointments, and medical tape. He dabbed at the blood on my face with a warm cloth, gently cleaning around the wound. He leaned in to inspect my injury, putting his face close to mine. I swallowed at the intimacy of the moment and was at a loss on where to focus my eyes. If I looked at him, I feared an immediate attraction or the peculiar heat sensation that had consumed me every time our eyes met. I had to admit, Bethany's observation of the man was quite accurate. He was undoubtedly the most beautiful man I had ever seen. His body matched his face in perfection, fit, hard, and muscular as if it had been carved from the mountain range itself. His silent demeanor added to his mysteriousness.

"You're trembling," he said quietly. "Are you alright?"

"Just a bit unnerved," I said. "I thought I was dying."

"You were." His words sunk deep into my soul as I realized the seriousness of the situation. I was drowning. I recalled the blinding light seconds before I sank beneath the cold, black darkness, and the sudden sensation of rain pounding on my face once again. This stranger whom I'd known less than twenty-four hours risked the dangers of the storm to save me.

"Why?" My thoughts became audible.

"Why, what?" He asked, as he opened a bottle of ointment.

"Why did you come looking for me?"

"Because you were missing."

I wasn't sure why, but the statement sent a wave of panic over me. The fear that taunted me at the lake unnerved me once again. *Missing.* He dipped a Q-tip in the ointment and dabbed it on the wound. The fragrance of the salve overpowered the fear, bringing me back to calm. "That smells very nice." He closed the ointment jar and folded a piece of gauze and then tore off strips of medical tape. "It's lavadin. It's a hybrid plant developed by crossing true lavender with spike lavender." He secured the gauze with one final piece of tape. "It's used for sterilizing. It's also known for its relaxing and calming effects." It worked. Leave it to this mountain man to doctor me up with some Native American plant poultice. He replaced the contents inside the leather case. "You should lie down and rest," he said, motioning to the bed he'd made a-top the sofa.

I was thankful for the suggestion. I relaxed on the smooth soft blankets and leaned against the comfortable pillows. As he walked past, I spontaneously reached for his hand, stopping him. "Thank you for saving me."

Travis looked at my hand lying across his wrist and then into my eyes. "It was my pleasure."

Thirteen

Mavis hobbled down the halls of the inn and knocked on the bedroom door while yelling over the warning sirens. "That siren means we go underground! To the basement. Now!"

Lillian bolted for the door, wide-eyed, but Bethany remained in the room. She pulled back the curtains from the window in a feeble attempt to peer outside. She hoped to see a returning Travis and Bronwyn. The sky was very dark, and the window was fogged over and wet. The only thing visible was the outline of bending trees that flashed into view each time the lightning zipped across the sky.

"Come on hon, let's get to moving." Mavis' voice carried across the room. Bethany knew she was right. She should be running for the safety of the basement along with Lillian, but she felt so guilty taking shelter when her best friend was unaccounted for and possibly out in this horrific storm.

Mavis walked up behind her. "She's a smart girl. I'm sure she's found shelter somewhere, and you'd best to do the same."

Hoping Mavis was right, Bethany let the curtain fall back in place and headed downstairs.

The inn's basement proved to be the most convenient place to ride out a storm. The room was designed for such an occasion, with bunk beds lining the far wall for Travis, Mavis, the kids, plus eight guests. There were two fully equipped restrooms with showers and tubs and a good-sized kitchen stocked with plenty of comfort food and drinks. Sofas and chairs provided rest, while bookcases filled with magazines, novels and various board games offered entertainment. There was also a large cabinet filled with first aid supplies, lanterns, kerosene, and matches.

Lillian was once again in tears, complaining terribly of the health and aging effects all the recent stress was having on her body. The wind howled overhead as the siren continued to blast. The inn creaked and moaned in protest. Thunder resounded with a deafening crash.

"Are we going to be alright?" Lillian asked, her voice quivering.

"You're in the safest place you can be," Mavis said.

"I pray Bronwyn is someplace just as safe," Bethany said hopefully.

"And Travis." Lillian added. "God protect him as well!"

Mavis smiled gratefully.

"I feel so freaking guilty," Bethany confessed. "If I had never criticized her writing, Bronwyn wouldn't have gone off alone. It's all my fault."

"No, it's mine," Lillian took the blame. "I should have insisted we go after her." "Then you both would be out in this," Mavis said. "Or we both would be here." Bethany's voice faded into her sadness.

A sudden explosion of thunder interrupted their conversation, rocking the foundation of the inn. The electricity went out, casting the basement into total darkness. "Shit!" Bethany reacted with a frightful scream and instantly apologized for her poor choice of words in front of the kids.

"No need for panic," Mavis's calm voice seemed to swallow the darkness. "We just lost the power is all. I'll light up a lantern."

The sound of a striking match penetrated the eeriness of the room as Mavis turned up the wick, giving light to the basement once again.

Fourteen

Travis lit the lantern and turned up the wick. The kerosene lamp gave more light to the basement than the small crackling fire could provide. The storm continued its relentless rampage outside, yet beneath ground level, in the shelter of the cabin basement, I began to relax. Travis had given me a steaming cup of tea and a bowl of piping hot soup. I only sipped at both, still a bit nauseous, being full of lake water. Travis settled down on the floor, his arms across his knees as he leaned against the overstuffed armchair that faced the sofa. My pulse quickened at the realization that I was stuck with him for a while and would have to make conversation or sit in a dimly lit basement in awkward silence. I could feign falling asleep but despite his rugged good looks, he was still a stranger, and we were alone in an underground room, so I needed to be on my guard.

He took a swallow of his tea. "What kind of books do you write?"

I didn't want to answer the question. I hated it when people asked. The response was always humiliating, taunting me every time. Romance novels were like soap operas, no one took them seriously. They were just brain candy. Yet, in all fairness my writing provided me with a living, and a good one at that, so why be ashamed?

"Well, presently, I write romance novels." I looked down, finding an interesting pattern to trace on my blanket. "But I hope to switch out of that genre one day. But for now, it pays the bills."

"What genre would you switch to?"

A bemused laugh escaped my mouth and the pattern on my blanket suddenly became very interesting. "I'm not sure what the genre is, exactly. If you asked me to tell you the story, I couldn't but I can feel it. I just don't know what it is. But it's real, you know." I quit focusing on the blanket and put my attention back on him. He was listening, nodding his head, as if he understood what I was saying. "I want to write about life, about living and the love that flows from that. I like romance but there's more to love than a romp in bed." I took a long sip of my tea, using my mug as a barrier to hide behind. I had no desire to look into his eyes with that thought in the room. It's what most men commented on once they found out. They expected me to be an expert in bed and all things sexual. "I want my stories to be life changing, the kind that sticks with you for years. The kind that makes you want to be a better person." I lowered my cup, still holding it between my palms. "It's there, somewhere in the far distance. I hope it will surface one day. I just haven't had the right inspiration I guess."

Travis stood and refilled our mugs. "Have you tried?"

I blew on the hot liquid. "I haven't written much of anything lately. Just sappy love stories."

"Writer's block?"

"To the nth degree."

He set his cup on the floor and gave me his full attention. "So, what's stopping you?"

I sipped my drink and let his question settle.

"I don't know. It all seems kind of useless, kind of...worthless in a way. I have a tough time writing about something I am not sure is there. I'm not certain heroes really exist. Not in the real world, anyway. In the real world, Sam would have betrayed Frodo and taken the ring for himself. In the real-world Jack would have hopped on the last lifeboat and let Rose go down with the Titanic."

The words had no more left my lips when I felt regret for what I'd said. How thoughtless could I be? He had just risked his life to save mine. He was a true hero and I'd just ignored that fact.

"Who let you down so much that you lost your faith in mankind?" His eyes bore into mine.

"I kind of got left at the altar." I picked at the blanket again. He was quiet and the silence was awkward, so as usual I tried filling it by spilling my story. "I met Ryan Reese two years ago, before he was famous. He and Lillian were cast in the same commercial. Lillian thought we would hit it off, so she introduced us. One evening, after watching a movie, we sat in a coffee shop critiquing the shallowness of the story and the predictability of its characters. He knew of my desire to write something more than romance junk, so we decided to write our own screenplay, the beginning of which was written on napkins.

The months that followed were thrilling. We created the story, developed the characters, and crafted amazing twists and plots. I thoroughly enjoyed our late-night writing capers. Whenever we experienced writer's block, we would venture out into the night, and find a run-down donut shop that stayed open until the wee hours of the morning. We would feast on sugary pastries and black coffee until an idea broke through. The night we completed the script, he suggested we celebrate by dressing up in our most elegant attire and treating ourselves to a nice dinner at an expensive restaurant. It was at the end of that dinner that he got on his knees, presented me with a ring, and proposed. We set the date and I began making wedding arrangements." I took another swallow of tea. It seemed more bitter than before, so I set it aside and stared into the fire. "It so happened that on the day I found the perfect wedding dress, Ryan's agent called with the news that one of his auditions had paid off. He landed a substantial role in a feature film. We were both thrilled for his good fortune, so we moved the wedding date back to accommodate his shooting schedule. The movie was an enormous success, skyrocketing him to instant fame. He was immediately signed to do the sequel. This time, the shooting took place in Australia. Again, I changed the wedding date."

Travis set his mug aside now and was leaning forward, listening closely.

"Ryan was gone for months, and his calls became scarce. I was faced daily with pictures of him and his co-star Gabriella Mendez, plastered on the cover of every magazine. Each article was accompanied by scandalous pictures that insinuated a steamy relationship. None of the articles mentioned his fiancé back home. I refused to read anymore. Besides, Ryan was never quoted in any of them. The reports were merely speculation, so I kept busy and continued with the wedding plans.

I decided to fly out and surprise him for his birthday. The visit was different than I'd envisioned. His schedule allowed us hardly any time together and as much as I hated to admit it, I sensed a noticeable distance from him. He introduced me as a friend instead of his fiancé. I forced myself to make it throughout the remainder of the week and was relieved when it was time to board the plane and return home. It was only a few days after I returned home that I received an email from him. His letter broke off our engagement... along with our relationship and my optimistic spirit. Anyway," I ended my long discourse, realizing I had told every detail of my personal life to a stranger. He probably didn't care to know it all, but he had listened as if he were genuinely interested. "I'm not even sure I can create amazing characters with virtuous attributes if I am not sure I possess them myself."

"Why do you say that?"

"Because everyone thinks my heart is broken over Ryan. And I let them."

Travis' mouth tightened along with his chest, yet he maintained a casual posture as he leaned against the hearth. His eyes narrowed asking for the explanation his mouth did not.

"I think I was using Ryan to fill the void inside of me. Writing the screenplay, planning a wedding, it took my mind off the strange longing in here." I touched my chest and sighed. "Don't get me wrong. I loved him, he was fun. But when he ended it, there was this part of me that was actually relieved. Hurt, betrayed, but a bit relieved."

He shook his head, knowing. His fingers raked the hair out of his face revealing more of those dark eyes. A soft smile pulled at the corners of his mouth but did not make it all the way to his eyes. They were still clouded in shadow. A loud roll of thunder shattered the silence and shook the ceiling as if nature were angry at what I had divulged. The eeriness I felt earlier tickled my spine and crowded in on me. The basement suddenly seemed isolated from the rest of the world. Like a trap I had stepped into and been ensnared. I shook and pulled the blanket even closer.

"You're shivering again." He stood and added another log to the fire. I shuddered from the inside and no added log or raging fire could warm the chill I felt within. I wasn't sure why I trembled. The raging storm outside offered no threat to me now that I was safe underground. I wasn't cold; the sofa and blankets offered enough warmth and a comfortable cocoon of safety. Travis certainly put me at ease. He was a kind and caring person, providing me with all the comforts I needed. Still, I shuddered and that frightened me. I reasoned that perhaps it could be some sort of post traumatic reaction due to my near-death experience. However, deep inside, I was conscious of a growing fear, a premonition of something that was soon to happen. I couldn't understand it. I could only sense it, but whatever the reason may be, I continued to shudder.

With each passing hour, the storm continued to build intensity. It was sometime past midnight, and I conceded to the fact that there would be no returning to the inn; at least not tonight.

Travis and I talked non-stop. He continued questioning me about my life. He was an excellent listener, never moving his eyes or attention away from me as I spoke. Most times, I would be the one to look away, especially when I was confessing an intimate part of my story that left me feeling a bit vulnerable. I would glance at my hands or find an interesting piece of lint on the blanket to pick, or stare into the flickering flame of the lantern. Whenever I returned my eyes back to his, I found him in rapt attention, his focus unwavering. Before realizing it, I'd poured out the entire story of my brief pregnancy and miscarriage, and the decision not to inform Ryan, when I surprised him in Australia, that I was carrying his baby. That's what the surprise trip had been about, yet

I couldn't bring myself to tell him, even after he had so coldly broken off our relationship. I confided to Travis of my fear in deciding to raise the child alone, and then the devastation of losing the baby after finally accepting the situation. The past couple of months had indeed been a roller coaster of emotion.

The fire in the fireplace burned down to a pile of glowing embers. The wick in the lantern was burning low as well. The light in the room was equivalent to the small flame of a lone candle, yet despite the dimness his eyes reflected the flicker, twinkling like stars in the night sky.

"I've never told anyone that story. Not my mother, not Bethany, no one." My confession was almost inaudible.

"Why do you choose to bear your burdens alone?"

I let out a soft laugh. "I choose to be strong." My voice grew louder. "It's a hard place to be though; when you're strong you tend to be alone."

"Is it strength or is it pride?" His accusing question took me off guard.

"Excuse me?"

"Pride secludes itself because it won't ask for help." The tone of his voice sounded more like a confession than an explanation. "Prideful people will not allow themselves to be vulnerable, nor will they let anyone know they're hurting. They're lonely because they refuse help. They want everyone to think they have it all under control."

"Sometimes you have to have it all under control, if only to save yourself the pain and disappointment of depending on someone who will only let you down," My words tinged with bitterness. He nodded in understanding and gave a smile that did not meet his eyes.

"So, tell me about Travis," I changed the subject from me to him. "You now know everything about me. Tell me your deepest secrets." I laughed.

His smile faded. "Not much to tell."

"I wouldn't say that. I think you're somewhat intriguing."

The smile returned, ever so slightly but it was there. "Intriguing? Are you sure?"

"Pretty sure. I don't really know you, but I have this gift, where I can read people pretty well."

I aroused his curiosity. "Read me then. What do you see?" He challenged.

I straightened up from my reclining position and leaned forward and gazed into his eyes. "I see wisdom, integrity..." I smiled, choosing my words carefully, playfully like a fortune teller looking into her crystal ball. "Oh, but there's some mischief, I see quite a bit of mischief..." He gave me a slight grin, but his eyes beckoned me, as if they were silently calling to me, inviting me. Like the song of the woman on the road last night. Her requiem drew me off the road and to something lurking beyond the tree line. His eyes were the unknown, the unfamiliar territory yet at the same time, they aroused a longing. I was lost in them plunging into those dark pools, seeing more than I expected to. My voice grew faint. "There are many secrets. You have repressed anger, and sorrow. There is an amazing amount of sorrow."

I was hypnotized by his stare. My head became dizzy as the strange heat sensation began again. Although I was sitting still, my heart began to beat as if I had just exuded an extreme effort of some kind, and I wondered if he noticed, or if he himself was feeling the same rush of heat. Our eyes stayed locked until a sudden clap of thunder broke my gaze.

The cabin was dark now, save for a few glowing embers from the fire. Travis lay on the floor, fully reclining on his back; his head propped on his arms, his eyes fixed on the ceiling. I lay on the couch and listened to the steady rain falling outside.

"Tell me about Mavis," I said quietly.

I had wanted to ask him that question for the past several hours, but for some reason could not drum up the courage. Now that we were in total darkness, it seemed easier to ask.

"What do you want to know?"

"How long have you two known each other?"

"Pretty much our entire lives."

"Really? Did you always like her?"

"No," He was matter of fact. "She was really quite a tease when we were younger." Although I laughed, I remained somewhat cautious. "What happened to her?"

Travis took a minute before he spoke and as much as I wanted the answer, a part of me wished I'd never asked the question.

"She was severely injured in a storm somewhat like this one. She didn't take cover soon enough."

"Do you love her?" I surprised myself by asking.

"Yes, I do."

There was silence, except for the popping and crackling of a few dying embers. I closed my eyes and began to doze of. "You're a good man Asa Colton," I said, yawning, drifting off to sleep.

⤬

Travis lay there a little while longer, his heart pounding with intensity while he stared at the ceiling. There was only one person who ever called him by his middle name, and he hadn't heard their voice in over six hundred years.

Fifteen

Falcon tossed aside the drenched cloak and made his way to the sink. He pushed the lever on the bottle, pumping out several squirts of creamy soap, and then scrubbed the blood from his hands. He grabbed a cloth from the cabinet and cleaned away the splatters that had sprayed onto his face. Leaning into the mirror, he examined the scar crudely cut beneath his left eye. It was his identity, his story, his proof of loyalty to those who might mistake his allegiance. He knew some of them doubted, but he didn't care. He knew where his faithfulness lay. He wouldn't waste time trying to prove his loyalties to those criticizers that constantly made assumptions about his motives. Besides, who were they to pass judgment? He was angry at them for losing track of her whereabouts earlier. How could she have slipped past them so easily? He had kept her in sight from the moment she stepped out of the car, following her as she walked into town, even watching the girls at the restaurant until he was summoned to a secret council. He hadn't thought twice about leaving since the entire town was watching them and would let him know if anything unexpected transpired. After the council meeting, the spies met him in the woods and notified him of new trespassers. He summoned his men and headed back into the forest; all the while expecting her to be closely watched.

The executions didn't take long. The men Abaddon was sending over were predictable which made him believe he was training them himself. Knowing Abaddon as well as he did, worked to his advantage, allowing him to calculate the men's moves with ease. After a quick kill he grouped the slain bodies together and wrote a single word across their foreheads before sending them back. A wicked grin spread across his face as he imagined the fury that would rise once the message was read.

He'd been warned not to live for revenge; nor, let the bitterness poison him, but for six-hundred years he had concentrated on nothing else but training for the day of promised retribution. He did consider his role in the matter vengeance and rightly so. He wasn't merely trying to get even with the one who wronged him, but he considered himself a warrior, and the way he saw it, warriors always ran into battle, fighting for a worthy and noble cause. This he would do. He would fight to set things right again no matter how many he must kill in the process. Even if the quest demanded his own life, he was ready to give it. Some said he was obsessed, and that his obsession over the matter had driven him insane, making him quite dangerous. He agreed in a way, there was a kind of madness inside him, pushing him, driving him, and since he was at a loss as to how to control it, he allowed it to control him.

He moved away from the mirror, ran his hands through his hair and secured it back in a ponytail before changing out of his clothes. Once dry, he lit up a cigarette, took a seat against the far back wall, placed his dagger across his leg, and took a long draw off his smoke. He would stay here the remainder of the night, riding out the storm. It was exactly where he should be, seeing as the lady scribe was below, in the basement, with Travis.

Sixteen

DAY TWO

I opened my eyes, confused as to my whereabouts. It only took a few seconds for my ordeal at the lake to resurface and remind me why I was alone in a dimly lit basement.

I sat up and glanced around the room. Travis was gone, and with no windows or outdoor light of any kind, there was no way to tell what time it was, or if the weather had improved.

Pushing the blanket away, I climbed from the couch, my muscles protesting with every move. Despite the pain, I decided to climb the cellar stairs to see what was waiting at the top, until I remembered I was only wearing a T-shirt and decided to get dressed instead.

An audible groan escaped my mouth as I glanced at my reflection. There was quite a bit of swelling and bruising around my eye where the canoe had rammed me in the head. The bandage was still intact; however, blood had seeped through the gauze and dried on my skin. Since there was nothing, I could do about it, I tried smoothing my curls with my hands since it had air dried a bushy mess, I laughed at the thought of what Lillian would say if she saw me, and for the first time, I wondered what they might be going through, not knowing where I was, or what had happened to me. For that matter, I wasn't sure how they had fared during the storm. Travis told me he dropped them all off safely, reassuring me that the inn had a protective shelter as well. He also told me Mavis would make sure they were all there and accounted for.

I reached for my clothes, only to discover they were still soaked. I couldn't bear the thought of putting them back on, so I left them in the bathroom and retrieved the soft blanket from the couch and wrapped it around my long naked legs, ascended the stairs, and climbed through the open trap door up into the main room.

We ran through the cabin so quickly last night; I hadn't noticed the furnishings. With sunlight streaming through the windows, the rustic cottage came alive with personality. Deep brown leather furniture offered comfortable seating. A massive stone fireplace covered an entire wall, and oddly enough, there were no animal heads of any kind hanging over the mantle. Instead, beautiful oil paintings of breathtaking scenery were the chosen decor. An antique desk sat in the far corner, holding a computer along with several potted plants. Noticing that the front door was slightly ajar, I pushed it open and stepped onto the large porch that was wrapped around the small cabin.

The fresh midmorning breeze swept across the lake and rushed upon the porch, gently kissing me on the cheek. I inhaled, taking in a deep breath of the invigorating air. Never had I been more thankful for a new day. The birds sang their glorious songs as they flew across the cloudless powder blue sky. All the pleasing scents and smells perfumed the day, as if the storm had never hit. Yet, the storm had indeed left its calling card. Broken branches and limbs had been ripped from their trunks and tossed about, littering the grounds. Debris floated in the lake, yards from the front door.

Travis was clearing away the fallen timber and placing it into a large pile. I wondered if this was every morning event for him. I watched him work, unnoticed. Again, he was shirtless, his sculpted chest corded with muscles. His shoulder length hair, already wet with perspiration and curling slightly with the moisture, hung in pieces over his face. If only Bethany could see him now. A slight smile curled on my lips. I could definitely write a steamy chapter on him. Travis hurled another broken branch into a pile of debris. I found myself envying Mavis. She was fortunate to have him. He had risked his own life in a storm to save a stranger; then had been so kind and caring, providing for my every comfort. He had remained a gentleman and kept his distance, sitting across the floor from me patiently, listening to all the ramblings that poured from my mouth. Not once did he turn the conversation to himself. That was unusual in the company I kept. My friends and acquaintances continually bragged about their income, their cars, their strengths, and talents, or how many people they had slept with. Not Travis.

A tinge of guilt began to manifest. He was married, yet I couldn't deny the feelings manifesting inside. I thought back to breakfast yesterday, avoiding conversation with him at all costs. Now, part of me wished the storm were still raging so we would be forced to spend more time together. But that was not the case. The sun was out and burning with intensity. I watched him hurl another branch into his growing pile of debris.

"Need some help?"

My words drew his attention from his task onto the porch. He wiped the sweat from his brow with his arm. "You're not dressed for it."

I shrugged and smiled. "My clothes are still wet." He removed his work gloves and headed for the front porch, while looking at the bandage over my eye.

"I need to change that."

I didn't follow him inside. Instead, I sat on the porch swing, pushing off with my feet, gently swinging back and forth. The scenery was breathtaking. The cabin faced one of the lake's many hidden coves. A small wooden dock stretched out over the water. Tree-covered hills encircled the area, giving it secluded privacy. The landscaping around the cabin was much like that of the inn, with varieties of flowering plants, vines and trees all emitting delightful aromas. Someone must take particular care of these grounds and for the first time, I wondered about the owner of this small cabin. Who was it? I hadn't thought of that until now.

He returned to the porch with the black leather case. He sat on the swing next to me and carefully removed the bandage. His hands gently swept back the hair falling across my face as he tenderly removed some of the leaves still entangling themselves in my messy locks. He caught my eye and smiled.

My throat tightened. Again, I wasn't sure where to fix my eyes. I gazed downward at his chest and noticed he wore a white stone pendant that hung from a silver chain around his neck. Deciding that staring at his naked chest was probably not the best place to fix my eyes, I shut them.

After removing the leaves, he began to gently clean the dried blood from around the wound.

"So," I said, trying to diffuse the awkwardness. "Whose cabin is this?"

"Mine," he reapplied the ointment. I opened my eyes, surprised.

"Yours? I thought you lived at the inn."

"I do."

"Oh," I closed them again before trying a little humor. "So, is this your vacation spot?" He unwrapped a new bandage and placed it on the wound.

"Thinking spot."

"Everyone needs one of those." I kept my eyes closed. He surveyed his work for a minute, studying my face much more than the bandage.

"Beautiful," he said.

Seventeen

Mavis hummed a mellow tune as she cracked open an egg, allowing the gooey substance to drop into the cast iron frying pan. She had risen early, leaving the confines of the basement for the kitchen, figuring her guests would be extremely hungry since the rush to safety had cost them their dinner. They had spent the entire night riding out the storm underground, snacking on popcorn, peanuts, crackers, and cookies.

The storm had been unusually severe; much like the one that hit the night before. It certainly wasn't one of those typical, relaxing thunderstorms that usually visited the mountains during mid-summer. Mavis was a bold spirited woman, but she feared these storms, feeling they had a distinct disposition, taking personal vengeance on someone or something. They arrived angry, sweeping through Moonshine like ghostly soldiers, riding their stallions, trampling anything and everyone in their path, looking for someone to kill. She hated them.

Bethany awoke and sat up fast, nearly bumping her head on the bunk directly above her. Looking around the basement, she noticed everyone was gone. Bronwyn! Perhaps she had returned, and everybody was above, listening to the story of her adventure. She jumped from bed and dashed

upstairs. Bursting into the kitchen, she eyed everyone at the table...
everyone but Bronwyn. Her heart sank. Lillian caught her eye and shook
her head sadly. Mavis continued to hum as she removed a pan of hot
biscuits from the oven.

"Did Travis come back last night?" Bethany asked.

"No honey, he didn't." Mavis dropped the hot biscuits in a cloth basket.
Bethany sighed, disappointed. "Did he call?"

"Phones are down again hon." Mavis took the basket to the table.
"Would you like a plate, dear?"

"No! This is crazy. I can't eat. Bronwyn's been missing for almost twenty-four hours. She could be...." Bethany stopped herself, not allowing the
words to be spoken.

"Hon there's no need to get yourself all worked up." Mavis' words
were soothing, consoling. "I'm sure she's fine, I'm sure they're both fine.
The people in this town all look out for each other. If something had
happened, there'd been someone on my porch early this morning to let
me know. In my experience, no news is good news."

Bethany wanted to believe her, but for some reason, her distrust suddenly grew. Travis' deep concern for Bronwyn's whereabouts unnerved
her. He was more than eager to go searching for her and refused to
allow her to accompany him. She had noticed Travis intently watching
Bronwyn more than once since their arrival. She neglected to mention it,
not wanting to alarm her friend, seeing Bronwyn had been going through
enough lately. She remembered Bronwyn's paranoid outburst at lunch
yesterday saying she saw someone following her.

Maybe she was right; maybe they all overlooked it, believing Lillian's
diagnosis of the progressions of a broken heart. A sick feeling hit her
stomach and she debated whether she should search for Bronwyn herself. She was certain Bronwyn would do the same for her. The lazy squeak
of the screen door interrupted her cascading thoughts.

Everyone in the kitchen let out collective gasps at the sight of me and Travis. The quietness of the morning erupted into laughter, applause, a loud "Hallelujah!" from Mavis, and delighted screams from the kids as they ran to hug Travis. An endless barrage of questions erupted from everyone's mouth at once. Lillian's voice overpowered them all.

"My God, I'm glad you're alright. I don't think I could have lived with the guilt."

"What happened to you?" Bethany gasped. "You look absolutely horrid!"

"Are you okay, honey?" Mavis asked.

Lillian hugged me lovingly. "You sure gave us all quite a scare."

"Girl, where were you all night? And where are your clothes?" Bethany asked, rather loudly. She stood frozen across the room, arms folded in front of her, relieved, yet angry.

"I'm in desperate need of a nice, long shower," I said, attempting to escape the onslaught of questions.

"Like hell you are!" Bethany said. "You stay out all night long, come walking through the door without your clothes, wearing nothing but a man's t-shirt, trying to hide your nakedness with a blanket. You owe us an explanation and it better be good!"

"Bethany!" Lillian tried to quiet her out of concern for Mavis, who had returned to the stove and continued to cook, her humming much livelier now.

"I went canoeing on the lake after I left the café. I fell asleep and didn't make it back to shore before the storm hit. My canoe capsized, hit me in the head and knocked me out." I pointed to my bandage.

"Travis found me just in time and pulled me from the water. The sirens went off, so we rode out the storm in town."

Lillian shook her head. "That's insane." She turned to Travis. "On behalf of both of us, thank you for saving our Bronwyn."

"My pleasure," he said, his eyes smiling at me. He crossed over to the stove and gave Mavis a quick kiss on her cheek before leaving the kitchen. I felt a bit of sadness as I watched him go. Feeling such a strong connection to him, I found myself wondering when I would have another opportunity to be near him. I quickly reprimanded myself. He was a married man, definitely off limits.

"Save you a plate hon?" Mavis asked. "Why don't you go take yourself a nice long bath. "I'll keep a plate hot for you."

I felt even guiltier. Mavis was so kind, offering me a warm breakfast, even after I'd been the cause of her husband risking his life in the terrible storm. Now I felt extremely selfish. My stubbornness, anger, and refusal to take constructive criticism nearly cost me and another innocent person our lives.

Nearly forty-five minutes later, I reluctantly pulled myself out of the water. I'd drawn myself a hot bath, adding in several of the elixirs from the welcome basket. Whatever these potions were, they brought complete relaxing comfort to my tired, aching muscles.

I toweled off and dressed in a clean pair of comfortable sweats and a tank. I was grateful to Bethany and Lillian for bringing my luggage back from the car.

Opening the door to the bathroom, I was surprised to see Bethany sprawled across the bed.

"Spill it sister!"

"Spill what?" I chose to be evasive. "I told everyone downstairs what happened."

"First of all, I am not everyone; I am your best friend. I get more than what you tell everyone. I get the uncut, uncensored version."

I began combing the knots from my freshly washed hair. "There is no uncensored version."

"Oh yes there is!" Bethany 's tone was a bit harsh, accusing. "I can see loads behind that smile you're attempting to suppress."

This time, I was pleased with Bethany's relentless prodding. I did feel a need to share the experience. It had been one of the most surreal, awkwardly romantic evenings of my life. I reasoned that if I talked things through, the feelings of a juvenile crush would subside.

I sat next to Bethany on the bed. "Alright, there is more. But I'm a bit ashamed to admit it."

"I knew it the moment you came in the kitchen door! Did you have sex with him?"

"Sh-sh-sh!" I glanced over my shoulder, making sure the door was closed.

"No, I didn't have sex with him! Good lord, Beth, he's a married man. We didn't even come close to that."

"Then why the guilt?"

I sighed. "Because I do have a slight, and I mean ever so slight, attraction to him."

"That's totally normal. It's some sort of damsel-in-distress syndrome. He gallantly rescued you, saved your life, and obviously doctored you up a bit. It's totally expected for you to feel close to him. Plus, it doesn't help that he is extremely handsome with a killer body."

I smiled. "It's not just his looks. We talked a lot last night, or at least I did. You know how I spill my guts when I get nervous..."

"Oh, no."

"Oh, yes. I was terrified of the storm, the sirens freaked me out, I was traumatized from nearly drowning, not to mention extremely tense because we were alone in a dimly lit basement."

"What basement? Where were you?"

"His place. He has a nice cabin on the lake. He said it was his thinking spot."

A cynical smirk crossed Bethany 's mouth. "More like his cheating spot."

"I don't know, Beth. He seems to have plenty of integrity if you ask me."

"All men cheat Bronwyn." Bethany's proclamation sounded bulletproof, certain.

I frowned at her assumptions and for a moment regretted confiding in her. This was how it had been lately, and why I had refused to divulge my feelings. Bethany couldn't listen without offering advice or her own perspective on the issue.

"Well, he kept his distance last night."

"Of course, he didn't try anything. You guys just met. But given time and the right circumstances he'll make his move. I saw the way he looked at you this morning." Bethany leaned back against the headboard, confident of her analysis. "So, what did you two talk about?"

"Like I said, I was pretty nervous, so I did most of the talking. I literally spilled my guts."

"No wonder he didn't try anything, you were pathetic."

I rolled my eyes, and then thought for a moment. "He was a good listener. He seemed genuinely interested in what I was saying. I told him all about Ryan and our breakup."

I stopped cold. I'd never confided to Bethany about the pregnancy, the lost child, or the fact I was relieved when we broke up. If Bethany knew I revealed this information to Travis and not her, she would be extremely hurt. Still, some things were easier to tell a stranger than a friend. I held the secret inside for almost three months, telling no one, not even Ryan. It had been quite therapeutic just to talk about it and get the emotion off my chest. I moved onward. "I told him about the screenplay we wrote, and how Ryan and his attorneys are harassing me to sign my rights over, so he can make the movie with Gabriella. I told him about my severe writer's block. He asked me a few questions and then deduced that I was cynical and a bit prideful."

Bethany grinned. "And you let him get away with that?"

"Well, it was storming outside. I couldn't just march away angry again, seeing that's what got me in my situation in the first place." I felt a little sheepish in my admission. "I sort of had to stay and take it. I kind of liked it, though. When he was talking to me, it felt as if he were looking into my soul."

"I knew it! He got in!"

I grinned slightly. "How so?"

Bethany sighed and grabbed my hand. "Because my dear naïve friend, the eyes are the window to the soul. If he got the chance to stare into your eyes long enough to see into your soul, then that means you two were entranced with each other and that you connected on a whole different level. This means you also got into each other's heads and hearts, for that matter. Pretty dangerous if you ask me. You're playing with fire."

I didn't want to admit it, but Bethany's evaluation was somehow impressive.

"There was this one moment..."

She leaned in closer, eager to hear.

"...when I was describing to him what kind of person, I read him to be. It was like I nailed it. Like I knew him, even though I didn't know him. Make sense?" Bethany nodded, wide-eyed. "Our eyes just locked in on each other. I don't think either one of us could pull away."

"I knew it!" Bethany said, nearly jumping off the bed. "So, what happened next?"

"It thundered really loud, I jumped, and the moment was lost."

"Be careful Bronwyn." She warned. "It won't be long now before he makes his move." I shook my head. "You're wrong. He loves Mavis. He told me so."

"I'm sure he does," Bethany said dryly. "All men love their wives, but given the right situation, they all cheat. Be careful, my friend. I don't trust him."

I shrugged. "Well, I do." I made my way back into the bathroom and continued combing out my very tangled hair.

I didn't realize how late I'd slept in. By the time Travis drove me back to the inn, and I'd cleaned up and endured Bethany's interrogation, most of the morning had passed. Now it was well into the afternoon, clean and in fresh clothes, I decided to explore the grounds of the inn.

A beautiful stone driveway led up to the main entrance. A large porch surrounded the entire inn, offering cushioned rocking chairs, comfortable swings, and a breathtaking view on all sides. The front of the inn was beautifully landscaped, with cottonwood, dogwoods, and magnolias lining the driveway, among others.

A peaceful river cut through the west side, with a wooden deck built over the waters. Large oak trees lined the banks; one offered a hefty branch with a thick rope to swing into the peaceful relaxing waters. Mammoth natural rocks lined the banks of the river, with a few covering the bottom, allowing the slow-moving river to wash gently over them.

The east side of the property was the site of a rather large garage that housed Travis' truck. Sitting behind the garage were three similar sized buildings, each mimicking the Inn's outer décor.

Directly behind the inn, small cobblestone paths led to a variety of gardens, each unique, each a particularly therapeutic destination unto themselves. I was intent on exploring everyone. A hedge or tall wooden fence surrounded all the gardens enclosing each one in privacy. I entered the first beneath an archway covered with hanging vines and took in the sights and scents. Once again, the relaxing perfume of lavender permeated the air. Numerous large trees offered ample shade, and a few provided a woven hammock. I followed the path to the center, where an exquisite fountain stood. Water trickled from the top, flowing quietly into a pool-sized basin. A couple of bathing birds took flight. A small table and two rustic bamboo chairs sat nearby. A fresh linen tablecloth covered the top, along with pitchers of iced water and lemonade. Empty glasses sat upside down on the table, awaiting their thirsty visitors. Mavis' many efforts to provide her guests as much comfort as possible really showed. I almost stopped to lay in one of the hammocks, sip icy lemonade, and wait for inspiration to strike. Nevertheless, I knew this was only the first garden; I desired to explore as many as possible before sundown.

All the paths I followed led to exquisite findings. Some gardens offered sweet floral scents; others offered earthy aromas of pine spruce cedar, mint, and refreshing eucalyptus. Each carried some type of relaxing noise, whether the trickling sound of a waterfall or the melodious sounds of various wind chimes, playing their tune in the gentle breeze. A couple of gardens were home to beautiful natural ponds, complete with jumping fish, frogs sunning on lily pads, and an occasional lazy turtle sleeping on a rock.

I enjoyed every garden, not able to decide which was my favorite. After walking at least three or four miles, I was surprised I didn't feel the least bit tired. Instead, I felt a renewed vigor with each garden I entered. My tender muscles no longer ached; the warm sun caressed me with a gentle massage.

I approached the end of the cobblestone path and the last garden, surrounded by a towering wooden fence. It was also the only garden without a gate. Instead, a colossal wooden door barred the entrance. Into its center, the letters BJC were elaborately carved. There was a brass knob on the door with an old-fashioned keyhole directly beneath it. I turned the handle. The door was locked, forbidding entrance to this secret garden. Stooping down I placed my eye over the small opening and peaked inside. Rays from the setting sun broke through the many vines and ferns, shading a tiny moss path, disappearing into a grove of thick trees. My sneak peek revealed nothing. Disappointed, I stood to leave but voices on the path motivated me to stay. Peering through the keyhole I saw two figures come into view.

My throat tightened when I recognized one of them as the smoking man from the café. He was walking alongside Travis. The two were engaged in a conversation but I was too far away to hear anything they were saying. The men came closer then stopped on the path to finish their discussion. I strained my ear, trying to pick up a word or two. However, they spoke in hushed voices and in what seemed to be an unfamiliar language... perhaps a lost dialect used by the mountain people.

My heart seized as the smoking man unexpectedly reached over and grabbed a black cloak clinging to a large rock. He put it on, pulling the hood over his head. My heart fell. Travis had lied to me. He did know of the cloaked figure! My head began to swim. What was going on in this town? Why were they stalking us or better yet, what were they protecting? The smoking man swiftly disappeared into the trees and Travis walked toward the entrance.

Regaining my composure, I quickly retreated, bolting down the path and entering another garden so he would not catch me eavesdropping. I waited just inside the gate, my heart pounding. Hearing his footsteps, I held my breath until he passed, then, leaning my head outside the gate, I watched as he disappeared down the path towards the inn. I sighed but the anxiousness did not leave; and once again I feared for my safety as well as that of the girls. Since Travis knew of the cloaked man, was he an accomplice to his murderous intentions? I argued with my thoughts.

I had an unexplainable trust for Travis. After all, he had risked his life to save mine, and had been more than a gentleman during the entire night. I had looked deep into his dark eyes and evil did not dwell there. Still, there was something secretive at play in this town and I thought it best to be on my guard.

The garden began to lose light as the sun sank lower in the evening sky. Mavis would be serving dinner soon; however, my appetite was gone. Realizing that Travis was more than likely at the inn by now, I ventured out of the garden, all the while unaware of the cloaked figure walking only a few feet behind me.

Eighteen

After a delicious evening meal, I followed Bethany to the inn's library for what she considered a much-needed conversation concerning my latest novel. Although we were technically supposed to be on a healing retreat, things hadn't gone quite as planned and there were deadlines with the publisher and matters that needed to be dealt with.

I pulled up a chair, and cozied up to the small desk, where Bethany was reading over some of my latest chapters. The desk lamp emitted a golden glow reflecting off the polished wood and lighting my manuscript. Bethany's pen was bleeding across the pages as she circled paragraphs, underlined words, and marked out complete sentences, all while scribbling notes in the margins. I was growing more defeated by the second. We had been discussing this book most of the summer. I felt a sick feeling in the pit of my stomach each time I was asked to fix the narrative. Bethany was right. The story was shallow and hollow. I couldn't argue the fact. This was not the kind of material I wanted to produce. I was ashamed and wished my name was not attached. I was relieved Travis had not followed us into the library. Despite my new-found suspicion of him, he struck me as such a deep, insightful, man. I didn't want him thinking of me as superficial and trite because of the ridiculous story birthed from my pen. I hoped he would stay away, knowing that if he did come in, Bethany would no doubt hand him the manuscript and ask his opinion just to drum up conversation. My stomach turned at the thought.

Bethany picked up the papers and read aloud. "Aspen gracefully stormed onto the alcove, approaching Trent. Why me? she demanded. Her chest heaving with the words. You can have your choice of any woman. Why did you choose me? I need to know!

How can you ask me such a question? Look at you," Bethany changed her voice from the melodramatic damsel to the dashing hero Trent. Her tone indicated the absurdity of what she was reading. "Trent's voice rode on its gallantry as he gently turned Aspen's face to the mirror. You see your reflection and still you ask?

Aspen stared at her likeness. Her blood red lips melted into a swollen pout. But one day, this reflection will be a small resemblance of what you see now. Time will take its vengeance and then what? Can you love what is left?

My love... Trent swept Aspen into his arms, pressing her against his form. Are you asking me if I love you only because of your beauty? Do you not realize, you are beautiful to me because I love you?" Exasperation framed Bethany's face as she read the line. "What are you trying to communicate here?" she approached the subject delicately, not wanting to offend me again.

I closed my eyes for a minute. I had no idea and to be honest, I really didn't care. "I want to emphasize the point that beauty, true beauty, is in the eye of the beholder. She asks him if he would still love her if she wasn't beautiful, and he is attempting to let her know that no matter how she looks, she will always be beautiful to him because he loves her." I paused for a moment; my eyes still shut. "His love for her only allows him to see her as beautiful."

I opened my eyes to see if there was a glimmer of understanding. Instead of seeing Bethany, my eyes fell on Travis, leaning on the back wall, arms folded across his chest. My stomach turned; my face burned. How long had he been standing there? What had he heard?

"It doesn't work Bronwyn because you've written Aspen as this beautiful ethereal goddess. Any man would love her. But if she were flawed in some way, the dialogue would have more meaning."

I desperately wanted to flaw Bethany's appearance for stating the obvious and calling attention to my poor writing in front of Travis, yet I knew she was right.

"Can you fix it?" She asked. Make her have an accident, or have a witch cast a deforming spell on her for a while. You can make her beautiful again in the end for your happily ever after. We just need to see if Trent's love is deeper than her appearance.

I wasn't sure I could fix it. Any other time, I would have answered with assurance. However, my inspiration for writing had abandoned me. It would be difficult to fix without introducing another plot and more characters. Nevertheless, I assured Bethany that I would work on a rewrite. Travis left the room.

Gathering my manuscript, I was ready to head back to the room when Bethany touched my hand indicating there was more to the meeting than I realized.

"Before you go, I have something else I want to talk to you about." I held my breath. Bethany was speaking with her agent voice, and I hoped my publisher wasn't thinking of dropping me. My last novella hadn't been any better than this one and sales had plummeted.

"The fact of the matter is you are a very gifted writer." She began. My heart fell. Starting with a compliment meant she had bad news to deliver next.

"I have always admired your work. Everyone at the publishing house is aware that you are experiencing some sort of writer's block, as well as a personal emotional struggle. So here is some friendly advice from your best friend, who cares deeply for you, and, also, your agent who knows a good business deal when she sees one."

I tried to swallow my sigh. It had been a long day and until now I had avoided Bethany's attempts to fix me. She was smart, working her schemes through being my agent as well as my best friend. Now I was stuck with a lecture I couldn't avoid.

"I'm referring to the screenplay you co-wrote with Ryan," she said.

"I don't want to talk about that." I drew a line.

"I am aware you don't want to sign your rights over for personal reasons. But think of the notoriety if you did; the prestige it would offer you. and it would obviously be a blockbuster hit, with Ryan and Gabriella playing the leads. Talk about a confidence booster."

At the mention of their names, I bolted upright and headed for the door.

"I said I didn't want to discuss this!"

"There you go again, stomping off like a spoiled child, not willing to listen to any advice. Just like you did yesterday, when you nearly got yourself killed, not to mention someone else."

Her harsh words stopped me in my tracks. Despite my anger at her interference, I had to admit she was right. I had developed a bad habit of running away when I grew uncomfortable with a situation or conversation. I turned back and slid into my chair. "I believe the best remedy for that is a little confidence booster. I'm listening." I said with a frosty voice.

"I care about you Bronwyn. And I certainly care about your future as an author. The notoriety would be great for you, as well as the Publishing house. Not to mention the money."

"So, is this what this whole conversation is really about? Money? Are you not making enough off me Bethany?" She ignored the insult. "Money is important. Not to mention necessary. Just think you could branch out and write for TV and film."

I sighed. "It's never been a dream of mine to write screenplays. That was a one-time thing, between Ryan and me. This whole thing is between us, no one else. This isn't just a script. It's personal and represents our time together. That is something I cherish. I cannot and will not put a price tag on that."

"Well, he obviously isn't as sentimental about it as you are." Her words stung. "I think you're upset that he wants Gabriella to star in it with him. You're letting him win by crippling yourself."

I took a deep cleansing breath and waited for my anger to subside before lashing out and saying something I would regret. "I'm not selling the script. Please never talk to me about it again."

"Alright." She sighed and gave a slight eye roll before following me upstairs. I did understand what she was trying to do, but I don't think she truly understood my pain.

Lillian was in the room dressed in shorts and a T-shirt. "Hurry and change clothes," she laced her shoe. "Travis is taking us on a moonlit hike to the waterfalls."

"He is?" my suspicion rose, remembering his private meeting with the cloaked smoking man. Perhaps they had been planning something devious that was soon to play out.

"I don't know. It's dark. Might be dangerous. Maybe we should stay here." Bethany glanced up at me, shocked. "You're serious?"

"I'm just remembering the wild animals, you know, bears feed at night."

"Oh, come on, please." Bethany released a sarcastic laugh. "Travis wouldn't have asked us to go if he thought we would be bear food."

"Hurry and put your swimsuit on." Lillian was giddy. "He said the falls are breathtaking."

My heart raced at the mention of his name. I reminded myself that he was married, not to mention the lack of trust I now held toward him. The offer was inviting despite my suspicions. The thought of a night hike to the waterfalls did seem thrilling. Sundown was my favorite, along with dusk. The heat of the day would lessen, the first star of the evening would appear, and the moon would enter the night sky in fullest brilliance. I loved the moon whether it was full or waning. There was always something peaceful about it, not to mention romantic... There I went again, obsessing over Travis.

I changed my clothes and joined Bethany and Lillian on the back porch, along with. Travis who was relaxing against the railing. Carla Jo was also there. Her presence eased my mind, dispelling any suspicion of malice. Surely Travis would not bring a child along on a night massacre. Mavis decided to stay behind with Molly, choosing to do their hiking in the light of day. Travis aimed his attention at me as I stepped out onto the porch. A smile turned the corner of his mouth. "Let's go."

"Shouldn't we take some flashlights?" Lillian asked concerned.

"The moon is brilliant tonight," he dismissed her suggestion. "You won't need them."

He led the way, skirting past the west side of the inn towards the river. We trailed him while laughing and talking. Carla Jo giggled thrilled to be coming along. We reached the river's edge, passing the small dock and grassy picnic area. Travis led us a bit further down the riverbank then stepped onto a narrow path that disappeared into the thick woods bordering the property. We were now forced to walk two by two down the dirt trail. Travis and Carla Jo led, and Bethany and Lillian fell directly behind them. I was left to bring up the rear. For some time, we wound in and out of the dense trees and down the sides of the riverbank. The river snaked deep inside the forest. At times, the path would be blanketed in total darkness, as the light from the moon was unable to penetrate through the thick foliage of the trees. The blackness became so thick, I could feel it. I placed my hand in front of my face. It was barely visible.

"This is why I wanted to bring a flashlight," Lillian whined, her nervous voice ringing out. The pace slowed as our confidence diminished. Within seconds, the path wound into a partial clearing, moonlight flooding the area. Each time, the light appeared more splendid in contrast to the utter darkness that preceded it. Sighs and gleeful laughter often escaped our mouths, only to be silenced by the path, as it again wound into total darkness. This pattern continued for most of the hike.

The last part of the walk took place in the shadows; it seemed to last much longer than usual. The chatter diminished altogether, and I sensed anxiousness within the girls. There was a noticeable air of uncertainty as the path narrowed even more, splitting up hiking partners forcing everyone to walk single file.

"Everyone grab a hand and stay close," Travis instructed. He took Carla Jo's hand, who took Lillian's, who grabbed Bethany's, who took mine. I desperately wanted to reach back and take Ryan's, but again, there was nothing but emptiness behind me. I walked along in total darkness, clutching tightly to Bethany. The woods were alive with chirping crickets, croaking frogs, an occasional hooting owl, and the lonesome howl of a coyote. The soothing sounds of nature being constantly interrupted by the whining cries of Lillian.

"You still with me?" Bethany whispered.

"Whose hand do you think you're holding?"

"Just making sure. I'm not certain what we've gotten ourselves into."

I heard the apprehension in her voice and admitted to feeling little like a sheep being led to slaughter. My thoughts traveled back to when I stumbled upon Travis and the cloaked man in the garden. What if they had met to plan out tonight's massacre? What if Travis was leading us to a hidden place, where a coven of knife-wielding hooded figures surrounded us and sacrificed us to some strange cult god of the mountains? But if that was the case, why bring along his little girl? The thought offered small consolation, but not enough. I reprimanded my vivid imagination. Maybe I should try my hand at suspense thrillers or horror. The darkness was now almost unbearable. I stiffened at a presence behind me that sent a shiver up my spine. I glanced over my shoulder into the thick blackness. My eyes could not focus on anything, yet I knew something was moving quietly along behind me. I inhaled the familiar scent that clings to the clothes of smokers, the stale aroma of cigarettes overpowering the pine and spruce. The cloaked man was nearby; I was sure of it. Uneasiness overpowered me. I expected to feel the cold blade of a knife dig into my flesh at any moment. I glanced behind me again. There was nothing but total darkness.

Lillian broke the silence, "How much further?"

"Almost there!" Carla Jo's cheerful voice answered from up front. Something in Carla Jo's gleeful response put everyone at rest. I envisioned Travis taking Carla Jo and the kids on many a moonlight hike. There was something quite comforting in the thought, dispelling my visions of Travis leading us on some psychotic slaughter. And then, my ears picked up on the sound of rushing water. "You hear that?"

"Hear what?' Bethany panicked.

"A waterfall."

No sooner had I mentioned the word than we reached a large clearing. The suppressed moonlight was released, illuminating the stunning view that lay before us. We all three stood in silence, gasping in awe. Lying directly before us was a picturesque scene that appeared to be birthed from a wondrous fairy tale. A dark turquoise pool of water lay at the base of three impressive waterfalls, reflecting the silver glow of the moon. On both sides of the waterfalls were two of nature's magnificent staircases made of rock, which led up to the top of the fifty-five-foot falls. The moss clinging to the rocks gave an iridescent green glow, giving the falls a fantastical look. Cobalt blue waters gently poured over them, emptying into the giant pool below. Steam and fog rose from the hot spring. The watery paradise was enclosed by tall black mountains silhouetted against the dark cobalt expanse. Seemingly millions of stars dotted the night sky, surrounding the full moon.

I stepped forward, speechless, my heart totally drawn to this magnificent place. A strange feeling invaded me as if I'd been here before. That, however, was impossible for I would have remembered such a place yet there was a strange familiarity, as if I had recently run into a long-lost friend or like a child at home in her own backyard.

Carla Jo was the first to remove her outer clothing and jump into the balmy waters. Travis peeled off his shirt and dove in, much to Bethany's delight as she flashed me her raised brows. A few others from the town were taking an evening swim as well. There were several handsome men, all with great physiques much like Travis. They appeared to be his friends and welcomed us with smiles. The cloaked man was not among them, and I saw no knives or threat of any kind. Just kind mountain folk enjoying nature. It took only one request from a blonde, green eyed gorgeous man, inviting them in for Lillian and Beth to peel off their clothing and jump eagerly into the water. I had no desire to join. I'd had my fill of water in the lake. Totally oblivious to the others who were frolicking in the pool, I decided to climb the glowing rocky staircase to the top of the falls. The moon's reflection off the water spotlighted a perfect path for me to follow.

All the fears and apprehensions that had manifested during the hike were gone. The excitement of exploring, accompanied by the unparalleled beauty of the place, erased all suspicion from my mind. The stony staircase led in and out of the trees, spiraling away from the falls and then back into view. The closer I came to the cascading water, the louder the roar, until the sounds of laughter and merriment were totally overpowered by the rushing waters. A fine mist sprayed my face. I didn't mind, the brisk walk had caused me to work up quite a bit of perspiration. The blowing spray came as a welcome relief.

The higher I climbed I was forced to crouch down and grasp sturdy boulders, as well as deeply rooted trees. I considered each step as I continued to climb with extreme caution. My path wound into a view of the falls one last time. Balancing myself, I turned and looked behind me. I'd ascended much higher than I realized. My friends were dwarfed by the loftiness of the falls. I thought that maybe I should have told someone where I was going, but the roar of the falling water was so deafening that they would never be able to hear me, no matter how loud I yelled. They seemed to be having fun and I figured I could climb to the top and return before anyone noticed I was missing. My overworked muscles burned, still sore from yesterday's bout with death. A few more feet, and I found myself at the top of the gargantuan falls.

I stepped onto the level ground. The scene before me was more spectacular than the one I'd witnessed below. It was surreal, like nothing I'd ever experienced, and it seemed as if I could hear the instruments of an unseen orchestra, playing an anthem of majestic music, swelling to a crescendo as I reached the top. The feeling tore into my heart causing inexplicable emotion and for a reason I couldn't explain, I began to cry.

The moon faced me directly and seemingly took up the entire sky. I had never seen it so enormous. There was little room left for anything else. The water lay still before me as if I were standing on glass. There were no trees, no towering mountains, nothing blocking this midnight canvas...only moon, stars and still waters. I stood frozen, with my eyes locked on the grandeur. All was quiet, save for the gentle melody of a pan flute playing in the unseen orchestra. Its soulful tune called to me, and I felt as if I were literally standing in the heavens.

I stepped forward; the tears continued to flood my eyes as my heart ached. My soul could hear a song, a tender voice of a woman singing a haunting melody. The language was unknown to me yet, strangely familiar. Each phrase, each note entranced me, calling as it did just two nights before. I felt as if my feet would leave the ground at any moment, allowing me to take flight, soaring past the moon, amongst the stars, flying with no regrets, no fear, no disappointments, only laughter and peace.

My legs began to tremble uncontrollably, and I found it impossible to remain standing. Giving into the weakness, I sat down and allowed the water to gently wash over me. It seemed as if it was cleaning away my past and washing away the broken dreams, along with the ugly bitterness of disappointment. It was as if I were being reborn in some way. I rested on my hands, and leaned my head back, drinking in the euphoric feeling. For the first time in my life, I felt true inspiration, as if my great story was climbing its way out of the rubble of my life where it lay buried. My heart raced, the heat sensation started again in the soles of my feet and rose upward through the rest of my body. It was much more intense than before. The feeling was so rapturous that it became frightening. There was an instinct to run as far away from this place as I could, yet an inner urge to remain close to this spot and never leave. The heat within continued to rise, the two opposing feelings began to wage a war inside me.

"What is this?" I whispered softly as my mind began to scramble. Good thoughts gave way to darker thoughts, evil and disturbing thoughts... terrifying thoughts. Then, just as suddenly, they snapped back to good, pleasant, and virtuous thoughts. my heart continued to pound, stampeding against my chest. I could hear it in my ears, count the beats as they hammered like thunder. The heat continued to rise, and I trembled uncontrollably. I wanted to scream, yet there was no air, no voice. Never in my life had I felt such terror mingled with peace. Opposing forces were fighting over me. Fear and darkness begin to overpower. It was strong, convincing, enticing. Its presence overshadowing to the point where I could almost see the invisible manifest itself before me. Terror and dread overwhelmed me as I saw a horrific shadow approaching.

"Enjoying the view?" Travis spoke from behind me. At the sound of his voice, the shadow dissipated and took with it the extreme distress. Relieved, I wanted to turn and face him, but my weakened state would not allow it. I tried to answer him, only to realize my voice was gone. All I could do was nod.

He studied me for a moment and then sat down in the water directly in front of me. His expression was stone cold, and I wondered what he saw as he looked into my eyes. Maybe my face had become paralyzed on one side, the exertion of the climb too much. This would explain why I couldn't open my mouth.

"Can you speak to me?" His voice seemed far away.

I opened my mouth; however, words would not come. I was only able to communicate a small shrug of uncertainty. He moved in closer, positioning his body between me and the moon. He gently brushed my hair out of my eyes and as he did his hand fell slowly, stroking my cheek. I swallowed hard as heat rushed into my face, the intimacy of the moment catching me off guard. He let his hand fall slowly down my neck as he continued to stare into my eyes. He reached into the shallow water and tenderly lifted my trembling hands. He clasped his strong palms over mine and looked directly into my eyes as he placed my left hand over his heart so I could feel the steady rhythm of his pulse.

"Shut your eyes and keep them closed. You will want to open them but don't. Do not open them until I tell you."

I obeyed and closed my eyes; deciding it might be in my best interest to trust him. My hand sensed the slow steady rhythm of his pulse beating against his wet sculpted chest. With every beat, his skin warmed until it was almost too hot to touch. A bright light shone against my closed lids, the warmth of it burning my face. My instinct was to pull free and open my eyes to see what was transpiring in front of me. He anticipated my reaction and gripped my hand tighter against his chest and whispered a solid "no."

My pulse resumed to a natural rhythm, my hands calmed, and my voice entered my throat once more. However, the heat sensation remained intense. This was becoming a normal experience with every encounter involving him.

"I am going to lift you to your feet and turn you around facing the other way. Do not open your eyes until I say." I nodded. He removed my hand from his chest but continued to hold it as he took my other hand and lifted me to my feet. My legs buckled as I struggled to stand. "Take your time." His voice was soft. "Your strength will return." Warmth still surrounded me, and I thought of the orb of light around the man in the road. The one I thought I had hit with the car. I wanted to open my eyes yet feared what would happen if I did.

"I'm going to turn you around now. Are you ready?"

I nodded and clutched his hands, allowing him to gently turn me in the opposite direction. I immediately regained strength, standing on strong legs again. He kept a tight hold on me until the warmth dissipated. He waited a few moments longer before giving me permission to open my eyes. The night was much darker. The view revealed a moonless sky covered in lofty pine trees, and mountainous terrain.

"What happened to me?" My voice quivering quivered, still a little shaky. "I heard music, and a song. I felt entranced."

He remained silent, offering no explanation. He only searched my face as I searched his. There were the secrets again, submerged in those dark eyes.

I felt the need to reach out and touch his cheek as he had done to me. I wanted to stroke the stubble that edged his perfect jawline. I wanted to put my hands back on his wet skin and trace the muscles and veins that mapped across his arms. I was drawn to him, but I could not give into my feelings. I must never allow myself to cross that line no matter how much pain I carried. I would not do to Mavis what Gabriella had done to me.

He cut his eyes away before answering. "You must have climbed too fast. The intensity of it, combined with the increased altitude and the cool waters, more than likely caused your temporary paralysis."

It was as if the wind had just been knocked from my lungs. His patronizing diagnosis irritated me. He was an innkeeper, not a doctor. I felt betrayed. Something out of the ordinary had just happened. Some sort of supernatural experience transpired. Even the treatment he had given was hardly standard treatment for paralysis. He knew something, yet he continued to hide secrets.

I released his hands suddenly.

"You don't believe me?" His grin was taunting.

"Why do you insult me by expecting me to?" I brushed past him, heading for the stony path.

He bit his lip, suppressing a smile that danced in his eyes. "Going back down the long way?"

I stopped, dreading the thought of a long, slippery downhill hike in darkness. Besides, I feared my legs might become wobbly again, causing a tragic fall on my way down.

"Is there a better way?"

He nodded to the falls. "It's a big jump, but you get there in four seconds." My stomach dropped, as I peered over the edge. "You're kidding me," was all I could say.

"It's the best way down."

I looked again, my heart now in my throat.

"I don't think I could do it."

"Sure, you can. It's easy; just let your feet leave the ground and fly toward the water."

Again, I sensed mystery in his words. Why was he encouraging me to jump 55 feet? He was baiting me, yet every time I asked a question, he was evasive. Why?

"I know you can do it." He said, positioning himself to jump. Then, gently, "I'll be waiting for you at the bottom."

The heat began to rise with intensity. This event had happened before. A strong Deja Vu. A vision flashed into my mind so quickly, I couldn't make sense of what it was. A dream perhaps and in it I could hear myself saying those same words... "I'll be waiting for you."

He dove from the cliff, and into the water. I watched him as he flew, gliding majestically like an enormous hawk. He broke the waters, resurfacing almost immediately. He looked back up and motioned for me to join him.

Part of me screamed "No!" Yet another part eagerly desired to fly off the cliff, soaring just as he did, breaking through the swirling waters below. My soul longed to be near him, to be where he was. His face, so inviting, so intriguing.

My feet left the ground. My body soared through the night air, cutting through the spraying mist and as I descended toward the water, my spirit soared upward. The unseen orchestra began playing its rapturous song once again. Its melody rose to a crescendo just as I broke through entering the dark balmy, swirling waters. The music was gone. Only silence. A strong hand clasped onto me, pulling me up.

I resurfaced to the pleasant sight of his black, mystifying eyes.

Nineteen

DAY THREE

The early morning breeze gently pushed the linen curtains away from the window, allowing the warm rays of the sun to make their grand entrance. Bethany and Lillian were unmoved, sleeping in after returning from the night hike after midnight. However, I had woken off and on all night with an anxiousness growing inside me. I couldn't put my finger on why I was so restless. Ryan usually occupied my dreams, but last night, each time I dozed off, Travis was the one I dreamt of, and I felt somewhat guilty about my night-time fantasies.

I lay in bed, staring at the spinning ceiling fan, trying to decipher the feelings inside. My heart continued to ache, and it was difficult to discern if it still hurt from Ryan's betrayal or was it an ache for a man, I could never have. Was there a danger in Travis that I should be aware of but kept suppressing because of his rugged good looks.

I climbed from the bed as the rooster crowed. I dressed and headed outside for an early morning jog to clear my head. I ran through the soft dewy grass alongside the riverbed, clicking off the miles. The brisk morning air filled my lungs with the perfume of mother earth. I always did my best thinking early in the morning, when no one was around to distract me. I tried to concentrate and plan the re-writing of the dreaded book. However, thoughts of Travis and the waterfall continued to invade my head.

The delicious aromas of breakfast wafted out to meet me luring me back to the inn after my long run. But after my workout I decided against the heaviness of country waffles, eggs, and biscuits and chose instead a glass of juice and a small bowl of fresh fruit which I ate alone on the porch. Afterwards, I returned to my room showered, dressed, and grabbed my computer just as a groggy Bethany and Lillian raised their waking heads.

"Hey, where are you going?" Bethany yawned.

"Re-writes."

Lillian noticed my wet hair. "How long have you been up?"

"Woke with the rooster. I couldn't sleep."

"So, what's going on with you and Travis?" Lillian asked as she stretched and sat up.

"What?"

Bethany gave a sarcastic laugh. "Don't act so surprised, Bronwyn. It's so obvious."

"What is so obvious?"

Bethany and Lillian exchanged knowing glances, and then Bethany said, "The obvious attraction between you two."

"I am not attracted to him." I lied.

"Maybe not, but he definitely is to you."

"Sh-sh!" I closed the door and then poised myself on the edge of the bed. "Why do you say that?"

Lillian's tired voice came alive with excitement. "Because he kept his eye on you all night last night. And he followed you when you took off rock climbing."

"You two sure were gone a long time." Bethany added sourly. "Just what was going on?"

"Nothing. I didn't know he had followed me. I thought I was alone until I reached the top. Then he showed up."

I paused, deciding not to try and explain what happened on top of the falls. How could I possibly explain such a supernatural moment? They would never understand. So, I told the girls Travis's explanation of the story.

"Did he have to give you more mouth to mouth?" Lillian teased.

"No" I pressed my lips into a straight line. "You two are terrible."

"You better watch yourself," Bethany warned. "All kidding aside, I think he is attracted to you."

"I think so too," Lillian agreed. I shook my head. "We've been alone twice now, and he's certainly kept his distance. He's been nothing but a gentleman."

"Give him time, Bronwyn," Bethany warned. "He'll find the opportunity. Then what will you do?"

I stood to leave and gave them a coy smile. "I'll do nothing. He is a married man, and as beautiful and mysterious as he may be, if he would cheat on his poor crippled wife, then I would not want him. That would take all the beauty of him away and place him in the same good-for-nothing, cheating scoundrel category as Ryan and a hoard of other common men."

"Hear hear!" Bethany gave me a high-five.

"I'm off to write," I said. "Wish me luck. I'll catch up with you guys later."

∞

Bethany leaned back against her pillow and stared at the door as Bronwyn left. Her stomach knotted. Her mind went back to the article Lillian had recommended on the progression of a true broken heart. She hated to admit it, but the foreboding predictions of the sequences of a broken heart were playing out. She remembered stage two, the desperate attempts for attention. True, Bronwyn had stayed out of sight during a storm claiming to have nearly drowned, and then last night, walking off alone, professing to have experienced some sort of altitude sickness. Both times, she needed the aid of the dashing Travis.

The thought of stage three sickened her.... the self-destructive stage. The one, as the article said, will justify affairs with married men. Bethany sighed. Her concern lay with Bronwyn's well-being. She knew first-hand what it was like to be involved with a married man. She fell quickly once, only to make the gruesome discovery that, unfortunately, never surfaced during months of long walks, lunch dates, endless conversation, and random intimate nights. It so happened that she ran into him leaving a local theater, one arm around a tall, beautiful slender woman, his other occupied by holding the hand of a ten-year-old girl, whom he promptly introduced as his wife and daughter. Even though Bethany had appeared strong, it damaged her more than she had ever revealed. She knew Bronwyn hurt badly from her broken engagement to Ryan. The last thing she needed was to give her heart away again, this time to a married man who would only betray her in the end. As Bronwyn's best friend, she would keep a careful watch on the situation, preventing any more alone time between the two, if necessary.

Twenty

I discovered a shady, secluded patch of thick green clover, far down the river, bordering the entrance to the woods. The sun burned intensely, casting its warming rays, and glistening on the gently flowing waters. A line of large trees offered a nice canopy shading me from the beating sun.

Several large boulders lay scattered in the grassy area. I noticed one of the smoother ones made an ideal desk. Scooting next to it, I opened my computer and the script file. Whatever inspiration had fallen upon me at the waterfalls was gone. I sat in the grass, staring at the screen, unmoved and uninspired. My attention wandered to a large hawk flying overhead, then back to the computer screen, and then back to a bird singing on a nearby tree branch... and finally back to the computer screen. The pattern repeated. Within a couple of hours, I had tracked a hawk, some blue jays, a vivid red cardinal, and several birds whose species I did not know. I dug the moss out of the corners of the rock, laid across the grass, followed the route of a strange insect, picked several wildflowers, pulled at the sticky sap oozing down a nearby tree, and became engrossed in the antics of my friends who had gathered at the river for some fun in the sun. I was too far away to hear their conversations. I was only privy to their laughter and playful screams.

My interest peaked when Travis and Mavis headed towards the river. Mavis carried a picnic basket, while Travis balanced an ice cooler on his shoulder. Mavis waved and called out to the girls as she spread two large cloths on the ground and unloaded the food basket. I could only imagine the amazing lunch she had prepared for her hungry guests. Mavis finished spreading out the feast and then, without warning, took a staggering run to the dock. Grabbing the thick rope, she swung far out over the river and fell into the water, causing an enormous splash and earning a round of applause from everyone. Travis watched Mavis; a genuine smile crossed his lips. Mavis must have challenged him because he removed his shirt and dove into the water, much to the kids' delight.

I felt a tinge of jealousy, which I immediately suppressed and scolded myself. I was not that type of person. I should be pleased to see a family so close-knit and a husband who continued to love his wife despite what fate had done. I wondered why Mavis had never replaced the missing tooth. I could understand the scars and even the limp, but a tooth could be replaced. I reprimanded myself again. Isn't this what my book was about? I turned my straying attention back to the computer screen and began typing randomly:

Does Travis love you, Mavis, because you are beautiful? Hardly, look what tragedy hath wrought. You are now a small resemblance of the girl you once were, the girl that stole his heart. Or my dear Mavis, are you a beauty to Travis because he loves you? Does Travis's heart not see your scars or the gaping hole in your mouth? Does he not see your body lean to one side, swaggering as you pull yourself along? Do your afflictions tell of a story deep inside of a woman that only Travis knows? Is it a story full of secrets revealed only to the one that holds your heart? Are they secrets that will not allow Travis to judge this beautifully written book by its cover?

With a sigh, I highlighted the entire paragraph and deleted it. My thoughts strayed to Ryan, wondering again why he had so easily stopped loving me and quickly replaced me with someone else. Thinking of him

I clicked on my email. A window immediately popped up on the screen informing me that the internet was not available. Figures. I'm cut off from the entire world here. I might as well be on the moon. I laughed at the thought. Moonshine, pretty close.

I absentmindedly clicked on my deleted files. Maybe I could dig up an old idea and run with that. I sighed. I had resorted to rooting through the trash. I scrolled down a list of my many failed attempts at stories and clicked on the first.

"Birds of Prey" "A group of top-secret agents, all possessing bird names, known as "The N.E.S.S.T." I immediately closed the file. Stupid, to think I could write espionage. No wonder I deleted you.

I scrolled the titles again, biting my fingernails on my left hand, stopping at, "The Covenant" "A young Baron falls prey to the wicked ways of the Teplem infiltrating the royal bloodline and causing his young wife's death...."

"Creepy," I muttered with a shiver and closed the file. I scrolled through the list before clicking again.

"The Eclipse" "During a lunar eclipse as the world sits in darkness, a warrior, who is an extra dimensional being comes to earth, as the gatekeeper. Guarding and keeping watch of the forbidden portal...."

"Dumb," I muttered with a shiver and closed the file. I scrolled and clicked again.

"Caught in the Whirlwind" After a tragic accident takes the life of her beloved, a woman finds herself raising her children alone in the new world, facing much more than the storms that took her husband's life." Don't want to write a period piece. Too much research.

"My Brother's Keeper" When her best friend is possessed by an evil entity, Kena goes on an incredulous mission to save him. What was I thinking?

I sighed, closing the file. Nothing. I ran my hands through my dark curls, twisting them and pulling my long tresses off my neck. I held my hair atop my head for a few minutes, letting the breeze cool me, before allowing it to cascade down over my shoulders. Closing the computer, I sat back against the tree feeling somewhat hopeless. I knew Bethany would expect something after dinner and I had nothing. My attempts for the past couple of hours had produced nought.

I turned my attention back to the happy swimmers. Everyone was out of the water, eating Mavis's lunch. I would join them at their festive picnic, but Bethany would inquire about the manuscript. I was too embarrassed to tell her I had nothing. Instead, I opted for an endeavor I had not attempted since I was a little girl. Earlier, I'd noticed a perfect tree for climbing. Its branches were thick and low and circled the tree like a spiral staircase. Leaving my computer on the rock desk, I entered the edge of the forest and approached the tree, grabbing the lowest branch and pulling myself up. Within seconds, I was climbing effortlessly like a young child playfully swinging across the monkey bars at recess. I climbed a bit higher before stopping.

The view of the river was spectacular. I stretched my neck, wondering if I would be able to peer into the secret garden at this height. I felt I could if I went just a bit higher. I pulled myself up one more branch, but my efforts were futile. The garden was much too far away. I rested on a wide sturdy limb, straddling it, allowing my legs to dangle on either side and leaned against the large trunk.

I watched my friends yet found myself focused on Travis and Mavis. Travis was sitting across the cloth from her, with Molly close beside him, leaning against his sturdy chest. He kept his arm wrapped around her as she ate. Mavis was sitting near Bethany, and I could tell by her gesturing that she was no doubt re-telling one of her many stories. Mavis seemed intrigued and soon took over the conversation. I wondered if she was telling the others about her injuries. I hoped so, Bethany would be sure to relay the information. Instead, whatever Mavis said caused the whole group to erupt in laughter. Even Lillian was red-faced, choking as she chuckled.

I noted Travis's expression, focusing on every word as Mavis continued talking. He, paid careful attention to what she was saying, just as he had done with me in the cabin. My heart ached even more. "Where were you Travis, when Mavis was injured?" I whispered to myself. "Why weren't you there to protect her as you were me? Do you stay faithful to her out of guilt? Or are you faithful because you have never known anyone other than Mavis because you've never been out of this small town? Has there never been anyone else to steal your heart?"

The sound of snapping branches interrupted my daydreams. Someone was here! Could it be the cloaked figure from the woods! My mind raced along with my pulse. I could climb down. No...that would draw attention to me. I could remain quiet, hoping the person wouldn't notice me so high up in the tree. I could scream for help, but if the girls didn't hear me, I would only give my hiding place away.

I leaned away from the tree trunk to catch a true glimpse of whoever was stalking us. The heavy footsteps drew closer, the rustling louder. I leaned forward, clutching the branch above me, steadying myself. A dark-hooded figure moved through the trees, the hood obscuring their face. What could possibly be going on in this secluded town?

I swallowed a scream that desperately wanted to escape my mouth. Ebony hands parted the tree branches, clearing a view of the river. I breathed a small sigh of relief. The shadowy figure was not aware I was high above him in the tree. The figure's attention was fixed on the picnic by the river. I leaned back against the trunk, trying to control my breathing, while collecting my thoughts. Was this man out to harm us? I had no desire to find out. I would ease myself down and make a mad dash for the inn.

Time to take my chances. I stretched out once more to make sure the figure was preoccupied watching my friends before attempting my self-rescue. Shakily, I rose, balancing myself by holding onto the branch directly above my head. I leaned forward. The cloaked figure was gone! How could it have left without me hearing? I scanned the surrounding area quickly... no sign of him. I leaned as far away from the tree as my body would allow. Nothing.

I sat back down against the tree trunk. The hooded figure was gone. As to where, I had no clue. Still, it was time to descend the tree and get out of the woods. Pulling myself up, I glanced above me before grabbing the lofty branch of the tree.

Ebony eyes stared at me from amongst the leaves. Sitting camouflaged on the branch directly above me was another hooded creature! His eyes pierced mine, his face was stoic, stern. Fear overwhelmed me, weaking my grasp on the tree branch. I let out a piercing scream as my body went limp and my grip loosened. I clawed for the other branches, but instead felt myself falling from the tree, plummeting into total darkness.

Twenty-One

The sandwiches disappeared, along with the soft warm chocolate chip cookies that Mavis removed from the oven only minutes before serving them. She laid out a spread of egg salad sandwiches, fresh tomatoes, slices of melon and a pitcher of ice-cold lemonade to wash it all down. The troupe had eaten well and was now relaxing while listening to Mavis' comical stories. The afternoon sun was at its peak, even making the shade of the massive oaks quite warm. Despite missing their intended mountain resort, their accidental trapping in Moonshine still offered rest and relaxing activities. A better vacation spot would be hard to find. Moonshine was proving to be one of the country's best-kept secrets.

A blood curdling scream from the edge of the woods pierced through the serenity of the afternoon. The unexpectedness of the scream startled everyone. Travis was the first to leap to his feet. Without hesitation, he sprinted across the grounds towards the edge of the forest. Everyone else followed. Even Mavis ran surprisingly fast on her crippled leg. None was able to keep up with Travis, though. He noticed the abandoned laptop lying on the large rock and charged into the woods, glancing to his right and then to his left. He spotted her body lying on the ground underneath a large oak tree. He sprinted to where she lay, placed his fingers on the side of her neck and felt for a pulse. Bethany made her way to the opposite side of Bronwyn, kneeling on the ground. "My God, is she okay?"

Travis gave no answer. He lifted her eyelids, checked the breathing, and felt down each arm and leg. Mavis caught up with the group, joining in the circle that now surrounded Bronwyn. She watched intently as Travis examined her.

Within seconds, she began to stir. A sigh of relief passed through the group.

**

I opened my eyes. The darkness cleared as I focused on a face leaning over me, then remembering the cloaked man, I gasped attempting to sit, but a firm hand on my shoulder prevented me, pushing me back to the ground. I fought against it, slapping the man who had a hold of me.

"Relax, Bronwyn, you're alright." I heard Travis' voice. I focused on his face, giving into his command, and allowing him to gently ease me back to a lying position. I looked around. "Where is he?"

"Where is who?" Bethany asked, puzzled.

"The man in the tree?"

"You okay hon?"

I tried sitting up again, but Travis prevented it. I lay back on the ground but continued to look for the man. He had been here. I had seen his face and locked eyes with him right before I fell. Lillian knelt beside me. "What happened, love?"

"I saw something and fell out of the tree."

"Were you climbing it?" She asked, a bit of laughter in her voice.

I offered a crooked smile and nodded.

"Girl, you are crazy!" Lil laughed.

"Is she okay?" Bethany asked. "I think she might have hit her head. She seems delirious."

"Are you in any pain?" Travis asked.

I shook my head again. "No, actually I don't feel anything."

"My God, she's paralyzed!" Lillian gasped, grabbing Travis' arm.

"No Lil,'" I tried sitting up again. "I mean; I have no pain. I'm sure I'm not hurt, just a little stunned.... maybe." My last words trailed off as I thought about the hooded man. I glanced cautiously around.

"Are you sure you're, okay?" Bethany asked again, curious as to my odd behavior. "Who are you looking --?"

"She's okay." Travis said and his interruption to Bethany's questioning seemed somewhat threatening. "There are no broken bones, no head trauma. She more than likely stunned herself when she fell."

Although Travis answered Bethany's question, his eyes stayed fixed upon me. There was something in his face that confirmed my suspicion... he knew of the goings on in the woods. His expression made clear he did not want me to inform my friends of the cloaked man. Reluctantly, I obeyed his stern gaze... I would question him later.

"We really need to have a serious talk, love, about the extreme measures you seem to be taking to get attention." Lillian said, winking, as she knelt beside me, placing her hand on my knee. "Good God, is this going to be an everyday event?" She gave my knee a final pat. "Glad you're okay." She stood and mouthed the words, "stage two," to Bethany.

I turned away from Travis, purposely avoiding him, and leaned towards Beth.

"Enough coddling. I'm fine. You guys can go back to your picnic; I'm not going to climb any more trees. I promise."

"If you're sure you're okay, love." Lillian said, offering me a hand. I grabbed it, allowing her to help me up. She immediately began brushing the dirt from my clothes and plucking a few bits of grass from my hair as well. "You need someone to carry you back?"

I was quick to protest, knowing the only person capable of carrying me would be Travis and I would have none of that right now. "I'm fine, really, I am." Once everyone realized that I was indeed alright, the group dispersed and casually walked back to the river. Travis stood to his feet and said nothing. He allowed Mavis to grab hold of his strong arm for support.

I retrieved my computer, taking my time to place it into my backpack. I made eye contact with Bethany, signaling her to loiter a bit. I waited until the others were out of earshot before I spoke. "How did you guys find me?"

"Heard you scream." Bethany's eyes widened. "Pretty chilling if you ask me." I slung the backpack over my shoulder, "Where was I when you found me?"

Bethany looked at me, puzzled. "Under the tree. Are you sure you're okay?"

"Did you see anything else?"

"No. Travis got to you first." Bethany gave me a nudge. "He took off running like a wild animal. His muscles pulsing, his hair flying in the wind. You should have seen that man run. I didn't know a person could move that fast."

"Stop it!"

"But seriously, you should have seen his reaction when he heard you scream. He didn't hesitate one second. He jumped to his feet and bolted. He left us all in his dust. I have this sixth sense, Bronwyn, I can tell when there's an attraction between two people."

I remained quiet. It was no use to continue. Bethany was not quiet long enough to listen to anything I had to say.

I lounged by the river the rest of the afternoon, staying close to the rest of the group. The rewrites would have to wait. Travis did not return to the river and was mysteriously absent at dinner.

Bethany canceled our meeting, completely understanding why the rewrite had not been completed. As twilight set, everyone was free to participate in whatever activity they chose.

I decided to stay close to the inn and visit my favorite garden, figuring it would be more enticing during the evening hours.

The magical feeling hanging in the night air was hard to resist so I left the porch, being drawn to the cobblestone path. Opening the gate, I pushed my way through the hanging vines. The romantic scent of night blooming jasmine filled my lungs. The garden was even more enchanting in the moonlight. Fireflies swarmed around the low hanging branches of the weeping willow tree, displaying their tiny glowing lights. The moon gleamed down upon the pond, its reflection casting the garden in a deep gray-silver. The quiet rushing of the waterfall accompanied by the croaking frogs and the chirping crickets, provided the evening orchestration. I sat in a soft patch of clover growing near the water and moved my hand gracefully over the leaves, reflecting on how as a child I would spend countless hours searching for a four leafed one. I laid back and gazed at the night sky. It was teeming with millions of stars, more than I'd ever seen at one time. The higher elevation made it seem as if I could almost reach out and grab a few.

Moments like this seemed so futile and empty without someone to share them with. My mind turned to Ryan. Literally no day had passed since our break-up that I hadn't thought of him, dreamed of him, pictured his face, and heard his voice. I imagined him in the clover, lying next to me, gazing at the stars. True I wasn't sure I had wanted to marry him but that didn't mean I wanted him out of my life completely. There was a time when I could slide my hand over, reach out and touch him, feel him lying next to me. I passed my hands across the clover once again. The emptiness was so real. My body longed for him, and I wondered if missing Ryan was the reason I was drawn to Travis.

Somewhere in the distance, the faint music of a dulcimer wafted through the trees. The melody was beautiful, although I did not recognize the song. Probably some old mountain ballad. I kept stargazing, hoping to see a shooting one, on which I could make a wish. The night was peaceful, serene...lonely.

I left the clover patch, walked to the pond, and took a seat on its bank, placing my feet in the shallow water. The garden gate swung open. There was not enough light to see who entered. I hoped it was Bethany and Lillian. Girl talk would be therapeutic right now.

The footsteps grew closer until the approaching figure stepped into the moonlight. My heart leaped.

Travis.

He sat next to me, and as much as I hated to admit it, I was glad he was here, despite the fact I was trying to convince myself I wasn't interested in him. I longed to be near him. Besides, I intended to interrogate him. I knew he was keenly aware of what lurked in the woods. He'd known the first day I questioned him, yet he avoided the subject, blaming it on kids or curious teenagers.

"What's going on around here? Who are the cloaked men stalking us from the woods?" I spared no time with a casual greeting. "And don't waste time with denial. I saw you talking with one of them in the garden yesterday."

Travis looked out over the pond. "There are secrets and mysteries that are not to be revealed to everyone."

My suspicion rose. "That's unfair."

"How is that?"

"We're obviously being stalked. Am I not allowed to know why?"

"In time."

His words frightened me. "What do you mean by that?"

"Exactly what I said. Time reveals things."

My agitation rose. "Maybe I won't wait for your time. What if I march right into the inn, tell everyone, and make a call to the local police?"

"Won't do you any good."

"Why?"

"I am the ruling authority in this town, that's why. It's also why you would do best by just doing what I say."

"Are you threatening me?"

"No." Travis hurled a small stone across the water. "I am protecting you." His words stunned me into silence. "How's the rewrite going?" He changed the subject as if to prevent any more discussion on the topic.

I wouldn't be put off. There was more to these hooded creatures than Travis wanted me to know, something strangely unusual at work in these mountains. I sensed it from the moment we arrived. If Travis was protecting me, that must mean we were in danger. If the cloaked figures meant us harm, then why was Travis having a private conversation with one of them?

"In time," he said quietly as if he were reading my thoughts and then repeated. "How is the rewriting going?"

I watched him, my emotions waging a war inside. I feared the man in many ways, yet my heart ached for him. There was no escaping the fact that I was unwillingly drawn to him, yet another part of me desired to run far away. I sighed.

"It's not going. I've been staring at a blank computer screen all day and have produced nothing. I don't know... maybe I'm done with writing."

"Do you think that you're wasting your time writing these romance novels, and putting off the story you want to write? Maybe you're burying it deeper by all the clutter you're allowing in your life."

"Yes," I answered quickly. "I know that for certain. But, these stories, no matter how cheesy, pay the bills."

"Then you might as well be writing for the National Enquirer." His words stung. I wanted to snap off a sarcastic rebuttal, but I had nothing. Travis took advantage of my silence. "You're making a living for yourself, instead of living the life you want to live."

Cued by his words, the heat sensation began rising within me again. My heart raced. I reached into the pond to cool my arms, splashing water over the top of my legs, and then repeated the action by splashing my neck and chest.

He pressed on. "You're attempting to write a love story, yet love is such a vast subject, and one with intense emotion. You're trying to write about that sentiment between two people, yet you have never really loved anyone on this earth except yourself."

My hands left the water. "What? How can you say that? You don't know me. I have loved. I loved Ryan deeply. Just because I wasn't sure I wanted to marry him doesn't mean I didn't care for him."

"You never really loved Ryan." He sounded certain.

I pulled my feet from the water and turned to face him, looking directly into his dark eyes. "Okay...explain yourself."

He stared back, and once again his eyes penetrated my soul.

"Can you take it?"

"Take what?"

"The truth."

"Why wouldn't I ?"

"Because the truth will always set you free and some people find it fearful to be totally free. For some reason, they seem to find comfort in the chains that bind them."

My eyes flashed as I leaned forward, my body closer to him than I intended.

"I'm not afraid of anything."

He tried suppressing another smile and I wondered just what it was about my declaration that he found amusing.

"You're a storyteller," He began. "You invent characters. You create them in your imagination exactly how you wish them to be. Correct?"

I nodded.

"You did the same with Ryan. You loved a man who did not exist anywhere but in your ideals. You loved a person that wasn't Ryan."

"Not true. I knew him very well. We lived together. You get to know someone that way."

"Then he suddenly changed and turned into someone you didn't know anymore. Right?"

"Yes, in a way he did." I couldn't argue with that.

"He didn't change. You were finally forced to see Ryan for who he really was. The true Ryan. Not your ideal created version of him."

I contemplated his ideology. His words seemed so obvious. I didn't want to think that I'd fallen for a self-absorbed, ego-driven, shallow person. I was smarter than that. Now I wondered if Ryan had ever loved me. Obviously, he hadn't. "I guess Ryan never really loved me. His true love was obviously fame and recognition."

"If all that had been offered to Ryan had been offered to you, would you have taken it?"

I thought a moment before answering. "Six months ago, I am sure I would have. I'd have been crazy not to. But I'd have taken Ryan right along with me."

"What if Ryan had asked you to turn it all down?"

"I never asked Ryan to turn it all down."

"That's not what I asked you."

My voice rose, all my suppressed anger for Ryan resurfacing. "It would have been very selfish of him."

"Would you have turned it all down for him?"

"No," I nearly shouted. "No, I wouldn't have turned any of it down for him. I would have seen him for the self-serving, egotistical, person that he is."

My voice trailed off as I realized my last statement…Seen Ryan for who he is… Travis was right. I had invented Ryan to be the man I wanted him to be, the man for whom I longed, never seeing him for who he really was.

I looked at Travis, realization shining in my eyes. He leaned forward and said softly, "If I say, I love you, Bronwyn. Do I mean I love you in the same way as I love these mountains, or the smell of the earth after a good rain, or the way I love music? Do I love you because the way you look ignites a passion inside of me? Is my love for you only contingent on the way it affects me? How it makes me feel? If so, then I only truly love myself. And I only love and want you for how it affects me." He moved close to me, his eyes reaching deep into my soul. "Or do I love you, Bronwyn? Do I love the person who looks at me from those emerald, green eyes? Do I love you despite the times you are angry, bitter, and unlovely? Do I continue to love you although you freely gave your heart to another? Can I send you away knowing I will never experience you, but you will experience all you've ever dreamed of? I can if my love is for you and not myself."

I was speechless, completely entranced by his words. I wanted to cry, to sob tears of regret of wasted time and loneliness. Everything within me wanted to lean against his chest. I wanted him to wrap his arms around me and hold me under the moonlight. I wanted to know what his lips felt like on mine, I wanted to taste his breath, his skin. I wanted to feel him inside of me. Despite my inner urgings, I turned away from him and went back to the water.

"True love is sacrifice," he said.

"Have you sacrificed a lot for Mavis?"

"Love never keeps count."

"Has she done the same for you?"

"Love never keeps count," he repeated.

An unseen tear escaped my eye and splashed into the pond. I quickly stroked the waters not wanting him to notice. The moonlight reflected off the rippling surface. "I couldn't imagine a more perfect place. It inspires me. I feel a strong urge to fight. To defy every odd stacked against me." My voice dropped to a near whisper. "I feel it here in Moonshine more than anywhere. This place calls to me, like last night at the waterfalls. I heard someone calling me, calling my innermost being. Label it altitude sickness or however you wish to explain it, but I have never felt anything like that before. It was unreal, yet more real than anything I have ever experienced in my life."

He listened to me but said nothing and the more I talked the more secrets I saw hidden in his eyes. What the hell was he not telling me?

I quietly pushed open the door, thankful it didn't creak, and crept into the room. Bethany and Lillian were both asleep, more than likely had been for quite some time.

I never intended on staying out in the garden so late, but once Travis showed up and our intriguing conversation went from intense to intimate, time melted away. I stole into the bathroom, politely closing the door, before turning on the light. I quickly changed from my clothes into my sleeping briefs and oversized tee, brushed my teeth and washed my face. Turning off the light, I opened the door and crept into bed.

"Where have you been?"

"Crap!" I breathed, startled by Bethany's whisper. "You scared me!"

"It's a guilty conscience that frightens so easily!"

"I'm not guilty of anything! Go back to sleep!"

"You guys can stop whispering. I'm awake." Lillian said, her head remaining on the pillow.

"You see Bethany, you woke up Lil' being all nosey."

Bethany sat up in bed. "No, you woke her up, sneaking into the room at an ungodly hour after your late-night escapades. "Bethany's accusation brought Lillian off her pillow and into a sitting position. "You're having exploits with Travis?"

"No, I am not."

"Yes, she is!" Bethany said firmly.

"Be quiet, or you're going to wake up everyone in the inn. Just go back to sleep."

"Not a chance." Lillian fluffed her pillow and leaned it against the headboard. "This is too good."

Bethany turned on the lamp. "So where were you? And why are you sneaking in so late?"

"Out with it, woman!" Lillian added.

"I was in one of the gardens...thinking."

"Were you alone?"

"Yes and No."

"What do you mean by that?"

"I was alone for a while, until someone else showed up."

"And who might someone else be?" Lillian mocked.

"Travis," I tried to be nonchalant.

"I knew it!" Bethany yelled. Lillian and I both quieted her.

"What were you doing?" She began her interrogation as if it were any of her business anyway.

"We were only talking."

"About what?" she demanded.

"Writing, writer's block, love."

Bethany 's eyes narrowed. "Uh huh."

"It's not what you're thinking. Real love, true love, sacrificial love."

"Sounds deep," Bethany rolled her eyes in sarcasm. "He's only playing the game, Bronwyn, setting you up for the moment."

"He's really not like that. There was plenty of opportunity tonight, but he never made a move." I could hear the disappointment in my voice.

"Are you falling for a married man?" Lillian asked.

"It's not what you think."

"Deny it then," Bethany challenged. "Deny that you're not attracted to him."

"I'll admit there is an attraction. I won't deny that. But it's more than just a sexual attraction. He's like no one I've ever known, yet there is something about him that is distantly familiar and comfortable. Like we were soul mates meant for each other, but for some reason we were born in two different worlds. Travis has been here, hidden away in these mountains, and I've been miles away in southern California."

"Yet fate has brought you two together!" Lillian sighed. "What are the chances of us breaking down here, in Moonshine, connecting you two at last?"

I sighed. "And who'd ever thought my soul mate would be married, keeping us apart forever?"

Bethany smiled showing compassion. "I'm sorry. You may not be able to have him, but I think you've found your rewrite. Think about it. It has everything. Leading lady meets a handsome mysterious stranger, her ultimate soul mate, who rescues her more than once."

"And they're forced to spend a long stormy night together in a hidden cabin," Lillian added to the story.

"There is a strong attraction between them that they both are denying." Bethany was rolling out the plot now. "He's married, and she is forced to stay at the inn that he, and his wife, own."

"He's an honorable person," Lillian chimed in, excited to be thickening the plot. "Very committed to his wife, despite the fact she's been scarred by a terrible accident."

"But" Bethany continued, "His love and commitments have never been tested, since he's never been out of the small hidden town where he was born."

Lillian blossomed with dramatic flair. "Until his world is invaded by the ever-beautiful, green-eyed temptress! Will he fall prey to his lusts and desires like every other man on this planet?"

I couldn't help but laugh.

"Oh, this is good!" Bethany hugged her pillow.

"How will you end it?" Lillian asked.

Bethany's mouth melted into an evil grin. "Time will tell,".

"I hope it ends well." Lillian's mood turned serious. "Mavis is a sweet lady and there are children involved. They are real people, not make believe. It wouldn't be right to destroy their lives."

I was touched by her thoughtfulness. "Lil' honey, I'm not going to do anything. I don't want anyone to get hurt. I wouldn't intentionally inflict the pain I have been going through on anyone. Believe me. I need the story to end with Travis as the hero. I need to believe there are some decent men out there."

I crawled under the cotton sheets. Bethany turned off the lamp as we settled into the massive feather bed. The night breeze blew the curtains back gently. The wooden chimes pealed softly below the window as a rocking chair creaked repeatedly, rhythmically. It wasn't the wind, however, that rocked the chair, but Mavis who sat on the porch below, rocking, hearing every word from the open window above.

Twenty-Two

"**O**nida" The summons caused me to stir. I turned over on my side and fell back to sleep, resting to the serenade of the frogs, crickets, and the continual hoot of an owl. I'd grown familiar with the quiet peaceful sounds of the mountains that filled my room each night.

"Onida." The gentle whisper fell softly upon my ear. My eyes flew open. I glanced around the room. Bethany and Lillian were sound asleep.

The room was empty and quiet; only the hum from the rotating ceiling fan penetrated the silence. I lay still, listening for a few minutes but there was nothing. I thought perhaps I'd been dreaming, so I closed my eyes.

"Onida." This time there was no mistaking what I heard. It was the same voice that called to me the first night in Moonshine, the voice of the woman singing the mournful song, beckoning me, into the forest, as it drifted through the trees whispering the word.

The heat began again, permeating upward. Pulling back the feather comforter, I climbed out of the bed, making my way to the open window, hoping the cool night breeze would cause the penetrating heat to subside. A dense fog hung in the air, obstructing my view of the inn's grounds and nearby river. Although I couldn't see if anyone was outside the window, I heard a faint melody of a pan flute, accompanied by the woman's enticing song. I wrapped my silk robe around me, tying it closed. I slipped out of the room, and crept down the staircase, stealing my way outside. I stopped cold at the porch steps, wondering why I would risk going out into the dark night alone, in search of the beckoning voice, especially since there were disturbing secrets at play. I had a fleeting thought to go wake Bethany and have her accompany me but decided against it when I heard the woman call again. This time there seemed to be urgency in her voice that empowered me with newfound courage; so, I abandoned the thought and entered the thick fog, and sprinted across the lawn. Reaching the edge of the river, I paused to listen. The woman's haunting voice grew louder, and even though she sung in a language I'd never heard, the lyrics brought overwhelming sorrow consuming me as the fog began to swirl and blow closer, nearly suffocating me in its thickness. It was then; I noticed the fog was not a fog at all, but a pale and ghostly woman with a strikingly beautiful face. Her long white hair billowed in every direction, swirling like a vapor along with her flowing silver dress. She spun around me, closing in, smothering me.

Certain that I must be having another nightmare I tried waking up. I wanted to step from the fog and run back to the inn, hoping to wake in my bed, but the mist was so blinding, so confusing that I was at a loss as to which way to go. I feared one step in the wrong direction would drop me in the river.

The vapor closed in as the ghostly woman stretched out her thin white arm and touched my lips with her finger.

"Silence your lips and put an end to your remorseful cries. Listen to Tiponi' whisper, deliverance is near. I am Tiponi ', listen to me my dear and begin to remember.... Remember...Hear my words and remember."

There was a familiarity in the woman's features and for a moment I thought I saw myself in her eyes. I reached out my hand, desiring to touch the woman's face, as a solitary tear fell down her ghostly cheek. The woman smiled and then swirled away from my reach. A deep sorrow invaded my heart. The heaviness of it buckled my knees sending me into the wet grass. My heart ached deeply for something, but what?

I lay by the water's edge, waiting to wake from the puzzling dream and trying to make sense of it. What did her words mean, and what was it she wished me to remember?

The mystical woman began fading from my view, dissipating into the air, taking the fog, the song, and my strength along with her. I lay in the wet grass, unable to move, my body weakened from the encounter. Again, I dreamed of Travis surrounded by falling water and in the vision, I could see his face, much clearer now. Noise and confusion surrounded him, yet he never removed his eyes from me. I wanted to go to him, be near him, but as I reached out, I began to fall, plummeting into darkness, emptiness, loneliness…and then, strong hands took hold of me, shaking me. I woke, surprised to be lying near the river. Travis was kneeling beside me. I looked around. No fog, no singing woman. Had I been sleepwalking?

I sat up quickly, shaken, and embarrassed to be lying outside in the grass. My silk robe, wet with dew, clung to my body.

"What time is it?" I noticed the sun had not risen.

"Four in the morning."

I didn't want to explain anything. I knew he would offer no insight into my strange experience anyway. He would only remain silent, keeping all the answers to the secrets that haunted me to himself.

"I've always wanted to sleep under the stars," I lied, attempting to stay as secretive as he did. "They were beautiful tonight, so I decided to sleep outdoors."

I felt silly for my lame excuse and by his expression, he didn't buy it.

"You didn't bring a pillow or blanket?"

"No. I didn't want to get anything dirty."

"Only yourself." He smiled and wiped a dirty tear-stained smudge from underneath my eye. My heart raced at the feel of his hand, and I wished he wouldn't entice me. Didn't he know what his touch did to me?

He offered his hand. "I'd feel much better if you slept indoors. No wandering off alone." his warning sounded more like a command.

"Why?" I baited him.

"Because it's not safe for you to be out here alone."

"And why is that?"

He watched me for a moment and my spirits lifted, thinking now might be the time he would finally allude to the cloaked man, the song of the woman, or any of the unexplained events that had taken place since our arrival. As terrifying as the answers may be, I wanted to know what was going on.

"The bears feed at night," was all he said.

I scowled, exasperated at his answer. "Bears?"

He nodded. "They come from the woods and raid the trash. You could be mauled."

I chewed my lower lip in frustration. Why must he continue to give evasive answers, especially when he knew I was aware of something? Why couldn't he just tell me the truth? In the garden last night, he said he was protecting me. Maybe not telling me what was going on in this elusive town was his way of keeping me safe. Maybe it was one of those, I could tell you but then I'd have to kill you, situations. If that was the case, then maybe it was best for me to play along and act as if I didn't care. But I did care, and my curiosity caused me to wonder why Travis was fully dressed and where was he going at four in the morning? I could hang back and follow him, but I had a sneaking suspicion he would know I was tracking him. I decided to play along; but wasn't giving up. "Thank you. I'll be sure to remember that."

I cinched the sash on my robe and headed back to the inn. I'd finish my sleep in the comfort of the grand feather bed, and come sunrise, I'd do some sleuthing and uncover the secrets of Moonshine.

Twenty-Three

DAY FOUR

My nocturnal wanderings robbed me of proper rest, so when Lillian and Bethany woke and went downstairs for breakfast, I took advantage of the big empty bed hoping to catch up on lost sleep. After fifteen minutes of staring at the rotating ceiling fan, I realized my mind was much too preoccupied to rest. Today I would walk into town and do some extensive research, and hopefully uncover what was going on in Moonshine. Who were the cloaked men hiding in the woods, why were they following us, and why did I need protecting? What secrets was Travis keeping?

I took a quick shower and then joined the girls for breakfast. Everyone gathered at the table except for Travis. Mavis was at the stove, flipping whole-wheat pancakes and slicing fresh fruit. She was humming again, as she did almost every morning.

Bethany poured a generous amount of syrup over her pancakes. "What is on everyone's agenda for today?" She started to fill her mouth. "Bronwyn, I assume you'll be writing?"

"I am heading into town right after breakfast. I have an idea, and I'm hoping to do a little research."

"We have a nice library in town," Carla Jo offered. "They have the internet there!"

"What are you writing about?" Molly asked while maple syrup dripped off her chin.

Mavis brought another stack of hotcakes to the table. "Now Molly, you're never supposed to ask a writer to tell their story until it is written. It is top secret until then. But I am sure it's something we'll all enjoy reading when it's finished." She gave me a gentle pat and then hobbled back over to the stove.

My stomach twisted and I suddenly felt full. I pushed my plate away and announced I was off to town. Bethany shoved in the last bite of pancake, wiped the dripple of syrup off her chin, and washed it down, draining the juice in her glass. "I'm coming with you."

"Me too." Lillian grabbed her plate and took it to the sink. I frowned at first, not sure I wanted their company, but thought it might be a good front for my detective work. Besides, if I uncovered something, they would be witnesses to it, and that would prove to them that I wasn't losing it, even though I knew they both suspected I was.

The walk into town did not seem as long and fearful as it had been a few days before. We enjoyed the beauty of the mountains and the peaceful existence it offered, though I could not stop thinking about the cloaked man since my fall from the tree. I knew what I'd seen but felt I should not speak of it to anyone. I also knew that I'd never hit the ground when I fell. I was still conscious when the strong arms of a man caught me and touched me on the back of my neck, causing me to drift into sleep. I didn't fear the cloaked man or men as much now, knowing they had every opportunity to carry me off yet didn't. Whoever he was, laid me gently on the ground for my friends to find. Still, there was Travis's statement that he was protecting me and his warning of the dangers of being alone. I was certain he was not really referring to bears.

We strolled down the middle of the road, and still not a single vehicle traveled the winding two-lane highway into Moonshine. This unnerved me as well, adding to the mystery of the place.

As we entered town, we were surprised at the bustle of activity so early in the morning. Many of the local residents lined the main street, constructing booths of various kinds. In the grand courtyard, workers were building a large wooden platform. Several firefighters were stringing up lights and hanging decorations from their ladders. Trays of warm fresh baked pastries and hot donuts flew out of the bakery free of charge for the volunteers. The coffee shop served mugs of steaming hot coffee and tea. Lively mountain ballads piped through the town's sound system, filling the street with folksy music.

A large banner flapping in the morning breeze explained the activity. The banner reminded me of the occasion Gil had brought to my attention the day of the fateful storm that nearly took my life.

Midsummer's Night's Cream

The residents merrily continued their duties. Everyone offered a smile, a friendly wave of their hands, a tipped hat, and a myriad of hellos. Each resident insisted that we attend their cherished event. Each invitation added the challenge that we would indeed enjoy the best ice cream we would ever put into our mouths. Yet, despite everyone's hospitality, the uneasiness washed over me once again. Moonshine affected me in strange ways. At times I felt happy and comfortable, however those moments were fleeting, and all too soon gave way to an unsettling anxiety that would overshadow without warning. The terror I experienced at the waterfalls and the bizarre dream last night, were the most unusual. It also unnerved me that I had been sleep walking, something I hadn't done since childhood. It was these things that made me wish the car was repaired, allowing us to ride away and separate from this place.

Bethany and Lillian seemed unaffected as always. They did not experience any strange sensations or phenomena. I wondered if I should try confiding to Bethany one more time about my suspicions of the strange goings on. In times past I had trusted my every secret to Bethany, save from the recent pregnancy and miscarriage, yet for some unknown reason, I felt estranged from her. As much as I hated to admit it, there was a growing rift between us. I anticipated that once we left this bizarre town, I might indeed take a long much needed vacation away from everyone. Maybe time away would help me put things in perspective.

It was the elegant woman with the auburn hair that unnerved me the most. Stopping her work in a booth decorated entirely with butterflies, she grabbed my hand, separating me from Lillian and Bethany.

"I'm so glad you have finally come to us." She whispered while squeezing my hand. "We have waited for so long. You've renewed our hope."

She held my hand so securely that the ring I was wearing left a deep imprint on my neighboring finger. The woman gave a final squeeze that I thought would sever my finger from my hand and returned to her booth, leaving her puzzling words echoing in my ears. "Did you hear what she said to me?"

"No. What?" Lillian asked.

"She said she was glad I had finally come. That they've been waiting for me for a long time. What did she mean by that?"

"Probably meant she's glad they finally have some visitors around here," Bethany said casually. "She probably gets bored of seeing the same people day after day."

There it was another level-headed, logical explanation from Bethany. I was angry with myself for even mentioning it. Even though Bethany's explanation seemed rational, I knew the woman meant more.

Bethany interrupted my tumbling thoughts. "Hey, you just passed the library."

"I'm not doing my research in the library. I said, pointing across the street to the local hair salon. "I'm doing it in the gossip center of every town."

Bethany's face broke into a large grin. "Good idea!"

"You'd trust them with your hair?" Lillian asked.

"Not my hair, my feet. I could really use a relaxing pedicure."

Bethany examined the ends of her hair. "I could use a little trim."

"Oh, I don't know," Lillian warned. "It's such a small, secluded town, I'm not certain they would be up to date on the latest styles."

"I'm not having it cut," she reiterated. "Just a slight trim."

We entered the salon. Any stereotyping of a small-town beauty shop suddenly flew out the window. The décor was much different than the expected vinyl chair and permanent solution odor. The ambiance was that of a jungle. Tall bamboo shoots and various palms grew from large basins scattered about the floor. Water trickled down the smooth black marbled walls, emptying into rectangular pools that housed many colorful fresh-water fish. Overstuffed chairs, upholstered in zebra and cheetah print fabrics, offered rest for the waiting clients. The ceiling, made entirely of bamboo and palm leaves, resembled a thatched roof. Recessed lighting gave a twilight feel. A small cabana, housing a reception desk made of bamboo, was placed in front of a beaded curtain, veiling the entrance into the parlor.

We introduced ourselves to the receptionist, who shook with delight and immediately escorted us into the servicing area where the rainforest theme continued. Three floor length mirrors hung on the walls with styling chairs set beside each one. There were no cumbersome hair stations in sight, just rolling carts equipped with the necessary tools to perform whatever service was requested. Each area had mosquito netting draped over it. Heavy old-fashioned ceiling fans turned slowly, offering a comfortable breeze and ventilation from the smells that accompany a salon.

Bethany was split from us and ushered to a hydraulic chair, draped, and left waiting for her stylist. The receptionist continued to escort me and Lillian into another room, seating us at what looked like a man-made waterfall. On top of each large boulder were soft cushions. Water fell from underneath our seats into stone basins filled with smooth pebbles of assorted sizes. Soft, relaxing music played in the background, interrupted by the occasional song of a bird.

Two smiling manicurists entered the room, positioning themselves at our feet.

"Hello!" The overly bleached blond woman said to me. "My name is Ashley."

Ashley appeared to be our age. She was pretty and tanned. Her hair was white from over bleaching yet didn't seem to be damaged. Her companion manicurist, Sherrie, appeared to be the same age. Her hair, a very unnatural shade of red, grew in curls that fell well beyond her waistline. Her pale skin was dotted with freckles, spreading onto her lips. Her blue gray eyes that seemed to house a freckle or two as well, were dancing in excitement. It seemed the two women were thrilled at the opportunity awaiting them. Lillian was right. The people here acted giddy, treating us as if we were celebrities.

"Are you enjoying your stay at Sandalwood Inn?" Ashley asked as she went to work on my feet.

"Yes. The inn is extremely comfortable, and the gardens are breathtaking."

"Isn't Mavis the best?" Sherrie chimed in. "She just adores that inn. It's her way of helping people. All Travis's patients stay there."

"Patients?" I repeated the word.

"Uh huh," Ashley casually glanced up at me while she trimmed my cuticles.

"Didn't he tell you? He's a doctor."

Lillian and I exchanged surprised glances. My plan was playing out. Not five minutes into the conversation, and I already received revealing evidence on Travis. I was sure to uncover my coveted information.

"He is?" Lillian was intrigued.

"Actually, he is a healer." Sherrie corrected Ashley's statement. "He travels the world and sets up clinics. He has a remarkably high success rate. Most of the patients that come to him have been sent home by their doctors to die. Travis treats them, and soon they return home cured. He hasn't lost a patient yet."

My mind was spinning. "Are you joking?"

Sherrie shook her head. "Why would we tease about that? You've seen the healing gardens where he grows all the herbs and plants to make his medications. That's what the big sheds out back behind the garage are for. They house all this special equipment to distill the oils from the plants. I can't explain the process; all I know is that it really seems to work, better than regular medicine anyway."

I was dumbfounded. Still, it all made perfect sense. Each garden was designed in a distinct way, each growing strange varieties of plants, offering comfort and vitality just by inhaling their aromas. I thought of the night in the cabin when Travis efficiently dressed my wound. He used a strange, yet soothing mixture of balms and oils with unique scents foreign to her, but apparently not to these manicurists.

"He is very generous, too," Ashley said. "He gives so much of his money away. Most of the clinics he's opened are in poor countries. He never charges anyone for treatment."

Lillian couldn't withhold her shock. "Travis has traveled the world?"

"Yep," Sherrie answered proudly, as if in some way Travis belonged to her personally. "That man's been all over this world. I'd say he pretty much knows his way across the planet."

I sat astounded, as Ashley took the smooth stones from the bottom of the basin and massaged my feet.

"I thought he was some lonely inn owner that had never been out of Moonshine," I heard myself confess aloud.

"He just doesn't seem the type," Lillian added.

"The type?" Sherrie laughed. "He's the type, alright. My type. He's near perfect if you ask me. I don't think there's a woman around here that wouldn't take that beautiful man if they could get him. Me included!"

"Sherrie!" Ashley said, her voice rising, "What would Martin say if he heard you?"

"Oh, he'd get over it." Sherrie began to massage Lillian's feet. "Besides, Martin doesn't have anything to worry about. Everyone knows Travis's heart belongs to only one woman."

"Lucky Mavis," Lillian said.

"Yep," Sherrie agreed. "That woman's been through some hard times, but all in all, I'd have to say she's blessed to have Travis."

My heart ached. All this added information, this research was proving to be more than I'd anticipated. The fact Travis was a doctor surprised me. That he was extremely wealthy, and traveled the world, opening clinics for the less fortunate, shocked, and stung a bit. The final blow to my heart was Sherrie's statement that he could have any woman he so desired, however his heart belonged to only one. Again, I reprimanded my pain. I should be delighted in the fact that Travis was proving to be the hero of whom I desired to write. Yet the pain was real, and I abhorred what it was doing to me. For the past six months, Ryan had contributed so much sadness, despondency, and sick feelings. Now, I had shoved most of my thoughts of Ryan aside and replaced them with Travis. Could I be falling for him, as Bethany so adamantly stated? Could I be infatuated with a man I'd known for less than three days? No. I was too smart for that. Yet, there was a strong undeniable yearning for him that far surpassed any silly crush. I couldn't understand why I desired a man so deeply, especially one I wasn't sure I could trust. I wished Larry would hurry and repair my car. Then I could flee far away from this place, and never think of him again.

"The people of Moonshine will surprise you," Ashley said proudly. "We have some of the most interesting characters you could ever meet living here."

The girls seemed talkative and eager to give out free information, so I took the opportunity to explore a bit further. "Were you both born here?"

Both girls concentrated on their task, dropping their gaze into the pedicure tub.

"No." Ashley answered but gave no more information. I thought it was somewhat peculiar since she was so chatty only moments before. I pressed the matter some more."

"Where were you born and what brought you to Moonshine?"

Sherrie took over. "Our families relocated here years ago, and we've been here ever since."

"You've never left?" Lillian asked, shocked.

"We've traveled some. But this is home for now anyway." Sherrie looked over at me. "Though I suspect I might be leaving soon." She smiled, and her grin unnerved me, and although their casual banter seemed honest, I sensed an underlying meaning.

I took a deep breath and asked another. "I've seen a man around here. He has long hair, which he usually wears back in a ponytail. He's unshaven, but easy on the eyes. He has a nice body, cool clothes. He wears dark sunglasses, and he smokes. Who is he?"

"That would be Falcon." Sherrie said, blushing. "I'm in love with the thought of that man!"

"Gosh, Sherrie!" Ashley reprimanded her again. "I feel sorry for poor Martin. You're lusting over every man in town but him."

Lillian laughed at the girl's banter. I quickly took back control, not wishing the conversation to phase into frivolity and the topic be dismissed before I found anything out. "Tell me about him."

Both girls remained silent for a moment, then a subtle glance between the two. I had stumbled onto something. Ashley finally spoke. "There's not much to tell. He's pretty mysterious, keeps to himself. He's some sort of secret agent," she said in a hushed voice, as if she feared the salon was bugged with listening devices.

I felt the heat. My pulse quickened. No doubt about it. This Falcon was the cloaked man! But, if he was some sort of secret agent, why was he following us?"

"He was stalking us," I blurted.

Lillian's perfectly arched brows raised. "He was? When?"

"On our walk the first day into town. It wasn't an animal in the woods. It was him. I saw him. Then he was at the café later when we were having lunch. I saw him staring at us from across the patio. He gave me the creeps."

Ashley laughed. "That would be Falcon alright. He always watches people. I guess no one ever told him staring was rude." She laughed it off, trying to divert the truth, but I knew there was more to him than poor social skills.

"He has friends that come to visit him from time to time," Sherrie added, also trying to make light of the subject. "They all have bird names too. I heard him call one of them Hawke, another Macaw, and there's one called Vulture. Talk about someone giving you the creeps!" Sherrie shuddered. "I guess they all work for the N.E.S.S.T. and someone known as the Great Owl, whoever that is."

My thoughts whirled inside my head. This was all beginning to sound vaguely familiar. I'd heard of this before, of secret agents with bird names. But where? I'd recently read about them but remembered dismissing the notion. It seemed so ridiculous. When and where had I encountered these people? Then it hit me, my deleted files! I read that synopsis yesterday while scanning through my discarded writings.

I shifted my feet in the water.

"I'm sorry did I hurt you?" Ashley asked.

"No. Just a nervous twitch, I guess. So, do these secret agents live in the woods and wear black hooded robes?" Sherrie and Ashley exchange knowing looks, it was my intention to press on with the questioning. "Is there some sort of secret society or cult up here we should know about?" For once, the two girls grew quiet.

Ashley removed my feet from the basin and promptly drained the tub. She toweled them off and then proceeded to rub an agreeable smelling lotion over them.

Ashley and Sherrie quickly finished polishing our toenails and cleaned up their supplies. They left us alone to dry.

"My God Bronwyn, why did you ask such a strange question?" Lillian asked. "I think you may have offended them. In any case, you learned quite a bit about Travis. I think your research was pretty successful."

I wished the polish would hurry and dry. My next stop in this town would be Larry's garage, to check on the status of the ordered parts. I wanted out of this place at once!

My pressing engagement was quickly forgotten when Bethany joined us in the pedicure room. Lillian and I were both caught off guard at the sight of her new mullet.

"Oh my God!" Lillian exclaimed, covering her mouth with her slender fingers. "What happened to your hair?"

"Can we just get out of here before I cry?" she asked.

I bit my lip, choking back my laughter.

Lillian's eyes flashed. "I warned you."

"I just asked for a trim!" Bethany said in a hoarse whisper. "I should have known when she suggested that I would look good in the Jennifer Aniston cut. I told her I used to have that cut, way back in the 90's when it was in style. Let's just get out of here."

∞

Sherrie placed the pedicure utensils in the disinfectant solution and washed her hands. "You really shouldn't smoke in here you know."

"So, you're in love with the thought of me huh?"

Sherrie smiled and turned off the water. "So, how'd we do?"

Falcon snuffed his cigarette and stood. "Pretty good. Keep it up and I might let you join the N.E.S.S.T." He flashed his impish grin and disappeared out the back door.

Twenty-Four

We spent the remainder of the afternoon helping decorate, much to the delight of the local townsfolk. I ran into Larry and questioned him on the status of the parts, only to learn that they had yet to arrive. The eight-to-ten business day estimate was proving to be the actual waiting time.

As the day wore on, the outdoor activities in Moonshine shifted from productive construction to gaiety and frivolity. With most of the work completed, the residents enjoyed a pre-festival party. As with every year on the eve of the festival, the café and other local restaurants treated volunteer workers to a buffet dinner in the courtyard. The bands took their turns at a sound check and a brief rehearsal, entertaining the dining workers. Dancing followed, along with homemade alcohol and soon the town came alive.

At sunset, the strung lights lit the courtyard and the grounds filled with people. Everyone either lounged on the grass or danced to the music. Several thespians approached the large wooden platform giving impromptu performances. Lillian had finally relented, due to the pleadings of Carlo Jo, and did a monologue. She decided on a comedy from one of her previous productions and as usual her stage presence was captivating. The locals enjoyed the performance, breaking out in spontaneous laughter at her wit, and standing to applaud when it was over. She took several bows and then bounced off the stage, her eyes glowing in excitement, pleased she had received such a rousing applause. Another band took the stage as she descended. The dancing started up again. I joined them on the grass and quickly learned the steps. This dance was obviously a local favorite, perhaps even legendary in these mountains. I enjoyed the fast-paced choreography, spinning from one partner to the next. Each face I connected with gave me a wide toothy grin. I was spun into the arms of the always-smiling Gil Peverley, the jokester and owner of the market. Sidestepping and shuffling, he gave a slight bow, "Howdy little lady."

This time I returned the smile I'd withheld at our first meeting. Gil spun me around and passed me into the arms of Larry the mechanic.

"Parts still haven't arrived," he said, grinning as he side-stepped, shuffled, and spun me into the arms of an extremely attractive man I hadn't seen in Moonshine before now.

He was olive-skinned with dark curly hair brushing the top of his shoulders. His eyes were a deep steel blue. He had a gentle face, and his speaking voice matched his appearance. He offered me a warm hello and an adoring smile. Slightly bowing his head in a respectful nod, he continued dancing while never removing his eyes from my face. Another sidestep and shuffle, and I was swirled into the arms of Falcon! Dark glasses covered his eyes. His impish grin frightened me. He said nothing as he twirled me along, nor did he pass me on, down the line. Instead, he purposely kept me to himself, spinning me out of the dance line, maintaining a tight hold as I was whirled forcefully across the lawn. Panic set in. Why had I let my guard down? Spending the afternoon with the friendly residents disarmed me to the point of second guessing myself, thinking that maybe I'd been mistaken about the place. But now, locked in Falcon's tight hold, my fears resurfaced. I tried focusing my eyes, but everything was a blur, as if I were riding some spinning carnival ride. The heat was rising uncontrollably now. My heart moved into my throat, stealing my breath. I tried pulling away, but his grip remained firm. He kept his body close, pressing into mine as he moved me along across the grounds. I tried once more to push him away, yet I was no match for his strength.

"Stay with me, scribe," his deep voice whispered in my ear. "Don't fight me."

Scribe? What the hell did he mean by that? He moved me swiftly through the crowd, his body creating a shield. I tried to look around for help, but he spun me with such force I could barely move my head.

"Don't." He placed his hand on the back of my head and buried it in his chest. There was no air and I struggled to breathe. I balled my fist and pushed against him, trying to get him off of me. It was futile against his crushing strength.

Then as suddenly as he had grabbed me, he let me go. I stumbled across the grass and tried to regain my footing. My head was still spinning, making it difficult to walk. He was not there. Where had he gone? I tried focusing down the line of dancers, yet he was not among them. I scanned the courtyard next. There was no sign of him. How could he have disappeared so quickly?

The band continued to play, their music blaring from the speakers. I felt trapped as if I were in the center of a gigantic carrousel, while everything spun around me. My legs wobbled and my heart raced at an alarming rate. The twinkling lights faded all around me and became as distant as the stars in the evening sky. Everything went black, and in the darkness, I heard a distant voice calling my name.

∞

"Someone wanna go get Travis!" Ashley yelled above the music.

The dancing stopped and soon a small crowd gathered. Bethany and Lillian pushed their way through and knelt beside their fallen friend.

"What happened?" Lillian asked. "Don't tell me she was climbing bloody trees again."

"I saw her standing there looking pale," Ashley offered Lillian the news. "Then she just kind of fell over."

A sudden gust of wind blew through the crowd, sending paper plates and napkins flying across the courtyard. Booth awnings billowed upward as a couple of makeshift stands collapsed. Bronwyn's eyes fluttered open.

A sea of faces stared at me from above. My eyes focused on Bethany.

"Bronwyn?"

"What happened?"

"You fainted, hon," Ashley said.

Bethany leaned in. "Are you okay? I think maybe you should see a doctor." She whispered her next words, so no one else could hear. "You're not on anything, are you?"

"No!" I said, giving her a disgusted look. "Of course not! You know me better than that."

"I just thought maybe you had gotten some anti-depressants or something. You know, because of Ryan."

I stood and dust myself off. "Didn't you see what just happened to me? Didn't anyone?"

Bethany shook her head. "No, what happened?"

"I was accosted, that's what! Something's going on around here and I want to know what it is." I made my accusations and demands out loud to the crowd who stared back at me. No one spoke except for Ashley.

"Maybe you should wait for Travis, you know.... just to make sure you're okay."

I hadn't seen Travis since early morning when he woke me by the river. He hadn't been at breakfast, nor had I seen him in town. Now that I had learned more about this mysterious mountain man, I decided the less I saw of him, the better.

"I don't need his help."

My refusal was too late. He pushed his way through the crowd and stood face to face with me. His hair was wet with perspiration and blood oozed from his bottom lip. His clothes were dirty and torn. His usual calm countenance was replaced by agitation.

"You alright?" his voice demanded an answer.

"I'm fine." I bit back. "But you don't look so good."

Sherrie stepped in close to him. "She fainted. Ashley and I caught her. We didn't let her hit the ground."

He never took his eyes off me, much to Sherrie's dismay.

I stared back, full of sentiments I didn't entirely understand. I was angry with him for causing most of these emotions and for hiding the secrets I was sure would unravel all these peculiarities. Yet, he kept these mysteries undisclosed. I had half a mind to shout out accusations and reveal tell-tale information of the cloaked figures that inhabited the surrounding woods. However, I felt as if most of the town already knew. Anything I might announce might bring a world of dread upon us.

"No need to worry about me," I clicked my tongue. "It's only altitude sickness, I'm sure."

I brushed past him and headed back to the inn. The girls caught up with me for the long walk back.

Travis removed the handkerchief from his back pocket and wiped the fresh blood from his knuckles and mouth. He made eye contact with Falcon and with a slight nod Falcon stole into the surrounding woods. Travis remained standing, watching, until the girls disappeared from view.

Twenty-Five

I lay in bed, staring at the rotating ceiling fan. Despite my long adventurous day, sleep would not come. For starters, Bethany had greatly annoyed me on the walk back. She had launched into a barrage of questions to support her growing suspicion that I was on drugs of some kind. Against my better judgment, I decided to confide in Bethany and tell her of some of the strange events. I mentioned nothing of my deleted stories, realizing it would be impossible to try and explain, seeing I had no explanation for it myself. I mentioned Falcon, the secret locked garden, and the covert meeting between him and Travis. Bethany barely listened, dismissing the stories completely, only to ask more questions about my psyche.

Defeated, I feigned exhaustion, and fell into bed to escape Bethany's constant advice. And now, here I lay, wide-awake listening to the heavy breathing of my roommates, my mind too active to sleep.

Quietly, I slipped from the bed, tiptoed down the stairs and walked out the back door. The night air was surprisingly cool. The mugginess of the evening had dissipated. I curled up on the cushioned porch swing, swaying back and forth with ease, hoping the rhythm of the swing, combined with the chorus of croaking toads and chirping crickets would be the sleeping aid I so desperately needed. The fresh air and change of scenery did wonders to relax the tension in my body and slow down the ramblings of my mind.

Voices from far down the cobblestone path caught my attention. Who else was up at this hour? I rose from the swing, tiptoed down the porch steps, and crept quietly down the stony path. The further I walked, the voices became clearer, whoever they belonged to was engaged in an intense argument. It was hard to tell which garden the disturbance came from, but as I walked, the commotion grew louder.

I stopped at the sixth garden, seeing the gate was unlatched. I pushed it open slowly, hoping it wouldn't creak. A splinter found its way deep underneath my skin, as my slender finger slid across the rough wood. I pulled my hand away, recoiling at the unwanted pain. It would take tweezers and much better light for me to remove it. Something that could wait until morning. Nevertheless, I slipped quietly into the garden. Large trees and vines created a canopy at the entrance, providing me with the perfect cover for my investigation. If Travis would not tell me what was going on, then I would find out on my own. I inched my way past the massive oaks, my slender body slithering through the hanging foliage of the weeping willows. I kept hidden in the canopy of leaves providing me with secrecy, while the soft earth beneath my bare feet allowed no noise, muffling my approach.

The ruckus grew louder. The angry voices were much clearer now. I moved from tree to tree, keeping under the weeping willows as I made my way closer to the center of the garden. Figures moved ahead. Reaching out I parted the hanging branches. The heat rushed in again, overwhelming me. The man in the road, the night of our arrival, was in the garden.

Poised to fight, he stood alongside Falcon, who held a man in a head-lock, his knife against his throat. One move and his head would be severed from his body. The prisoner appeared to be composed even though Falcon pressed the knife hard against his neck. I swallowed and my throat constricted at the vicious scene.

A third man stood with Falcon and seemed to be interrogating their prisoner. He too was muscular, well-built and wore his blond hair fastened back in a ponytail. He was one of the men in the pool the night we hiked to the falls. I remember his eyes were turquoise, much like the water he was swimming in.

"Answer me!" His eyes were no longer placid but rather a whirlpool of a torrential current.

"Surely you know." The captive man choked, despite the knife pressed against his throat. "Abaddon's realm is spreading, growing in strength. His power is more than you can imagine. You can kill me, but more will come. Your tower of safety has fallen. We found your hiding place and the information has been released. We know the scribe is here, somewhere. We will find them and when we do, they will be destroyed. Every one of you will return to captivity again. It's just a matter of time."

The bronze warrior spoke. His voice was vast, haunting as if a woodwind instrument were playing along with him. The sound of it was captivating, drawing me into each word he said.

"Know that we will not miss a move. We are aware of every step you take in these mountains. Your sole purpose was to make a name for yourself and receive your reward. However, the only prize the one you serve will offer for your allegiance is death. Your foolish choices have trapped you in a dead end. Death is now the payment you will receive for your betrayal."

Taking a step backward, the warrior gave Falcon a nod. Falcon's hand moved swiftly across the man's neck. Blood spread quickly, soaking into the fabric of his shirt, as he slumped to the ground. A gas gasp escaped my lips at the sudden brutality.

All heads turned in my direction. The warriors' eyes glowed as they pierced across the garden, cutting through the foliage. I ducked taking cover under the tree but was sure he had seen me. My legs wobbled beneath me. I'd witnessed a murder! If they found me, would I receive the same punishment?

I needed to run and wake the girls but where would we go? How could we defend ourselves? Bethany hadn't brought a gun. Strong hands grabbed me from behind and pulled me out of view. Terror rose inside as I anticipated the cold steel of a knife slicing through my neck. I could scream, perhaps the noise would wake the girls.

Before the cry could escape my lips, a hand pressed firmly over my mouth. "Stay quiet." I recognized the voice of the one holding me. My heart throbbed, pumping up the invading heat.

"Sh-sh." His voice was stern. "Don't make a noise, or they will find you." He spun me around, still keeping his hand across my mouth. "I warned you not to venture out alone. From here on out you'd do best to listen to my instructions."

The only thing visible was Travis' dark eyes lit by a streak of moonlight shining through the foliage. He removed his hand from my mouth and before I could demand information, he gently pulled my face toward his and placed his mouth on mine. I inhaled his breath, tasting his scent as he whispered, "what am I to do with you?" He tenderly kissed me on the lips. I felt his fingers press into the back of my neck. My legs buckled and all went black.

Twenty-Six

DAY FIVE

I woke to the gentle hand of Mavis on my back.

"Seems you did your sleeping on the porch last night," she said cheerfully. "I've done that a time or two myself. There's nothing like the night air to hypnotize you and put you in a deep sleep. The only side effect is that it can bring on some strange dreams and, might I say, you were definitely having one. You woke me up last night with your hollering and carrying on."

Mavis poured a tall mug of steaming coffee and handed it to me. "This should clear up the haziness I suspect is clouding your mind right now."

I sat up, confused by my surroundings. I looked across the property. The sun was just making its way over the mountains, striking the ground glistening with the morning dew. The pungent aromas from the gardens wafted in the morning breeze. I reached for the coffee, and sipped the strong brew, nearly choking at the bitterness of it.

"I woke you during the night?" I asked.

"Sure did. My window is directly above this side of the porch. I heard you scream. Sounded like you were scared out of your wits. I ran out here and found you having a fitful sleep on the swing."

I took another slip of the awful coffee. I vaguely remembered leaving my room last night. Could I be sleep walking again? Steam rose from the mug and filled my nose with the earthy aroma of my drink. The events of last night gradually made their way back into my head. The memory of the intense argument began to emerge, and within seconds all the images raced back into my mind. The warrior, Falcon, the blond man, the murder and then Travis under the tree...The kiss!

I raised my hands to my lips at the thought of the kiss before I noticed Mavis watching me intently. I quickly lowered my hand.

"Must have been some kind of dream." A sly smile pulled at the corner of her lips while she gave me a suspicious look.

I sensed her distrust and wondered if it stemmed from Mavis' wariness of me and Travis. Maybe she could sense a mutual attraction as well.

"You want to tell me about it?"

My heart picked up its pace. "Tell you about what?"

"Your dream hon."

"I don't think it was a dream." I said boldly. "I think I stumbled on something I wasn't supposed to see."

"Sometimes it helps when you talk out a disturbing dream. Even though it seems so real at the time, you realize how absurd it is when you hear yourself telling it to someone. You realize it couldn't have possibly happened."

I stared back at her, seeing through her pretense. Despite Mavis's outward appearance as a country mountain woman, beaten down by a hard life, she held as many secrets as Travis, and the rest of these peculiar town folk.

"I left my room because I couldn't sleep. I was upset about something that happened in town earlier. I came out to the porch and that's when I heard a heated argument in the garden. I followed the voices just in time to witness an execution."

"An execution! My lands that would cause anyone to scream. No wonder you were scared. Who was executed?"

"I don't know. I've never seen him before. But the sight of him unnerved me. He spoke in a foreign language and said a lot of bizarre things, like a tower of safety falling and finding some heirs and a scribe and destroying them."

"If he spoke in a strange language, how is it you were able to understand what he said?"

I felt color enter my face, realizing the impossibility of my statement. "I don't know how I understood, but I did."

"You're a writer, aren't you?" Mavis asked. "Maybe you're stressing over your re-write so much that your dreaming people want to destroy you."

I remained silent for a moment before speaking again. I was certain what I experienced had not been a dream. However, Mavis' friendly interrogation was beginning to cause me to wonder. After all, the man had said he was looking for the scribe. A scribe is another word for a writer. I shook my head.

"No, it was real. I saw it all. There was this very tall man who was dressed like a warrior...." I stopped cold, realizing how absurd my story sounded. "The man who did the killing was someone I have seen here in Moonshine. I think they call him Falcon."

Mavis remained unaffected. "What happened in town earlier that upset you?" She sounded like a psychiatrist.

"Falcon got pretty forceful with me last night."

"How so?"

"During the dance, he pulled me away from everyone and spun me into the crowd. When I tried to get away, he called me 'Scribe' and told me not to fight him."

Mavis smiled. "But he didn't hurt you. That's the way some of these mountain men are, but you, being from the city, wouldn't understand our ways. No wonder you had such a frightful dream about him."

The diplomatic stare down between me and Mavis continued. Each one's distrust for the other hovered just beneath the surface, unspoken.

I broke her gaze and looked over towards the gardens and then back to her before I stood.

"It seemed so real."

"I'm sure it did." Mavis smiled. "How did it end?"

I sipped the coffee, only to hide my face. How could I tell the part where Travis kissed me? Mavis made me uncomfortable. Despite her supposed concern for me, I felt she already knew the answers to the questions she was asking.

I forced the bitter coffee down and handed the mug back to Mavis.

"I don't remember. It's all still a little sketchy. I guess you're right. It was just a dream. Thanks for the coffee. I think I'll go take a long hot shower to work out the kinks in my neck."

∞

Mavis waited for Bronwyn to disappear inside of the inn before pouring the remaining coffee in the grass. She grabbed the shovel leaning against the side of the inn and limped out into the gardens.

∞

The steaming shower relaxed me, soothing my aching neck and back. The porch swing didn't make a comfortable bed. I hated to think I was sleep walking again after all these years. It used to be a problem for me as a child, resulting in my parents taking such extreme measures as alarming our house and adding bolt locks on every door. My dreams as a child were night terrors, and although I could not remember any of them, my mother had documented almost everyone. I prayed they weren't returning, but my dreams of late had been quite vivid and disturbing, and I hoped that maybe the cause was the higher altitude. Once we left this God forsaken place, I hoped the nightmares and sleepwalking would end.

I massaged the shampoo into my hair and felt a painful stinging in my finger and discovered a splinter embedded under my skin. The events of last night had not been a dream! The splinter was proof I'd witnessed a murder! My mind reeled with questions. I let the warm waters run over me as I tried to focus. I thought back to the garden, the words of the murdered man. He spoke in another language, yet I understood, even though what he said made no sense to me. However, he had evoked the wrath of his three captors when he mentioned a tower of safety falling, and that his people had found the hiding place.

His next words unnerved me. He mentioned finding a scribe and destroying them. Could he have possibly been referring to me? After all, that is what Falcon called me, and Travis admitted he was protecting me. Then, under the tree, he warned me not to make a noise or they would find me. Who are "they?" I was more confused than ever. How could I be this mysterious scribe? Our visit here was an accident. We weren't supposed to be in Moonshine, so no, they couldn't have been referring to me. Maybe we just stumbled on to some kind of mafia crime ring or something and because we are innocent, trapped victims, Travis was just trying to keep us out of harm's way.

However, the events in the garden were powerfully overshadowed at the recollection of his kiss. He kissed me! I could still feel this touch as he brought my face to his and the feel of his mouth tenderly placed on my lips. My stomach tightened at the memory. It had been quick and unexpected, yet more passionate than any kiss I'd ever received from Ryan. Travis gave the kiss. He had not stolen a kiss from me under the privacy of the weeping willow. He had not satisfied his desire by taking a kiss; rather, he had given me a kiss. He had placed a kiss on my lips, for me. But then he'd placed his fingers on the back of my neck causing me to slip into unconsciousness, just like the cloaked man when I fell from the tree.

Twenty-Seven

The only reason I showed up at breakfast was to see if Travis was present. He wasn't. I picked at my food, my inner anxiousness suppressing my appetite. I ignored the idle chatter at the table and gazed out of the window, thinking it would be a smart move to return to the garden and collect any evidence of last night's slaying. Surely there would be blood in the grass, something to prove to everyone I hadn't dreamed it all up.

Bethany interrupted my thoughts to ask again about the rewrite. I sighed. My mind was far from the plot of a cheesy romance. However, to satisfy her, I mentioned that I'd been contemplating the idea, of instead of doing a simple rewrite, I would rather scrap it and try an entirely new story. To my surprise, she endorsed the idea. She lovingly confessed that my latest manuscript had not been one of her favorites, going as far as to say that she absolutely abhorred it, finding it was full of cynicism, bitterness, and a bit apathetic, and admitted she would be delighted to read brand new material. Then, she told me she was pleased with our recent turn of events, saying she was happy that the car broke down when and where it did. Despite the fact she and Lillian had lost their deposits at the mountain resort, she realized that we needed this little sabbatical. Had we plowed through our carefully planned schedule there would have been no time to discuss the book and no time for rewrites. I appeared to be listening to her ramblings, responding with an occasional smile and nod, but my mind was far away.

After breakfast, I slipped off and settled on the porch swing. The grand veranda provided a pleasant view, and a large spinning ceiling fan generated a nice breeze the summer day would not.

I opened my laptop, to my dormant files, the last place I'd visited. I thought back to the pedicure room, the stories told by Ashley and Sherrie. I paused for a moment, debating on whether to open the file again. If the stories the girls told were identical to those I'd written some time ago, I wasn't sure I could muddle through the strong emotions.

But I was desperate for more information about Falcon. After all, I'd witnessed him commit a murder. If there was some clue in my files as to what was going on, I was intent on finding it. My slender finger clicked on Birds of Prey. The file opened once more, displaying the short synopsis. Taking a deep breath, I scrolled down to my character list and read the typed names:

Falcon, Macaw, Hawke, and Vulture, all agents of an elite top-secret organization known as the N.E.S.S.T, a group of top-secret agents, all possessing bird names and working for the Great Owl. Falcon, the leader of this group, is sworn protector of a Prince who is being hunted by an evil assassin. Falcon, and the other birds of prey, have made their NESST in the branches of The Tree of Life.

I leaned into the swing and thought back to when I received the inspiration for this story. A vivid dream jolted me awake at 2:22 a.m. one morning. Its images were so real that I stumbled from my bed and sleepily typed the brief synopsis. By the next morning, I'd forgotten about the dream completely. A few days later, I read my rambling notes and dismissed them as incoherent babble. Besides, I wrote romance not espionage.

I read the brief synopsis again. If this was true, then possibly Falcon killed to protect a Prince. But how could this be? How could I've known this and written about it? And what was the tree of life? Was it some kind of fountain of youth? Could this be what the cloaked men were guarding? Could the Bible's mysterious Tree of Life be hidden somewhere in Moonshine?

I shut my eyes and took a slow, cleansing breath. I closed the file and nervously clicked on, My Brother's Keeper, and read the synopsis once again:

A woman is forced to face life, raising her children alone, when a tragic murder claims the life of her beloved husband....

Nervously, I scrolled down to view the character list letting out a small gasp when the name Mavis appeared on the screen. My heart pounded. How could the people in my stories be real? What did all this mean? Was Travis destined to die?

I felt as if I would vomit at any minute. I was hyperventilating. I needed to breathe. I needed to talk with someone. But who? Who could begin to understand the craziness of all this? Bethany? Maybe I should try talking with her again. This was too much to take in alone. Maybe I should talk to Lillian. Show her the files. After all she believed in so many conspiracy theories, I doubt she would dismiss my information as bullshit. My stomach churned. I knew the person I must talk to, the person who hid volumes of secrets behind his dark eyes. The same person who had pulled me to safety last night whispered a warning and kissed me.

Travis.

I closed my laptop, deciding I would find him and demand an explanation. If not, I would threaten to write a disparaging story, revealing the location of a supposed fountain of youth. The entire world would read it, blowing wide open the deep secret of Moonshine and the clandestine deeds they were hiding.

A strong wind swept across the back lawn, toppling over chairs, and vigorously ringing the chimes hanging overhead. The back screen door slammed shut, as a cold chill raced up my spine. An overwhelming feeling of terror washed over me, as an unseen presence swept across the gardens. The sudden fear was paralyzing.

"Here you are!"

I spun around, startled at the sound of Bethany's greeting.

"You, ok?" Bethany asked. "You look pale."

"I'm alright," I breathed, relieved at Bethany's arrival. However, I could still feel the malevolent presence roaming about.

"You're shaking!"

"I'm cold."

"You're kidding me!" Bethany laughed. "How could you be cold, it's at least 90 degrees in the shade. Are you sick?"

She walked forward and placed her hand on my forehead. "You feel fine. Are you sure you're not taking meds?"

"Damn it, Bethany! Quit asking me that. I am not nor have I ever taken anything!"

Her eyes widened at my reaction. "Alright! Calm down! I won't ask you again. It's just that you haven't been yourself lately. You're not sleeping at night. You leave the room at all hours, you have fallen from trees, and last night you fainted. Now you look terrified, you're pale as a ghost and are trembling. I just want to know what's up with you."

"Do you really want to know?"

"Yes, please tell me."

I glanced above, remembering Mavis' comment about her window being directly over this part of the porch.

"Come with me."

I led Bethany off the terrace and into the gardens. Confused, she followed me down the cobblestone paths until I stopped at the sixth garden. I took a deep breath before pushing open the gate.

"What..." She began to protest but I held my hand up to silence her. I led her past the weeping willows and headed toward the open grass, where I'd witnessed the slaying. I focused on the spot and clenched my teeth. "I should have known."

A freshly planted tree stood where the condemned man's death sentence had been carried out. There was no evidence of blood. The ground had been broken and the soil turned.

"What?" Bethany repeated her question.

I looked around cautiously before whispering. "Beth, I saw someone killed in this garden last night." She stared at me, at a loss for words. "I know it sounds crazy, but I saw a man get his throat slit right here. Right where this tree is. I think it was planted to cover up the spot where he bled out."

"I'm sorry," Bethany said. "But I have to ask again. Are you taking pills?"

"Damn it Bethany! You insist I tell you things and when I do, you completely disregard it. Why do you do that?"

She suppressed a laugh. "Come on Bronwyn. You really don't expect me to believe you witnessed a murder. I'm not Lillian you know."

"Yes, I do." The frustration seeped into my voice. "Why wouldn't you? Have I ever lied to you before?"

"No. But before you weren't...."

My eyes flared. "Weren't what?"

"You weren't depressed and upset and going through the phases of a break-up. C'mon Bronwyn. You have to admit you've not been yourself lately. Even Lillian thinks..."

I rolled my eyes. "Since when do we take what Lil says seriously?"

"Well sometimes she makes sense! Besides, if you did see someone get murdered, why did you wait so long to tell me? Why didn't you wake me during the night? How could you have simply fallen back asleep after something like that?"

I couldn't disclose that Travis kissed her under the willow tree. I paused a moment before offering a feeble answer: "I fainted."

Bethany looked intently at me, suspicion pulsing from her eyes.

"Okay" I sighed. "Someone grabbed me from behind and did something that caused me to lose consciousness. I woke up on the back porch swing early this morning."

She still looked skeptical. "And you never told anyone about this? You were just going to let all of us be bludgeoned to death in our sleep?"

"I didn't think any of us were in danger. They could have killed me too, as an eyewitness. Instead, they laid me on the porch swing."

"And they didn't think you would tell us or the police when you woke up?"

I dropped my voice to a whisper. "Mavis tried to dismiss it as a bad dream. She said I woke her during the night screaming. In her words, I was having a fitful night's sleep. I think she is in on it."

Bethany sighed sympathetically. "In on what Bronwyn? I am sure Mavis is right. You were having a dream. I hadn't mentioned it earlier, but I've noticed you have been leaving our room during the night. Maybe you're sleepwalking again like you did when you were a kid. Dreams can seem so real at times."

I ran my fingers through my long dark tresses and surveyed the garden. The splinter in my finger was more than enough proof that what I witnessed had not been a dream. A definite cloak and dagger conspiracy was unfolding among the residents of this puzzling town. Should I dare mention the fact I was suspicious that the tree of Life may be hidden somewhere in Moonshine? After all, I hadn't seen one senior citizen during my entire stay, and no one in the town looked any older than forty. Bethany's reaction to everything else so far, answered that question. It did seem absurd to say the least. However, I knew it was very real. I would continue to keep it to myself, and only discuss it with those who knew what was truly going on. At the festival, I would search for Travis. Once I found him, I would demand answers.

Twenty-Eight

The girls spent extra time dressing for the whimsical festival. Lillian appeared as a mountain blossom coming to life, wearing a soft pink halter dress, cascading into several layers of powder pink and white airy fabrics. The sheerness of the fabrics would have undoubtedly been see-through, had they not been layered one over the other. Her luxurious platinum hair hung loosely down her back, with random strands of pink ribbon braided periodically throughout her massive mane. She did her makeup to its usual perfection. Silver sandals adorned her dainty feet.

Bethany's greatest challenge was disguising her new haircut. Lillian and I both suggested several different styles, yet nothing seemed to work. Much to our surprise, Carla Jo entered our room with a pair of razor-sharp scissors, and quickly and artistically turned Bethany's mullet into a classic shoulder length bob. Even though Bethany grieved over losing her long locks, she much preferred the bob to the hideous mullet. She quickly chose a turquoise tank style dress, accessorizing it with silver bangle bracelets and hooped earrings.

I pulled my curls over my left shoulder, securing them in a very loose low ponytail. Several pieces escaped their clutches and fell around my face. I chose a simple white linen halter dress and accessorized with turquoise jewelry and silver sandals. I resembled a Native American princess.

We trekked into Moonshine on the two-lane highway. The more frequently we walked this path, the less the distance seemed. The melodious tune of a dulcimer drifted over the mountains and through the trees, as it had throughout the week. The night was clear, beautiful. The magnificent moon gave off enough light to illuminate the dark road. Millions of stars filled the sky like loose diamonds scattered across a piece of dark purple velvet. The cool breeze swept gently over the mountains, stirring against the trees, and casting the aroma of spruce, firs, pine, and cedar into the air. It evoked a sense of protection, a sacred feeling that seemed to empower me, filling me with renewed strength.

As we walked down the center of the crooked highway, Beth, and Lil each took turns recounting events of the past five days, telling various stories of the curious people they had met thus far. Bethany occasionally pointed out the unique lifestyle and forgotten dialect of the mountain. I enjoyed this moment, listening to my friends describing their adventures. Their stories gave some sense of normality to our situation. What I did notice was that all their stories were typical, average. Neither of them spoke of uneasiness, or gave mention of any peculiar events, apparitions, cloaked figures, or murders in the gardens. They simply experienced everyday common behavior. I envied them in a way.

Country mountain ballads could be heard on the outskirts of town, along with laughter and gaiety. The festivities were in full swing. As we rounded the final curve, the streets and courtyards were ablaze with activity. Each decorated booth erupted with color and offered a tasty treat or trinket of some sort. Strung lights and blazing lanterns gave off a fairy tale ambiance. Vendors were dressed in what resembled medieval masquerade, most of their identities hidden by peculiar masks. It seemed to be a combination of a Renaissance faire and Carnevale in Venice. In keeping with the theme, young children, dressed as charming fairies, ran through the crowd throwing glittery pixie dust, and giving out small bags of delicious candies. Molly, a winsome little fairy, eagerly brought her bags of goodies to each of us.

The delicious aromas of sweets and baked goods overpowered the natural scents of the mountains. Booths offered home-made waffle cones, warm baked brownies, and oversized cookies, all of which could be covered with mounds of the delicious frozen treats.

We strolled amongst the kiosks and various stands. Everyone eagerly offered us ice cream samples. Not yet ready to begin gorging, we graciously declined.

Tiny lights blazed all over the hills, giving indication of homes hidden deep in the trees. Judging by the enormous turn out, Moonshine appeared to be much larger in population than I'd had originally thought. All these people, hidden from view, nestled in the mountains and still I saw no one over the age of forty,

The courtyard bustled with activity. A group of dancers, dressed in silver and blue angelic costumes, performed a beautiful interpretive dance in the grass outside the church grounds. Another large group of people danced to the lively tunes of the band.

A masked figure approached, offering each of us a single rose. He bowed slightly, and without a word, disappeared back into the crowd, giving away more flowers. This carnival-type atmosphere was nothing I'd had ever experienced before. It was as magical as a page out of a fairy tale book.

Lillian grabbed my arm, "Look! Is that Falcon?"

My heart leaped into my throat. He was leaning against a tree with a cigarette clenched between his teeth, and appeared to be in deep thought, unaware of each drag he took. He kept his attention on the crowd, not watching anyone in particular. He was wearing his sunglasses, despite the late hour. He seemed totally indifferent to the fact he had recently slit someone's throat. I shuddered at the thought of his forcefulness last night and the extreme fear and discomfort he hurled upon me.

"It's him," I said, steering us in the opposite direction. I didn't wish to draw his attention our way.

We continued to walk past the booths, stopping only once for a giant blue cloud of cotton candy. I unwound a strand of the fluffy confection from the paper stick. "I'm really missing Ryan tonight," I confessed, before popping the sugary substance in my mouth.

"Really?" Bethany's brows raised, joyful that I had opened and shared a rational feeling. "Why?"

"I don't know. The ambiance maybe, the sultriness of a warm summer night. The fairy tale atmosphere of the festival. The perfect night sky. It all seems so surreal. Like some sort of a dream. It's moments like this I wish I had someone special to share it with."

"What are we then?" Bethany attempted to sound offended.

I laughed. "You know what I mean. I enjoy spending time with you both. In fact, I am glad we're here together. It's just..."

"There's no need to explain," she confessed. "I totally understand. I am desperate for some sort of romantic interlude myself."

We spent most of the night sampling ice cream, feasting on sweets and baked goods, even trying our luck at several challenging games. We took in a few impromptu performances of various dancers, magicians, poets, and watched the strange antics of a mime.

Masked figures would approach from time to time, presenting us with flowers or placing colorful beads around our necks. Some simply took our hands and kissed them. Occasionally, I would glance over my shoulder to keep a close eye on Falcon, who dutifully maintained his attention on the crowd. I'd also glanced around, searching nonchalantly for Travis. He was not among the gathering. I chewed my lip in disappointment. I had not seen him since last night. I feared he was staying hidden, more than likely avoiding me, so he wouldn't have to answer any questions concerning the events in the garden.

Three nervous teenage boys approached us, interrupting my musings. Timidly, they asked for a dance and soon we were being whirled about in the grass. Although I was dancing and laughing, I felt it impossible to relax and enjoy the evening. A bitter feeling gnawed in the pit of my stomach, as my attention was drawn to the large banner hanging over the bandstand. I'd seen this banner on my first day in Moonshine and had read it several times since. This time a certain portion jumped right off the canvas and punched me in the face.

Saturday August 16th

There hadn't been a day in the past year, especially the past three months that I hadn't thought of August 16th. It was embossed on hundreds of discarded invitations and napkins. The day Ryan and I were to be married. My stomach knotted, a lump formed in my throat, blocking a cistern full of tears that would certainly burst forth if given the slightest chance.

I left the dance floor, making my way through the crowd, and across the busy courtyard, heading as far away from the festivities as I could. Another masked figure approached, placing a small decorative cylinder in my hand.

"I am delivering a message just for you my dear," He whispered in my ear.

Blowing me a kiss, he bowed slightly and twirled away, disappearing into the crowd.

I shoved the small cylinder in my dress pocket, before I discovered a small path leading towards the lake. I followed the trail until the music and laughter transformed into croaking frogs and singing crickets. Tears stung in my eyes, yet I held them at bay. I refused to cry. I would not allow myself to give Ryan any more of my tears. I picked up the pace, wanting to run for miles and never stop.

I slid off my low-heeled sandals and contemplated whether to toss them into the lake or to hang onto them. They were one of my favorite pairs, but at this point I didn't care. I hurled them one at a time into the dark silvery waters and continued to run. Soft pine needles provided a carpet, cushioning my bare feet most of the way. Still, a few splintery sticks and sharp pinecones pierced my soles. I didn't feel the stinging as much since the pain in my heart overcame all other senses in my body.

Then from behind me, I heard snapping branches. Thoughts of my mourning disappeared, burning away with the realization of what I'd done. How could I have been so careless? Why did I put myself at risk by running through the woods late at night alone? Should I dare stop and look behind me?

A cold chill snaked its way up my back. I was lost and had no idea where I was, or how far away from the festival I had run. I wanted to turn back but feared if I did, I would only come face to face with Falcon and imminent doom.

Snap!

Terror consumed me as I ran. I kept as close to the lake as possible, hoping I wouldn't lose my way. I entered a clearing and saw a cabin. I knew this place...Travis's cabin! Maybe he was there. Yet it was dark. No lights glowed from the inside. I bolted up the porch steps and headed for the door. On the night of the storm, Travis opened it without a key. I doubted these mountain dwellers ever locked their homes. I would seek refuge inside, bar the door, and perhaps find a knife or something I could use to defend myself.

I grabbed the knob and turned, pushing hard. It didn't budge. I turned the knob again and pushed harder. Nothing! Maybe there was a back door. I whirled around. A scream escaped my lips as I crashed into Travis.

"I told you not to wander off alone."

I bent over, trying to catch my breath. "Were you following me?"

"I've told you no to wander off alone." He crossed his arms and leaned against the porch railing. "Yet you still disregard my warnings. Why did you leave? You seemed to be enjoying yourself."

He had been watching; but from where? I chose not to answer him right away. Instead, I remained aloof as he was. I looked into his dark eyes. I had a myriad of questions I intended to ask him before the night was over. However, before I interrogated him, I would play along and answer his questions first.

"I was having fun until I happened to look up and see the banner. And for the first time, I read what it said. And there it was staring me in the face: August 16th. My wedding date."

He tensed. A single muscle flexed in his jaw as he bit down. "Ryan and I were supposed to be married today." My voice dropped until it was nearly inaudible. "A day hasn't gone by for the past three months that I haven't thought of that date. And now, for some unexplained reason, it slips my mind, and I don't think of it for days, and then suddenly, there it is mocking me, staring at me in the face from a ridiculous ice cream banner." My voice rose with the telling. "Now instead of being surrounded by my family and friends at my seaside wedding, I'm surrounded by strangers in a small town somewhere in the southern Appalachians at an ice cream festival. And you know what, Travis? I don't even like ice cream." His stern expression gave way to a slight smile. "All I could think about was Ryan, and I was wondering where he was tonight and if he remembered what today was, and I wondered if his heart ached at all. I contemplated going to the beer garden and getting drunk. But I knew that would solve nothing, so I decided to go for a walk and have a good long cry. But for some reason I couldn't cry. And that's what scared me the most. I've been brooding for a while now and you know what? It's not about Ryan. I keep trying to convince myself that it's about him but in truth it's not. There is this emptiness, I can't explain it. But it's painful. I feel lost. Beth's probably right. I think I might be going crazy. So, I decided to run until I fell off the face of the earth or ended up somewhere else. That's when I heard someone behind me, and despite the fact you do not think I listen to your warnings, I remembered what you said last night. I was scared, so I kept on running. Before I knew it, I was here, and you know the rest."

I studied him as I finished my long discourse. There was something about having a conversation with him that kept my eyes engaged. He was always attentive, a rare thing in my social circles. There had been so many occasions where I had met seemingly nice men but as we talked, I would notice how their eyes would either wander below my face, only interested in one thing, or wander completely over the top of my head, surveying the room, to see if someone more important had entered. Someone who they felt would be better to talk with.

Travis was different. His eyes absorbed every expression, every syllable. I appreciated that. Deeply.

He took my hand. "Come with me."

His fingers curled around mine. His hand was surprisingly rough for a physician. It made perfect sense though; he worked the earth, growing, and distilling the many plants he used to treat his patients. Not to mention clearing away rubble after the storms.

Favoring my bleeding aching feet, I carefully descended the porch steps, following him on a path leading to the lake. A boat rocked in the waters, softly knocking against the dock. He helped me into the vessel. I chose a seat near the back of the boat, slightly behind the captain's seat, while Travis opened a cabinet door and removed a plush blanket and passed it to me. I wrapped it around my bare shoulders, grateful to have something to cut the chill coming off the water. I had no idea where he was taking me or his plans, nor did I care. My life had been changing so much recently that everything was completely opposite of what I anticipated. Tonight was supposed to be my night. My wedding night. The night I was supposed to wear a white dress. The night all eyes would be on me. The night I danced in celebration with friends, the night I was to become Mrs. Ryan Reese.

My hopes had not come true. My dreams of my future had been disrupted. So tonight, I had no plans. I was not in control, nor did I desire to be. Tonight, I would allow life to happen.

Travis started the engine and guided the boat across the glassy waters. He pushed the throttle back and the boat picked up speed. I pulled the blanket closer and eyed him. His hair was blowing away from his face revealing his sharp peppered jawline and for the first time, I noticed a small silver earring in his ear. I wanted to keep looking, to map out every detail of his face but quickly turned my attention away before he could catch me looking.

The lake was much larger than I'd anticipated, with no end in sight. Travis had been driving full speed and there was still so much ahead. The water reflected the glow of the moon, while the hills and trees were black silhouettes against a deep purple sky. He pulled back on the throttle, steering around a corner and into a large hidden cove. He drove the boat to the center of the inlet and turned off the engine. There was complete silence except for the woodland noises and gentle kisses of the waves against the boat as it rocked slowly in the wake.

My thoughts raced, competing with my thundering heart. We were hidden, completely alone. What would happen next? He turned and looked at me, offering his hand once more. I took it, allowing him to lead me to the center of the boat. Without a word he stood next to me and then released my hand.

Suddenly the whistling sound of an object being hurled across the sky broke the silence, followed by a thunderous pop and explosion. I gasped. Colorful embers of fireworks exploded directly overhead, raining down around us, and falling into the water. The night sky shimmered. Another whistle tore across the sky, followed by another explosion, and more colorful embers. I was stunned at the brilliance and beauty of the firework display and by my host's graciousness. Travis had taken me to the best spot in Moonshine to see the festival's firework show. Another explosion as blue, lavender, silver and green embers burst around us. The experience was magical, breathtaking, exhilarating. The kindness he had shown was amazing. He had no selfish ulterior motives, only the desire to give me a magical moment.

Overcome with emotion, the dam holding my tears at bay for months finally broke, allowing a single tear to escape and trickle down my cheek. Another followed, and then another. Soon I was sobbing uncontrollably, my soul cleansing from the pain and disappointment, the shock, the betrayal, the bitterness, the abandonment, the miscarriage... the emptiness. Each tear seemed to have a name as it poured down my cheeks and splashed off my face. I felt the heaviness leave my body. I collapsed on the cushioned bench, shivering and watching the enchanting display through burning eyes. I tucked the blanket closer. Travis sat down beside me, and wrapped his strong arm around my frame, pulling me against him. I scooted in closer, leaning my head upon his shoulder.

The fireworks continued to fall, and Travis continued to hold me as I cried. He never moved, spoke, or interrupted my personal moment of healing. He simply sat there, patiently, his powerful arm cradling me, offering me a shoulder to lean on, and a private place in which to escape.

The night grew quiet once again. The fireworks stopped. The music no longer played in the distance. The sounds of laughter and carefree frivolity dwindled away. The festival had come to an end.

The only audible sound was the gentle rocking and creaking of the boat. The lake had become somewhat darker, the moon now high in the sky. I was heavy-eyed, fatigued. The steady swaying of the boat nearly rocked me to sleep. I should move, to allow Travis to take the boat back to the dock and return home before Mavis worried. He had been so kind to bring me here, to allow me the privacy to grieve. I wouldn't take advantage of his thoughtfulness, yet I wished to remain exactly where I was as long as possible.

My mind went back to earlier in the day, the uneasiness, my desperate need to speak to him and my urgent desire for answers. That was one of the mysteries of Moonshine. Some experiences were so bizarre, so supernatural, leaving me weak and in an emotional panic. Yet within moments, the episodes would give way to the ordinary, almost causing me to forget the urgency I'd felt earlier.

Finally, I broke the silence. "You're a doctor?"

"A healer."

I smiled at the strange way he responded. Then, "Who did Falcon kill in the garden last night?" There was no reply. "I know what I saw was real. I wasn't dreaming."

Still no reply.

"Part of me tells me I should fear you, yet another part wants to trust you completely. I am not sure which one I should listen to." I couldn't see his face from where I was leaning. I could only feel his rock-hard body. His chest tightened when I asked the questions. I pulled myself away from him and looked into his face. His eyes were fixed across the water.

"Am I the scribe the murdered man spoke of?"

He continued to fix his gaze across the lake. His mood was somber. His throat bobbed. I studied his expression, contemplating his silence. Time to press the matter. "I know there is something very out of the ordinary going on here. Something supernatural. I've felt it from the moment I arrived. From the moment we met on the bridge, I've experienced strange sensations. I'm not sure what they are, but I know what they aren't. They are not symptoms of altitude sickness, so please don't insult me with that explanation again. I need answers and I know you have them."

"Not tonight," he said.

"Why?" I pressed.

"Because you've gone through an incredible amount of emotion tonight. You could not handle what I would tell you."

Although his words frightened me, I found a reason to trust in them. His eyes burned with sincerity. He was right. Tonight, had been emotionally exhausting. I couldn't take much more. My body was drained. There was a sense of satisfaction in knowing that there was something going on. At least I wasn't losing my mind. Only one question left to ask. "When? When will you tell me?"

He took his gaze off the water and turned his eyes back to me. "Soon."

Twenty-Nine

DAY SIX

My intention of sleeping late was thwarted by rolling thunder and a gentle rain tapping on the window screen. Fluffing my pillow and re-adjusting my position, I dozed back to sleep, only to be reawakened by the continual slamming of the door, as Mavis and the kids headed out to church. I lay in bed for another half hour, hoping to drift off again but my mind suddenly became crowded with thoughts of the boat, the lake and…Travis.

I gave in to the fact that I was indeed wide awake, so I grabbed my laptop and headed downstairs. Mavis had left behind a continental breakfast for her guests, so I poured myself a cup of coffee, grabbed an oversized blueberry muffin, and headed for the back porch. I curled up on the swing, sipping my coffee and enjoying the smell of the warm summer shower.

Bethany joined me on the porch and settled down in a rocking chair beside the swing. I set my computer aside, realizing there would be no writing as long as she was there. I could sense she was full of questions seeing I'd left the festival without giving her or Lillian any notification.

Bethany rocked in the chair, sipping coffee, and nibbling at her croissant, while I relayed the entire story of the walk, how I ended up at Travis's cabin, the boat ride, and the spectacular fireworks display. At that point, Bethany removed herself from the rocking chair and joined me on the swing.

She curled her legs up underneath her, anticipating a more secretive accounting. However, that's where I ended my story.

"So, you're saying nothing happened between you two?" she asked skeptically.

"Nothing at all. I told you he is a good man. He is in love with his wife. Even Ashley said it at the salon. Everyone in town knows Travis's heart belongs to only one person." I ended my last statement with a sigh.

"It just doesn't make sense. He seems to be attracted to you. He's always following you around or at least showing up where you are. He followed you up to the top of the waterfalls. He obviously was watching you at the festival because he followed you to his cabin. Then he took you out on his boat to a secluded private cove on the lake to watch fireworks... and he didn't make a move?" she shook her head in disbelief. "Something's not right here."

I smiled. "Just admit it, Beth. There may be a few good, trustworthy, faithful men out there."

"That's just it." She pointed out. "He's not that faithful, or he would have taken Mavis out on the boat and had some happy times away from the kids. Maybe you intimidate him."

"I don't think so." I chuckled at the thought. Bethany was wrong. Travis was faithful. What was faithfulness anyway? Being loyal? Steadfast? Dedicated? Committed? Travis was certainly all those things to Mavis.

"You promise me, nothing happened?" she asked again, eyeing me suspiciously. "He didn't hint at anything; accidentally touch your leg or something?"

I laughed again. "No, he didn't. He did put his arm around me when I started crying. He literally gave me his shoulder to cry on, but that was it."

"AH HA!" she yelled, nearly spilling her coffee. "I knew there was something! He's just a slow mover, but he's making his moves alright, setting up opportunities, getting you to trust him, to relax around him. That scoundrel!" She shook her head, feeling she'd achieved an inner victory.

I smiled, unmoved. "You're wrong Beth. You're way off on this one." I reached for her mug and exited the porch to refill our coffee, only to return to more questions.

"So, what happened after the fireworks? You didn't come back to the inn for a long time after the festival was over. I'm seeing a time gap here. How did you fill it? Bury more victims?"

I gave a courteous laugh and proceeded to tell Bethany how my sobbing had taken its toll, leaving me heavy-eyed and drained. I explained how the stillness of the night and the gentle swaying of the boat nearly rocked me to sleep. How Travis had sat there patiently, allowing me all the time I needed. Then when I was ready, he took the boat back to the cabin and returned me to the inn. I purposely neglected to tell Bethany of our conversation that transpired, understanding it was not for Bethany to know. She could never comprehend the meaning of it all.

She leaned her head back against the swing, watching the light rain falling outside.

"I'm glad he was there for you last night. I'm proud of him for behaving himself. He could have easily taken advantage of a distraught bride, abandoned on her wedding night. For that, he's a good man."

I watched Beth sip her coffee while contemplating. Her concern was entirely for my well-being, combined with her own heartbreaking experience. Even though Bethany's relationship had only lasted a short six months, I knew her pain, from that experience of deception, was more than she showed.

Thirty

THE The rain began to lessen, the clouds having completed their duty of giving the thirsty earth its morning drink. The sun broke through the gloom just as the local church was dismissing. The few dedicated worshippers, faithful enough to attend services on the morning after the festival, exited the sanctuary, and milled about outside. They discussed assorted topics, from the relevancy of the lesson to the antics of the previous night's celebration. Mavis descended the steps of the church, carefully holding tightly to the pastor's hand.

"How are those big city guests of yours?" the benevolent minister asked, as he helped her off the bottom step.

"Doing just fine." She smiled.

The pastor beamed. "They seemed to be enjoying themselves last night."

"Didn't we all!" Mila, a tall thin woman with copper hair, eagerly wedged herself into the conversation. "I think it was the nicest festival we've had in a while."

Mavis forced a smile, excusing herself. She yelled to the kids to head to the car. She knew if Mila joined the conversation, there would be no getting away anytime soon. Her guests were sure to starve before she would be able to return and prepare a meal. However, Mila had other intentions.

"Mavis dear!" Mila's long nails scratched her elbow as she tugged for her to stop.

"Where are your guests this morning?" She was panting, her face already red with the energy she exerted to catch up with the hobbling Mavis. "Not churchgoers I assume? That's how it is with big city folk. They're so busy; they never make time for such things."

"I suppose." Mavis continued limping to the truck.

"Well, I can only assume they were plenty tuckered out from last night," Mila continued. "As the pastor said, they all did seem to enjoy themselves quite a bit. Especially one of them. I'm sure you know whom I am referring to. I saw Travis taking her in his boat late last night."

"Really?" Mavis answered, somewhat perturbed. "And how could you have seen that, seeing as Travis's boat is docked at his cabin, which we all know is not visible from the courtyard?"

"I wasn't in the courtyard. I'd taken a little walk," she tried sounding naïve. "I was near the cabin when I noticed Travis helping her into the boat. It just surprised me is all I'm saying."

"I'm surprised to know you were at his cabin instead of the festival. Pray tell what caused you to end up there?" Mavis' eyes narrowed before her left brow raised in an accusing question.

Mila's long fingers covered her heart. "You know I think the world of you and that man Travis! I saw her leave and I followed to see what she was up to. I'm just looking out for the both of you. She may seem sweet and innocent but...."

Mavis swung the truck door open and climbed into the front. She glanced back to make sure the kids were inside. Molly was safely buckled in the back seat. Carla Jo was standing outside, still talking with her friends.

"Thank you, Mila." She grabbed the door handle. "Travis is a wise and decent man. He can protect himself if need be. I'm sure he knows what he is doing. I trust his judgment completely." With those words, she slammed her door shut.

"Carla Jo! Let's go!" she yelled.

Carla Jo jumped in. Mavis sped away leaving a disappointed Mila behind her.

Thirty-One

Mavis returned from church, prepared a quick simple lunch, and disappeared for the rest of the afternoon. Bethany and I decided to clean up our room and do some much-needed laundry. Sunday was the one day of the week that Mavis neglected to make the beds and clean the rooms. It was her day of rest. Usually, when we returned to our room, we would find the bed made, clean towels in the bathroom, fresh flowers in a vase by the window, and some sort of treat on our pillows. Once, we received a plate of her famous chocolate chip cookies; on another day, it was a bowl of chocolate dipped strawberries. Then there was a plate of chewy brownies. It was always a treat to see what Mavis would leave. In all of my travels, I'd never stayed in a placc as inviting as Sandalwood Inn.

I tossed the last pillow back onto the bed and then retrieved my dress from the floor. I'd come back to the Inn so late last night, and with no desire to wake the girls, I quickly disrobed, leaving my clothes on the floor. As I grabbed the dress to add to the pile of laundry, I noticed a bulging in the pocket. I shoved my hand inside and retrieved a small cylinder tube. The cylinder was carved from smooth wood. I ran my thumb over the intricate design and the detailed engraving as I admired the beauty and antiquity of the object. Detailed cuttings were etched around the tube. An elegant letter E was carved in the center. A golden cap sealed the contents. I barely remembered the masked figure that placed it into my hand. "I am delivering a message just for you," he whispered before he kissed my hand, bowed, and backed away, disappearing into the crowd.

I'd been so overcome with emotion at the time, I had paid little attention to the event, let alone remembered it. Curious, I pried open the end of the cylinder, emptying out a parchment rolled into a scroll, and tied with a blue ribbon. My fingers carefully uncurled the paper. Handwritten in beautiful calligraphy were the words, Isaiah 42:9.

"A bible verse." I mumbled. Probably a gimmick of the church, handing out scriptures and telling everyone to repent or they will go to hell. I spoke from experience, having been a victim of that methodology before.

"What did you say?" Bethany asked, as she sorted through her clothes, deciding what items needed to be laundered.

"Sorry. I was just thinking out loud. I opened my cylinder, thinking it was Moonshine's version of a fortune cookie. All that was in it was a Bible verse. Probably a gimmick of the church."

Bethany looked at the ornate cylinder. "Where did you get that?"

"One of those masked, trinket-bearing figures gave it to me. He said he was delivering a message just for me."

"Weird," Bethany said. "I didn't get a cylinder."

I twirled it around my fingers, wondering if there was significance.

"What's the message?"

"Just a Bible reference," she replied. "Probably telling me to repent or go to hell."

Bethany laughed. "They're onto you and your late-night escapades."

I tossed a soiled towel her way.

"Look it up and see what it says."

"You got a Bible?" My voice matched the sarcasm of her question.

"As a matter of fact, I do," she raised her chin in a haughty manner. "Back home."

"A lot of good it's doing you there."

"Go look it up," She urged. "I'm sure Mavis has a Bible somewhere around here."

"I'll do it later." I returned the scroll to the cylinder, which I placed in the pocket of my shorts.

Thirty-Two

After dinner, I retired to the back porch swing to work on the new book. Bethany and Lillian sat with me, relaxing in rocking chairs, sipping blueberry and lavender iced tea, and enjoying a calm Sunday evening. Mavis joined us, occupying another rocking chair, and reading the paper. I was listening to my music to drown out any conversation on the porch.

"You girls enjoy the fireworks last night?" She asked from behind her paper.

"Yes, they were amazing." Bethany answered, somewhat startled by the randomness of the question.

"What about you Bronwyn?" Mavis asked, her face still hidden.

The music piping into my ears prevented me from hearing Mavis's inquiry.

"Bronwyn!" Bethany raised her voice trying to overpower the music, but I was busy searching the Bible, looking up the message in Isaiah 42:9.

"What?" I pulled out my airpods.

"Mavis just asked you if you enjoyed the fireworks last night." she said, glints of warning in her eyes. I threw a quick glance at Mavis' way whose face remained concealed behind the paper.

"Yes, I saw them. They were beautiful."

"That's good." She casually turned the page. "I was hoping you had a good view."

Bethany's eyes widened as she looked at me. My stomach fell. Mavis had to be suspicious. Why hadn't she asked Lillian the same question? I wanted to blurt out "Nothing happened!" Instead, I returned to my search for Isaiah 42:9. I flipped through the many smaller books, Psalms, Proverbs, Ecclesiastes, Song of Solomon, and Isaiah. I found the book. My hands began to tremble from the adrenaline rush that had accompanied Mavis's question. I was only seconds away from reading the message that had been delivered just for me. I wouldn't at all be surprised if it said something to the effect of, "Adulterers will burn!" My finger scanned the pages, Isaiah 39...40...41...42... Verse 9. I read silently:

"See the former things have taken place, and new things I declare. Before they spring into being, I announce them to you."

The heat sensation began to invade again. The message was nothing more than another riddle; another enigma to muddle through. I scribbled the verse on the back of the scroll before returning it to the cylinder.

The melodies of the late evening dulcimer player began drifting through the trees, as they did every evening. This was becoming clockwork. The winsome melody was soon accompanied by the song of the woman, drawing my attention away from the crowded porch and into the woods. Curious, I decided to follow the voice. I laid the Bible and computer aside, stuffed the scroll back into the pocket of my shorts and left the porch.

"Where are you going?" Bethany asked.

"I'll be back in a minute," I called over my shoulder and hurried away as Mavis slightly lowered the paper and peered at me as I headed for the river.

I found the small trail that led to the waterfall. I was sure I could follow the path and find the idyllic spot on my own. I gave a quick glance over my shoulder towards the inn before slipping into the tree line. I breathed a sigh of relief. I was too far for anyone to see where I was headed. The distance, accompanied by the dark of the night, hid me from their view. Happy that no one would join me, I stepped further into the woods, my feet connected to the soft path. The moonlight glistened through the trees, providing enough light to illuminate my way without the need of a flashlight. Confident, I walked at a brisk pace, following the trail for quite a way before the crackling and snapping of leaves and twigs caught my attention. There was movement to my right. I let out a small yelp as a frightened deer bolted across the path and disappeared in the darkness. I stopped for a minute to regain my composure and for a second time, I remembered Travis' strict warning not to venture out alone. I had done it again, when was I going to learn?

And then my mind began to taunt me with thoughts of dark-hooded, knife-wielding men, hiding behind every tree. I even conjured up the visual of hungry grizzlies   descending to feed. I scolded myself for running off without thinking first or at least grabbing a flashlight. The trees thickened during my walk, obscuring the moonlight. I remembered these little bouts of darkness from our hike a few nights ago. We wound in and out of light and shadow for quite some time. If I could stay on the path, it would only be a matter of time before I had light again. Using my hands as eyes I felt my way down the winding path continuing my determined walk, but unfortunately at a much slower pace, uncertain if I still remained on the path. I stumbled over rocks, low lying branches and felled tree trunks as I groped my way along. A seed of terror began to grow inside. The fear was not brought about by my present situation, despite the fact I wished I had been a bit more prepared. The fear that manifested within was of a threatening horror overtaking the woods. The same malicious presence I felt at the falls. I could feel it, sense it. Although the darkness was blinding, I was aware of dozens of eyes, on the prowl, stalking and watching. My courage left me. I would visit the falls another time but for now, I would abort this mission and return to the porch.

I glanced around to get my bearings. A futile task, seeing it was as black as pitch, the darkness so dense I could barely see my hand in front of me. North, south, east, west, it made no difference. I was disoriented and unsure I could retrace my steps. I did an about face and continued to feel my way back through the dense forest, grabbing at branches, hoping for a break in the trees, which would allow the moon to give a bit of light.

I groped along a little further before the trees cleared, releasing the bright glow of the moon. Finally! But the path beneath my feet dropped, sending me toppling over the side of a deep gulch, doing several somersaults as I careened down the side of the hill. Sharp branches and jagged rocks sliced into me tearing at my flesh. The fall deposited me into the darkness once again dumping me in what seemed to be a bottomless pit. I lay there covered in mud and in too much pain to move. The distant hoot of an owl pierced the black silence surrounding me, for the dulcimer and the song of the woman had ended.

"Damn it!" I cursed out loud, angry over my extreme stupidity. I rarely ever cursed. I found swearing to be the sign of a poor vocabulary, and as a writer, I preferred more descriptive appropriate words to describe life events. However, there was always a time and a place for everything, and this certainly was the time to curse.

"Mother Fucker! I crawled to my knees, feeling around for a root or a stone, anything that would help me climb up the steep embankment. My fingers tore into the wet clay, but the slippery mud could not hold me. My feet slid, I lost my grip and to my horror I slipped a few feet further down. I didn't waste my breath on any more expletives, although the words were racing through my head. I didn't have the strength to say them. Exerting every effort, I pulled myself back into a standing position and reached my hand into the darkness, feeling the side of the cool muddy wall for a solid root, a rock.... anything. I grabbed a protruding root and attempted the climb, only to become part of a mudslide when the soaked wall gave way, escorting me to the bottom once again. "Shit!"

My heart was beating like a drum and pounding in my head. I'd heard stories of people hiking in the mountains, becoming separated from their party, never being heard from again. These mountains were massive. The woods were vast. If I could just lie here for the night, perhaps in the morning there would be enough light to find my way out. But thoughts of a bear or a mountain lion, or some other hungry animal that would soon feast upon me as their midnight snack compelled me to try again.

I reached out into the forbidding darkness, grasping for anything. My hand touched something slick, warm, and moving. I screamed fearing I had grabbed a sleeping snake but before I could pull away, the object wrapped itself around my wrist and with incredible strength, pulled me up out of the pit, placing my trembling legs on level ground.

I could barely make out the outline of a shadowy figure. It uttered no sound but continued to hold onto my wrist as it guided me deeper into the woods. I stumbled along, trying to keep my footing as whoever had a hold on me dragged me through the pitch darkness. They walked with ease as if they possessed some sort of night vision. I was breathless, my legs waved, buckling, too weak to continue. And just when I thought I wouldn't be able to take another step, we came upon a small clearing, cast into soft silver light by the moon. I was in the custody of one of the cloaked men. His masquerade gave an eerie presence. His face concealed by the large hood didn't allow me to see who he was. I didn't think it was Falcon. I didn't smell smoke and although he practically dragged me through the forest, he wasn't as rough with me as Falcon had been.

He led me to a broken-down shack, camouflaged into the side of the mountain. A dilapidated front porch housed a single weathered rocking chair. A dulcimer lay nearby. My pulse quickened. I was not going to go into that dirty shack. The cloaked man's grip had lessened during the duration of the walk. I figured a sudden jerk of my hand would surely release his grip, allowing me to escape. But where would I run? Back to the pit from where I was pulled. I took a deep breath and uttered a small prayer, as the cloaked figure led me into the darkness of the cabin. A smoldering wick of a candle offered little light, but I could make out a small fireplace, a cot type bed with worn coverings, a rustic wooden table, and a single chair.

Keeping his grip, he led me into the far back corner. The shanty was built much deeper into the side of the mountain than I had expected. What could be waiting for me in the deeper recesses of the room? I didn't want to know. I stopped and planted my feet firmly. The cloaked figure paused only for a second, never turning to face me. He continued to walk, gently pulling me along. I pulled against his tugging. "Where are you taking me? He said nothing, he only tilted his head, hidden beneath the hood, motioning further into the recesses. "I can see that." I fumed. "Talk to me!" He didn't say a word as he continued to pull me further into the darkness. I couldn't see anything now. The air was cold and stale as if we had just entered a cave. I felt the cloaked man reach high above his head and pull on some sort of lever. The ground beneath my feet shook, as the entire rock wall began to slide to my left. A sudden gust of frigid air blew through the opening, sending shivers through me. A dimly lit corridor appeared in front of me.

I planted my feet, this time much more firmly, fearing if I ever entered that corridor, I might never see the light of day again. "No!" I shouted, trying to pull my wrist from his grip. The cloaked man turned his head slightly. Only one saffron eye was visible behind the fabric of the hood.

"Trust me," he said quietly. I recognized the distinctness of the voice. The woodwinds that seemed to speak along with it. This was none other than the warrior from the garden.

"Why should I?"

He gave me another sideways glance. "Isaiah 42:9." His answer was a password of some sort, and I supposed possibly the key to every riddle and secret lies just on the other side of this passageway. So, against all reason, I followed him into the corridor. We had no longer stepped through the door when the rock wall closed behind us. There was no turning back now. The cloaked man took a lit torch fastened to the wall to light our way. The path descended deep underground and connected to a subterranean river flowing in a bed of white marble and cutting across the cavern floor. The icy cold waters rushed over my aching feet as we crossed.

We continued to descend until the path grew rocky and suddenly elevated at an increasing rate, like the shaft of a coal mine. I paused. I had exuded so much effort trying to climb out of the pit, that there was nothing left within me to climb this gargantuan staircase. As if he read her mind, the warrior clasped his arm around my waist and lifted me from boulder to boulder with great ease.

Within a few minutes a beam of moonlight pierced the darkness and spot lit the end of the long corridor.

The warrior placed the torch in another holder and led me out through the opening. An immense silver lake lay before us, reaching as far as my eyes could see. The tranquil waters were surrounded by trees of every variety, all silhouetted against the deep purple sky. Two intricately carved gondolas floated near the shore. My cloaked guide removed his dark robe and placed it at the entrance of the cave.

My guess was right. It was the warrior; the man I'd seen the night of our arrival standing in the middle of the road as we skidded towards death, and then again in the garden with Falcon two nights ago. His bronze skin glowed under the light. The moonbeams casting their glow across the water highlighted his silver dreadlocks neatly fastened into a ponytail. as if he had plucked the strands from the waters themselves. White linen pants clothed him from the waist down, however his well-built chest was bare, revealing his powerfully defined muscles rippling with every move. This was no doubt the source of his amazing strength. His saffron eyes smiled as he offered his hand.

I climbed aboard the floating vessel and relaxed in the comfortable cushioned chair, as the mysterious man pushed off from shore. I couldn't fathom what awaited me, and what was soon to be revealed. I was more certain than ever that the answers I'd been seeking, the answers Travis had promised, were coming.

The ride was silent, both the warrior and I were immersed in deep thought. He stood at the back of the boat and paddled through the placid waters while I rested comfortably, taking in the view that lay before me. The lake narrowed on several occasions, once taking a thin passageway behind a magnificent waterfall, another time entering a dark cave and riding the swift current until we emerged from the other side. My fears had long subsided, I trusted the warrior, certain he meant me no harm. My only anxiousness derived from what I still didn't know, and my part in the whole of it.

Half an hour later, the boat arrived at its destination. The shoreline was splendid. Snow white sand covered a small beach. Tall trees grew in rows, providing a leafy archway over a smooth stone path, each tree trunk covered in leafy vines, producing colorful exotic flowers. I noticed many rare and beautiful plants that were not indigenous to these mountains. I followed the warrior down a sandy path, winding through even more exotic plants. At the end of the trail lay tall, sculptured hedges, growing in a vast maze with numerous entrances, I noticed five or six. He led me to one of the many openings and we proceeded down another trail, surrounded by a hedge wall, taking many sharp turns and corners. The only visible sight was green leafy walls, and the night sky overhead. I was Alice falling down a rabbit hole, caught in some crazy maze.

We stepped into a clearing. I was speechless at what my eyes beheld. A majestic castle made of smooth white stone and glass stood directly in front of me. The architect of this dwelling had created a masterpiece. I had never seen anything like it, nor could I have ever imagined something this exquisite in my writings. It was surrounded by a sense of awe. The walls appeared white yet as I approached, they seemed to change colors depending on whatever way the moonlight reflected. I wondered how beautiful these iridescent walls would look under the full light of the sun. Towers rose from the corners, their spires reaching into the inky expanse as if each point were crowned with one of the many stars scattered across the night sky. A crystal-clear river, reflecting the glow of the castle, like a mirror, provided the perfect moat. A drawbridge seemingly made of various colored crystals, each shimmering and reflecting the hues of the iridescent walls, lowered slowly, offering us entrance.

We crossed the bridge and arrived at a large blue door, carved from a star sapphire, which barred entrance to the astonishing citadel. One push of the door and we were inside this magnificent palace.

The interior of the home was just as awe-inspiring. The floors and walls were fashioned from white marble. The furnishings were elaborate, from intricately carved tables to chairs covered in a luxurious midnight blue fabric. Ornate mirrors decorated the walls, as well as paintings of beautiful scenery, just like the ones hanging at the inn. Lush green ferns hung from the ceilings, and plants of every kind grew from large planters.

Bypassing the double staircase, the warrior kept me on the first level, escorting me down a long corridor, with many doors lining the passage-way. Stopping at one, he invited me inside.

"You can clean up here. Make use of anything you find. If you wish to change from your soiled clothing, there are gowns in the wardrobe. We will begin when the council arrives." With those words, he exited the room and disappeared down the hallway.

I walked about the large suite. An artistically carved canopy bed, cov-ered in vibrant jewel tone pillows and satin blankets, invitingly stood in the center of the room. A bombe chest, with a hand-painted swollen front, sat nearby. Large glass doors led outside to a courtyard filled with giant palms and ferns. In the middle of the courtyard an overflowing fountain emptied its water into a pond filled with beautifully colored fish. On the opposite side of the room, marble steps spiraled down into a sunken tub, hewn right into the marble floor.

Turning a golden lever, I watched in awe as a waterfall poured from the ceiling down into the basin. I tried a small lever to my right. Violet colored cream squirted into the tub, causing the water to foam and on a lavender-scented, milky appearance. Delighted at my discovery, I pushed the lever to the left. The waters bubbled and threw off a hot, steamy, Jacuzzi feeling. I couldn't get out of my clothes fast enough, tossing the filthy pieces aside before I made the spiral descent into the warm milky waters.

"I'm in heaven." I breathed, and then thought that maybe this was the entrance to heaven, and Mavis must have shot me in the back when I left the porch. Perhaps, I had died on the grounds of the inn, and didn't know; like in the movies, when a person dies and is not aware of their demise for some time. Besides this fantastic castle was indeed other worldly.

Maybe the warrior was some type of gate keeper and just as the thought entered my head, I recalled my deleted story.

"The Eclipse " The world sits in darkness, during a lunar eclipse, as an extra-dimensional arrives as the gatekeeper.

My stomach ached. The heat sensation rose as thoughts scrambled through my mind. Enough basking in the scented waters, I needed answers, now. I grabbed a nearby wash cloth and quickly started cleaning the mud and crime from my body. I paid careful attention to the gaping cut on my leg. It stung in the perfumed water. I dabbed at the sticky blood, clearing it away. After I cleaned and inspected all my wounds I washed my hair in the sudsy waterfall, rinsed and quickly exited the tub. Wrapped in a towel, I picked up her soiled clothes. I dreaded putting them on again now that I was clean. Then I remembered the warrior mentioning the gowns in the wardrobe. I pulled out a long silk robe and held it in front of me. It seemed to fit so I pulled it over her head and gazed at myself in the mirror. I resembled some Greek mythical creature, my long dark hair falling over the aqua silk empire waist robe. This is crazy, I breathed, fighting my way out of the dress as quickly as I could. I returned to my soiled clothes, deciding not to buy into anything just yet. Once dressed, I ventured out of my room in search of the warrior, and for an explanation as to why I had been brought here.

Thirty-Three

I managed to lose my way in the castle as easily as I did in the woods and just like before, the warrior found me wandering through the labyrinth of hallways and offered his hand.

"Are you ready?" The voice that once sounded like many waters was calm, soothing, almost normal. I wondered what kind of person he was to have such an indistinct tone that could change, at will with his disposition. "The council is waiting."

"I think I am," I hesitated, wondering to whom he was referring when he mentioned the council. I knew better than to ask, I would get nothing from him, so I followed along figuring I would find out soon anyway.

He led me outside, through a grove of trees, and into another court-yard that contained several palms and ferns, along with blooming jasmine, deep purple hydrangeas, pines and palms, the latter not indigenous to the mountains. We passed a reflecting pool, which was home to exotic fish, ducks, geese, and a couple of elegant swans. I followed him up a set of stairs, to a large patio surrounded by white pillars, standing tall and proud, covered in vines and wisteria. Their tendrils reached out, entwining each other in a graceful embrace as if they too were guarding this sacred circle, protecting intimacy and seclusion. The moonlight filtered through the foliage; the only intruder allowed on this starlit night. A low fire burned inside a rectangular pit, running the entire length of the terrace. The quiet crackling and popping of embers combined with the gentle rustling of leaves created a soothing harmony. On any other occasion it would be one of the most relaxing places I'd ever visited, but one look at the eleven ornate chairs, and their inhabitants and all sense of tranquility was shattered. Only one chair was empty, reserved for me.

The warrior introduced me to the first council member. "Neveah Quinn," she stood, towering over me by at least six inches. She was thin with bronze skin and ebony hair that hung down her back in dreadlocks accessorized with silver diamonds like the morning dew clinging to the ground. She gave me a warm smile and bowed her head in a silent greeting.

"Mila Harper." Mila stood, not quite as tall as Neveah. Her hair was russet, and her eyes matched the color almost perfectly. Her ruby red lips painted to perfection formed a straight line as she stared at me. There was no nod, nor any glint of a smile in her eyes. Only a slight tip of her chin, as if to inform me she was someone of importance. I didn't care.

"Violet Paisley." Violet's smile was pleasant and her eyes, matching her name, danced in accordance with her grin. Instead of offering a nod or an arrogant stance, she grabbed my hand and squeezed. "Welcome, Bronwyn, is it?" I nodded.

"Jace Miles." Jace stood. Like all the men here he was quite handsome and well built. Golden hair to his shoulders and green eyes that neither smiled nor frowned, but narrowed in on me, suspiciously. I didn't look away. I had been dealing with Ryan's attorneys over the past couple of months and learned not to look away or appear weak. So, I kept his gaze, tightening my eyes on him until the Warrior introduced the next council members in the circle.

"Nolan Easton, Mateo Issacs, Oaklyn Paisley," The warrior continued the introductions, each standing as they were introduced.

"Adam Colton." Adam stood; a pleasant smile spreading across his face. I remembered seeing him before. He was the beautiful man, with whom

I'd danced, the night of the pre festival activities. I'd been twirled into his arms for a moment. Colton, he must be related to Travis.

Adam's obsidian hair hung past his broad shoulders in waves. His face was sculpted as beautiful and his body. Deep set aqua eyes, lantern jaw, sharp cheekbones, and full lips which he placed on the back of my hand, giving me a gentle kiss. He bowed, and when he did, a silver chain with a white stone pendant, like the one Travis wore, was revealed from his shirt.

"It is my extreme honor." he said, reverently.

He too remained standing as the warrior introduced me to the man sitting beside him.

Crushing his cigarette underneath the heel of his bare foot, Falcon removed his dark glasses, allowing me to get a glimpse of his sapphire eyes. To my surprise, they were quite pleasant, not the color I expected. A deep scar cut through his eyebrow, continuing underneath his right eye, and stopped just above his cheek. He grabbed my hand, bringing it to his lips. He kissed it, more gently than I'd imagined him capable. He gave me a slight wink and remained standing as the warrior introduced the last council member.

"I am sure Travis needs no introduction."

Travis took my hand as if it were the first time, he'd ever met me. He lifted it to his lips, keeping his eyes engaged on mine, and kissed it tenderly. At the touch of his lips the air escaped my lungs, stealing the breath from me. I tried lifting my chin as Mila had, giving a nonchalant response, so he didn't see the effect his touch had on me. He dropped my hand, and reverently bowed his head. The warrior took my hand, and for the first time announced his name.

"I am Barak," he said, before kissing it. He didn't take a seat as the others did but rather moved behind the group and kept watch. It was then I noticed sentries wearing hooded robes standing in the shadows keeping guard. What was this place?

The council bowed and then returned to their seats. I swallowed hard and took mine along with them.

"How did you end up in Moonshine?" Jace Miles asked. His question was direct, almost accusing as if I had breached national security and trespassed on government protected land. "We do not get many visitors here, if any at all."

"It wasn't intentional. My friends and I were headed someplace else. I missed my turn and then our car broke down and we ended up here. I assumed everyone knew that."

"Where were you headed?" He asked another.

"The Fiery Dragon. It's a mountain resort. You've probably heard of it."

Mila played with the bracelets covering her wrist and raised her eyes towards mine. "Why were you going to The Fiery Dragon?"

I gave a soft chuckle and clicked my tongue. "Why all the questions?" I bit. I could easily say a girl's retreat but in truth it wasn't anyone's business, and I hoped my broken heart and engagement would not come up in this inquiry. "Am I being accused of something? Because if I am, I would like to have an attorney present."

"Is there a reason you do not wish to answer the question?" She baited as if I were hiding secrets. Fury began to boil inside. I was becoming annoyed and would stomp off as I had a habit of doing but in truth, I had no idea where I was or how I would get back to the Inn.

"Just that it's none of your business."

Falcon let out a husky chuckle as Mila stiffened. The council remained silent, increasing the awkwardness of our little gathering. Now my turn, whether they agreed or not. "Why the interview? Why was I brought here?" My voice walked a tightrope between demanding and frustrated. "You're not explaining anything to me. I want answers, not questions. I want to know where I am, what this place is, what it is you're hiding, why you're stalking me, and who the hell are you?"

"Who do you think we are?" Falcon's eyes pierced into mine holding my gaze captive.

"How should I know who you are?" I choked out. "We've never met and believe me I would have remembered someone like you." He smirked as if I had given him a compliment and then exchanged glances with Travis which did not go unnoticed despite the dizziness in my head.

Falcon took advantage of the awkward silence. "You wrote a book of sorts when you were ten, did you not? A book that your parents eventually asked you to stop writing. You named your story Moonshine."

A memory surfaced, clawing its way through the years of suppression, defeating the force keeping it hidden. He was right, I partially remembered this story! My pulse quickened even more, laboring my breathing. The intensity of the heat rose within me along with a familiar terror. There was a reason I'd forgotten about it...why? And then, as if he were privy to my thoughts, he answered the question.

"Disturbing things began to happen as you wrote your story. Nightmares, sleep walking... such things prompted your parents to take you to counseling. The therapist told them your story was taking its toll on you and insisted you stop."

No, I wouldn't listen to this! I couldn't listen. Everything inside forbade me from remembering. There was a reason the chaos was buried. "How do you know all of this?" My question was barely audible.

"We've done some extensive vetting this week. You are Bronwyn Grace Sterling. Born to Martin and Madison Sterling on January 4th, 1990, in Arlington Texas. After extended counseling," he continued, and I wished he wouldn't. "Your parents took your story away. It was then they enrolled you in piano, dance and acting, steering you toward other interests, keeping your mind busy and away from the book."

I wanted to wake up from this ridiculous, haunting dream. Who was this man, and how did he know so much about me? A whirlpool of thoughts ensued. He was right in what he was saying. It had been twenty-three years, and I hadn't thought of the story, or its aftermath in all that time. More memories began forcing their way back, as if he opened a door that had been locked for years. Terror pushed its way forward, along with a deep sorrow filling my soul, as the tears pooled in my eyes, spilling over, and streaking down my cheeks. I wanted to leave, to get back in that damn car and go back to a normal life with my friends. I would much rather choose the pain of Ryan's betrayal, than the craziness I was experiencing now. I swiped the tears from my face and stood to leave, intending to bring an end to this bizarre confrontation. The emotion was too much. My legs buckled beneath me. Several council members reacted however Falcon reached me first. I wanted to push him off, push him down on the marble veranda and stomp his head in the ground for digging up personal and painful memories. What gave him the right?

"Maybe it's not the time," Adam said kindly. "It's proving to be too much for her."

"It will never get any easier," Travis said. "And we need to know. We must know." He reiterated. "She has shown innate curiosity. Let her hear what Falcon has to say. She has already heard and seen too much to stop now."

He was siding with Falcon. I should have known, seeing they were consorting with each other in the private garden. Aside from feeling betrayed, something inside told me he was right. It was for this reason he refused to tell me anything on the boat last night. Whatever this council was attempting to reveal was immense. I was somehow involved in something much more significant than I'd anticipated. I couldn't leave. As Travis said, I had heard and seen too much already. No matter how terrifying the ordeal was, deep inside I knew I had to stay and hear them out.

Falcon still had a tight grip on me, so with what little strength I had I pushed him off. Again, a smirk exchanged with Travis did not go unnoticed. "I just became a bit overwhelmed." I cleared my throat attempting to sound stronger than I felt. "I can continue."

"If you're certain you're alright?" Adam needed assurance.

I nodded, offering him a faint smile for his kindness.

"I suggest we take a less threatening approach," Falcon said. "Why not let the lady scribe ask us the questions? We can take it one step at a time. The whole story should unveil itself." The council agreed that this might prove to be the best way to approach the subject.

"Alright," Falcon took back over. "What would you like to ask us?"

I contemplated where to start. There were so many questions. "You asked me who I thought you were. I would think you were figments of my imagination since I found stories in my old writings that are quite parallel to some of yours. Even the names are the same. Can you explain that to me?"

There was a brief pause as Falcon lit up another cigarette. "No. We were hoping you could explain that to us."

"Well, I can't." I crossed my arms in front of me.

He took a long draw, eyeing me as he blew out a thin line of smoke. "Ask another."

"Who are you? Why a council, and what the hell is this place and why was I brought here?"

"Too many at once. Narrow it down." He let out another puff.

"What an ass." I mumbled, hoping he could hear and not the rest of the council. I closed my eyes. It was easier to block out the scrutiny and Falcon's penetrating stares. I took another route. "The other night in the garden, I witnessed you kill someone. Before the person died, they mentioned a tower of safety falling, and your hiding place being breached, a scribe and that you will all return to captivity soon. What was he talking about and why did you kill him?" I opened my eyes and glared back at him, not sure if I had just exposed his crimes or if the council knew he had slit someone's throat a few nights ago. "I know that's more than one question, but I don't care."

He flashed me an impish grin while smashing the butt of his cigarette. He glanced at Travis who gave a slight nod.

"The place we are from," he began, "is another earth, somewhat like this one. But different, better."

"You're aliens?" I interrupted; certain I was dreaming now.

"Not, aliens. We are just like you, but different, better."

I rolled my eyes at his condescending remark.

"We are from earth, but from another dimension. We are extra-dimensional beings. Our world is existing right now, right here, just in another facet. Our domain is somewhat like yours, as far as the earth is concerned, but our time is measured differently as well as other facets. Like I said, like yours but better. "Each person," he continued, "contributes and administers their talents and gifts to others. We understand honor. We all live, learn, and love."

"Sounds great. If it's so much better, why are you here?" I said, realizing something dire must have happened, because they were here, in my dimension, and not theirs. There had to be a reason.

"For centuries we were governed by three brothers," Mateo Issacs took over the story. "The three Princes of Eden. They were great men, governing our world with compassion and mercy. Each endowed with unique gifts which helped our people. They reigned for years, protecting our world, our borders, from universal threats. However, the darkness crept in, and influenced some in the royal line. The promise of power and secret knowledge tempted the leader of the Barons."

"He promoted himself and his ideas among the people." Adam picked up the narrative. He extolled himself higher than the three Princes, betraying and assassinating his best friend, Ariston, my father, and the eldest of the three ruling Princes. And, for the first time, murder took place and blood was spilled in Eden."

"This wicked Baron gained incredible influence and spoke lies to the people, making untrue charges and accusations against all three Princes." Jace Miles shared the next part of the tale. "Unfortunately, he happened to be a very well-liked and popular man, so his worthless ideals seemed intriguing to many. Our world became divided. His selfish ambition produced nothing but chaos and dissention. The wicked Baron took over, bringing in his regimen and exiling all the heirs of the royal city of Eden, to a mountainous island in the middle of the sea. It was a prison we could not escape. The remaining peoples of our earth, who were not citizens of Eden, were forced to become followers of the destroyer and his new ways. If they refused, they were immediately executed."

Travis rested his ankle across his leg and spoke for the first time. "Three ancient prophecies were given by the virtuous realm millions of years ago. They were foreign to us at the time. We didn't know what they meant, seeing our world never had a need for redemption until now. Some saw them as a premonition, others thought they were simply instructions should the dark realms ever infiltrate the royal bloodline. The first one stated that one day a scribe would emerge and write a story that would exonerate the character of our Princes, against the false charges of the destroyer. This story will validate something especially important to all the inhabitants of our world and beyond. This story, once written, will allow us to reclaim our world and our way of life. What the writer writes will happen."

There was complete silence. All the council members seemed relieved that the story was out, the story they had contained within themselves since their exile.

I tried wrapping my mind around the entire thing... a futile effort. "So, you believe I am the writer...?"

"We know you are the writer," Falcon said. "You fulfilled the prophecy."

"How?" I was flabbergasted at the thought.

"You ended up here, a place no one has been able to find or penetrate without an invitation. You opened the door to our hiding place. Only the prophesied Scribe can do that."

"I'm sorry," I scanned their faces. "I have no answers...I don't know how we ended up here. I am pretty sure, I'm not who you were expecting."

"No, you're certainly not." Mila's lips curled in disdain.

A sudden thought hit and although it seemed ludicrous, I had to explore the idea. "Am I being punked? Did Bethany set this entire thing up just to provoke some inspiration for me to write? This is just like something she would do. She and Lillian, conspiring together, set up this entire girl's trip and an accidental wrong turn." I was on a roll. It would be like them to go to this extreme measure to shock me out of my slump. Lillian was an expert party planner and with her money... I was sure all the council members were some of Lillian's acting friends. The elaborate costumes... I stood and glanced around the engraved pillars to see if they were hiding behind them, watching the entire scene unfold. "Okay, you guys got me! Come on out."

Some of the council were looking at each other, as if I had lost my mind, others were shaking their heads, figuring their return was futile if it were in my hands. Falcon grabbed my shoulders, forcefully turning me to face him. "This isn't a fucking joke." He was unyielding, not letting me derail this.

A heaviness fell upon my shoulders. The heat sensation was forced out by a cold chill that made my teeth chatter. I pushed him off. "Prove it or shut up!"

No one moved and Falcon said nothing. I smirked. "I thought so."

"She obviously doesn't want to help us." Mila snapped.

"Of course, I would help if I thought any of this was real or if I thought I could." I sighed, overwhelmed. "You mentioned being governed by three brothers. You said one was murdered. Where are the other two? Can't they figure something out?"

Again, the council grew quiet, an aching silence spread across the terrace.

"Sadly, my father wasn't the only Prince who lost his life." Adam spoke. "We lost another one as well. There is only one Prince of Eden remaining."

"Where is he?"

"He resides in Moonshine, and he is here among us tonight. You know him as Travis."

I swung my head to him. His dark eyes looked back with a helplessness in them that confirmed his need for me. I went numb. My stomach twisted in knots and my heart ached more than ever.

"I've had severe writer's block for some time now. I can't even produce a simple sappy novella. On top of that, I know nothing about your world. I think maybe you should keep waiting for your prophesied scribe. Maybe I was simply the person to open the door. Someone better can still come."

"Tell her the first prophecy." Falcon said. The others shifted in their seats, and I wondered if it was too sacred to be recited to just anyone.

"Either she believes or doesn't." Mila smoothed out her skirt and fumbled with her bracelets again. "And by her actions, I'd say she doesn't. I'm not sure her ears are worthy."

Travis ignored Mila and stood, maybe out of respect, I didn't know. "This is the first of three oracles given by The Utterance. There is great devastation. Sorrow sweeps across your horizons like clouds being tossed in the tempest that created them. Those dwelling in the darkness hunger for the light, yet in time, they will bend, consuming what is vile, malnourishing themselves with the bread of fools until there will be no remembrance of the virtuous. The overshadowing of evil will continue to spread until hopelessness gives way to decay, honoring the death that charmed it. Wailing and mourning come with the realization of the great deception carefully plotted by the one who hisses lies, then wipes his mouth and moves on through another watergate.

Do not be disheartened, for the sun continues to rise and with dawn there is hope of deliverance. Only one possesses the skill to survive against the cunning of the darkness. A sacrifice is required for one must plant in order to reap. A seed will be sown, and when it reaches maturity, it will take possession, discovering riches unknown, and destroying the all-consuming evil. Only then can rebirth take place.

The one who came from Amadahy will accomplish this. They will rend the veil of obscurity, arriving on the scene unannounced. They will pass through the Sipapu at the appointed time to deliver the words of The Utterance. Write the vision and make it plain that he may run who reads it. For the vision is for an appointed time, though it tarries wait for it, for it will surely come.

My head continued to swim as thoughts raced across my mind. "I came here from California not Amadahy, wherever that is."

Travis didn't try to explain or convince me. They had all said enough and by the look in his and Falcon's eyes, there was no convincing them I hadn't fulfilled the prophecy. "You said there were three prophecies. What do the other two say?"

"Unfortunately, we do not know," Travis confessed. "No one has ever seen them. They are veiled, hidden so the dark realm cannot acquire access. They will be revealed at an appointed time. It's a race to see who can get to it first. We believe the second prophecy could be hidden in your original manuscript."

I didn't say anything. I wasn't even sure where it was or if it still existed. Besides, the last thing I wanted was to dig up that old bastard of a book.

"Writing the story will be extremely dangerous." Travis' eyes bore into mine, wanting me to grasp the severity of what he was saying. "The dark realm does not want it written. They will be defeated if it is. Now that you have opened the gate, they are searching for you. Their solitary goal is your destruction. The storm that hit your first night here was one you wouldn't have been able to track on the weather radar. The portal was reopened. Spies were sent. If they find you, they will kill you. You must always be on the defensive. This is why I have asked you time again, not to venture out alone. Understand that your way of life can never be the same again."

He had been warning me all along. Even the night in the garden when he caught me spying under the willow tree, he had told me to be quiet or they would find me. Now his words took on an entirely different light. He was no longer the soothing voice of a wise man of the mountains. He was royalty, a Prince once ruler of an entire world and his words rang with authority.

"Not to worry, lady scribe." Falcon chimed in, noticing the distress carved into my face. "I will be your personal bodyguard, your secret service so to speak. I will give my very life to save yours."

His declaration caught me off guard. The distrust I felt for him earlier began to fade. He was nothing more than a rebel rogue, a fighter for a world and way of life stolen from him. He was a bit unorthodox, but the ultimate in passion for his cause. I will give my very life to save yours.

"That's why we danced so close the other night." He flashed his impish grin. "The spies were searching for you, asking questions. Your friend Lillian pointed you out. I shielded you and hid your face, so they couldn't identify you. But not to worry, as far as those spies are concerned, Travis and I disposed of them. You saw the last one lose his life in the garden."

I sat in silence, dumbstruck. The murdered man said they will find the scribe and destroy them. Fear began to manifest. He and Travis killed someone to protect me. My stomach knotted.

"Are you sure?" I focused my attention on Travis this time. "Are you one hundred percent positive it's me? It all seems so ludicrous. I am not anybody really, I'm not some famous author or wise philosopher. I'm just...me, Bronwyn Sterling..."

"It's you." His voice rang with conviction, and I didn't want to challenge his certainty, but I gave it one last shot.

"What makes you so sure?"

The council all looked at him as if they wanted to know too. "There are a couple of things. One being the night in the basement, during the storm, you spoke of wanting to write an epic story. That desire from deep within was stirring, awakening, ready to be written. It is a part of your soul. That is where it has been buried for years. You know the story. You've known it your entire life."

"And the other?" I asked.

He stayed quiet and his silence told me he wasn't going to let that secret out, not just yet. I sighed. I finished talking. I longed to lay down somewhere and bury my head under a soft blanket and sleep for hours.

Content that the council's work was done for now, Travis suggested that I retreat to the room for a few hours of sleep before heading back to Sandalwood Inn. Barak offered me his hand, ready to escort me back to my room. I didn't object. I was exhausted, my mind full. I needed to withdraw to a quiet place, where I could meditate on all that had been said to me.

Barak stopped at the door to my room. "Sleep well, my dear Bronwyn. In a few hours you will be escorted back to the inn. You must return before sunrise, to dispel any questions or suspicions." He closed the beautifully ornate door behind him as he left.

I undressed and climbed under the silk covers, extinguishing the small lamp on the bedside table. The room remained filled with the glow of the moonlight filtering through the glass doors. I lay there sinking deep into the feather mattress, the silk coverings feeling heavenly against my naked skin. I stared at the ceiling, hoping to fall asleep and wake up back at the Inn, realizing the whole thing had been a dream. I could imagine re-telling the events to Bethany and Lillian as the most bizarre insane dream I'd ever had. I sighed, realizing I could never breathe a word of this to either of them, all the while knowing I would more than likely have a lot of explaining to do in the morning. Bethany was a light sleeper and certain to notice I'd been out all night again. She and Lillian would profess without a doubt that Travis and I were having "escapades," as they so often called it.

My heart fell with the thought. For the entire week, I'd allowed the girls to convince me that Travis, with all the time and attention he devoted to me, was somewhat romantically interested. Now I realized the entire reason for his concern. He was only protecting his interest in the whole equation. I was his gateway back to Eden, and as a Prince of Eden, it was his duty to protect that passage. His heart, did, only belong to Mavis. That is why he never took an opportunity or made an advance when we were alone together. Even the kiss under the tree was nothing more than a tender gift. Travis and I were literally from two different worlds, and he was not interested in me in any romantic way.

A tear escaped my eye, finding its way down my cheek and rolling onto the silk pillowcase. I'd never felt more alone. I desperately missed Ryan and the normalcy of what we once shared. Another tear slid silently onto the pillow that cradled my head. My eyes became heavy, and soon I fell asleep.

I was still sleeping when Falcon entered my room, so I didn't see him smile in approval as he gazed upon my form, bathed in the glow of moonlight streaming across my bed, giving an iridescent glow to my ivory skin. He picked up my discarded clothes from the floor and tossed them onto the bed.

"Scribe," he whispered. "It's time to head back."

I stirred but remained asleep, spellbound in comfort.

"Scribe." This time he was much louder.

I opened her eyes and groaned at the sight of him.

"Good morning to you too," he said sarcastically. "Get dressed. It's time to head back."

I reached for my clothes, making sure the covers were pulled high enough to cover my nakedness "Turn around!" I demanded, before rising to a sitting position. He laughed lightly, turning to face the opposite direction.

"Why don't you wait outside the door?" I suggested.

"Time to start trusting me scribe, you're going to be seeing a lot of me." He gave the command, "three minutes," before leaving the room.

Heaviness invaded me with the realization. Last night's events had not been a dream. I dressed quickly, my body shivering from the coolness of my chamber, the marble floor like ice on my bare feet. My clothes were now crusted over, the mud long since drying. Bits of dirt crumbled to the floor as I slipped them on.

I made quick time, joining Falcon in the hallway. Together we headed outside into the damp darkness of the early morning. He led me back through the hedge maze, knowing every turn to take, navigating just as expertly as Barak the night before. We reached the line of trees, strolled through the leafy tunnel, and within minutes arrived at the white sandy shoreline.

Adam and Travis were waiting beside the gondola. In a way it was a relief to see them, knowing I wouldn't be taking the thirty-minute boat ride alone with Falcon. But in another way, being in close proximity to Travis produced an aching that I wasn't ready to deal with so early in the day.

Adam offered me his hand along with a welcoming smile as he helped me into the vessel. "Were you able to get some rest?"

"Yes," I managed to return the smile. "I did sleep well, thank you."

"Good to hear it."

He did seem princely. I smiled at the thought of what Lillian would say if she met him. He was strikingly handsome, not to mention royalty, if all they fed me last night was indeed true.

Travis remained silent, not even a greeting as we arrived at the water. My heart ached over it. Just as well, I thought.

A brisk wind blew across the water, carrying with it the rustic smells of autumn. The season would be upon us before long, fall always came earlier in the mountains. I pulled my bare legs up into the seat, curling them underneath me for added warmth. Travis removed a blanket as he had done the night of the fireworks show and draped it over my shoulders. Our eyes met briefly.

"Thank you," I muttered before looking away.

Falcon steered the vessel across the still lake, his eyes searching the water and the shorelines, watching for anything that would threaten his passengers. We glided along in silence; the only sound was the oar quietly cutting into the water. The tranquility of the early morning ride was like weights on my eyelids. I shifted in my seat, fighting the drowsiness, but the comfort of the blanket, and the gentle swaying of the boat rocked was the perfect sedative to rock me to sleep. I was dozing off when the harsh cry of a nighthawk ripped through the silence. Had I been alone I would have thought nothing of the bird call, but when Falcon cupped his hand to his mouth and sent back a series of convincing whippoorwill cries, I knew otherwise. Within a matter of seconds, the call was returned. As usual, no one offered me any information, and no words were exchanged among the men. Yet, when all three smiled at once I knew they were communicating in some way. My heart skipped a beat. Could they read minds? If that was the case, then Travis knew every thought I had about him. The assumption made me sick enough to contemplate jumping overboard.

"How do you do that?" I yawned, my sleepy voice breaking the silence. "Can you read minds?"

Falcon cocked an eyebrow and grinned; but it was Adam that put my fears to rest.

"We can, but only if the other person allows it. We call on each other through meditation, much like you do when you make a phone call. When the other person responds to the beckoning, we exchange information with our thoughts."

Intriguing. "Then why the bird call?"

"Because Falcon has been talking to Travis the entire ride and their conversation cannot be interrupted."

His answer annoyed me although I tried not to show it. If I was expected to fulfill the prophecy and write their story of redemption, then it might be nice to be let in on what was going on. The time of confidentiality should be over and the fact that they continued to hold secrets only fueled my distrust. I hadn't agreed to author their story and even if I wanted to, I doubted I could. How can someone write about something they know nothing about? Once more, how can you learn, if others refuse to inform you? A flame of anger ignited inside. As soon as the car was repaired, I would leave this place and never give it another thought.

We arrived at the opposite shoreline where the opening of the cave appeared like the mouth of an angry beast ready to swallow us whole. Falcon grabbed the torch and led the way. The descent was a bit more treacherous in this direction. I remembered several different levels of boulders upon which Barak needed to lift me so I could ascend. Falcon jumped from the first boulder without effort like a mountain lion on the prowl, leaping great distances with little exertion before landing lightly on his feet. Adam followed suit, gracefully descending to the lower levels, always landing noiselessly while exuding minimal effort. Travis followed with the same prowess, same result. Without hesitation he turned back and raised his arms high, offering to help me.

I wanted to descend as the men had and was almost certain I could make it. However, I feared slipping on the muddy surface, and landing hard on my ass, possibly breaking a bone, and then needing to be carried the rest of the way. To save myself from extreme embarrassment, I decided to take his offer. He placed his hands firmly around my waist, and with amazing strength and control, lifted me into the air and then steadily sat me on the ground below. This act was repeated seven more times as our trail descended deeper underground.

We walked in silence. At least I wasn't talking. They, however, were probably having quite an interesting conversation in their minds but I wouldn't know. I wasn't included. We crossed the marble riverbed, the icy water cramping my feet as we sloshed across it. Falcon replaced the torch, and then climbed a few feet up the side of the wall, where he pulled a small lever. Once again, the ground beneath us trembled as the rock wall slid slowly to our right. The musty smell of dirt welcomed us. We crossed through the beaten down shack, the wall closing slowly behind us.

Adam retrieved a hidden sword, then donned a black hooded cloak, as he stood on the broken-down porch of the cabin. He took my hand in his.

"Bless you lovely Bronwyn. It has been an honor. Until our paths cross again." He kissed my hand, and then nodded to Travis and Falcon. He jumped from the porch and ran into the woods, disappearing like a frightened deer.

"I'm turning the scribe over to you. You have it from here," Falcon said to Travis. He gave me a slight wink. "I'll be seeing you around." He too slipped into his hooded robe, darting off into the woods, disappearing into the thickness of the trees.

Travis and I were left alone on the porch. He took my arm. "Stay close beside me." We made our way through the woods back to the inn. Neither one of us said a word.

Thirty-Four

DAY SEVEN

I woke up earlier than planned. Despite my body's protests, I crawled from the bed, wanting to take advantage of Bethany and Lillian's absence. I was glad they weren't in the room. I didn't have the energy to make up a story explaining where I was last night, and why I had snuck back into the room at five in the morning. I splashed cold water on my face, brushed my teeth, ran a comb through my tangled hair and dressed. While the others were eating, I quietly took my leave.

The sun was at work again, radiating its warmth, making me grateful for the beauty of the morning. The gently moving ripples on the river glistened under the rays of the sun, and seemed to smile at me as I walked past, uplifting my spirits from the feeling of dread overwhelming me last night. I skirted past the river, scouting for a place to escape. I needed solitude, a private corner to collect my thoughts and pen the many questions invading my mind. I slipped across the property and onto the small narrow highway. This time instead of heading into Moonshine; I decided to venture in the opposite direction and strolled down the highway until I arrived at the old, covered bridge where we took shelter the night of our arrival, the same bridge where I first laid eyes on Travis The place was perfect. No one would ever think to look for me here.

I hiked down the grassy hill, leading underneath the bridge, and found a delightful place near the river's edge to sit and collect my thoughts. My mind had been jumping from one subject to another since I escaped the inn, and now sitting in solitude, I mused at the implausibility of last night's events. What Barak and the others told me defied all physical laws, all logic, all sense, and yet, for some bizarre reason, I believed it, my heart did anyway. Throughout my life I usually followed my heart rather than my head. I'd learned from experience, if my brain told me it was impossible, then my heart knew it to be true and right now, my heart was telling me this was the very reason I was here.

I dared to wonder about my earlier writing of Moonshine. Thoughts of the old manuscript evoked an anxious feeling that did not sit well with me. I began chewing my fingernails, something I hadn't done in years. My memory of the story was vague at best. Falcon was right when he said my parents insisted I stop writing. I was sent to counseling for several weeks before I was allowed to come back home. My parents visited me often yet when I returned home, my writing desk was gone as was my manuscript. I remember a hollowness that cracked inside of me. Like a pet that had run away, and I couldn't find it. I didn't cry or ask for my story. I knew if I did, I would be sent back to the hospital, so I left it alone. But a part of me longed for something I couldn't explain. I hadn't thought of the incident for twenty-three years. A gnawing dread surfaced, there were suppressed memories concerning the story, events I'd been compelled to forget. With my curiosity peaking, I decided to find my old writing and shed more light into all of this. Besides, as Travis mentioned, the second prophecy might be hidden somewhere within the pages. Hopefully, mother had not destroyed the book, but stored it somewhere in the attic. I would make a surprise visit to my parents on the way home from this trip and search for the manuscript. With the conclusion of that matter, my mind settled on the subject, and then sporadically jumped to the next.... Travis.

He was a Prince, the ruler of another world, a man of wisdom and power. He seemed compassionate, caring for everyone alike, yet as I noticed on our night in the basement. There were secrets, even more than were revealed last night. There was also a fierceness that frightened me in a way. I felt silly thinking he had been attracted to me. His concern lay in who he was, his solemn duty, it was what he did as a benevolent ruler. I should've never read any more into his actions other than that simple fact. My heart ached. Not again, I could not go through another heartbreak, so I immediately forced it from my mind, but it didn't leave willingly. Instead, it attached itself to thoughts of Mavis, and I began to speculate why Mavis asked about the fireworks show. Did she know I had watched them with Travis?

I felt a twinge of guilt but then dismissed it. Nothing adulterous happened between us. I thought again about Mavis's injuries, wondering if they happened during the uprising. There were so many more questions. I thought of Lillian, and Bethany, and the rewrite I had yet to start, let alone finish. Today was our seventh day in Moonshine. It was just a matter of time before the parts arrived and Larry repaired the car, accelerating our departure.

Leaving seemed like an escape back to normality. The idea of heading back to civilization seemed like a visit from an old friend. The thought of being home in my condo on the beach, visiting my favorite coffee house with my friends, and the other activities that usually consumed my life, seemed so appealing. I watched the flowing river smiling at the thought of it all.

"How's our Lady Scribe today?" A voice broke my gaze and brought my eyes to Falcon sitting on his motorcycle.

"I never heard you drive up."

"You need to become more aware of your surroundings. I followed you the entire way." He lit a cigarette, took a draw, and expelled the smoke slowly, all the while keeping his eye on me.

"Didn't Travis warn you about going off alone? Yet, for some reason you continue to neglect his instructions. Why is that?"

I let out a defiant chuckle. "I'm not used to asking permission to take a walk."

He drew on the cigarette. "It's not about asking permission; it's about letting us know where you are."

"Am I in danger?" I rolled my eyes. My nonchalant attitude didn't sit right with him.

"Always."

I rolled my eyes again. "It was you following us the night we arrived, wasn't it? I saw you moving in and out of the trees."

He took a long draw exhaling the smoke slowly before he answered. "I knew you noticed me, I saw the fear in your eyes, as I do now." He didn't take his eyes off me. His stare was cold.

"I'm not afraid of you." I swallowed.

"Yes, you are." The smoke billowed from his mouth when he spoke. A shudder crawled up my back and for some reason a seed of distrust began to take root.

He took one last draw, and then tossed his cigarette to the ground. "You don't trust me?"

The heat wrapped around my neck. Was he reading my thoughts? I pressed my lips together, "I have a hard time trusting men in general."

He stared at me a few seconds longer, and then continued with the previous conversation, as if we had never strayed from it in the first place. "Abaddon was notified of your arrival that night. He sent many of his men through the portal as soon as you opened it. It took all of us to fight them off."

I shuddered again at the thought. "How did they know I was coming? Our arrival was an accident. I took a wrong turn that night."

"According to you." He dismounted his bike.

I studied him. He was in excellent physical shape, as were all the men I'd encountered here. Moreover, like the others, he wore his hair long, the ebony strands hanging over his azure eyes not allowing anyone a true glimpse inside his soul. He sported a slight five o'clock shadow adding to his rugged and unkept look. He was always barefoot, dressed in torn jeans and a muscle shirt, his ensemble adding to his rebellious unorthodox vibe. He too wore the same white stone pendant around his neck as I saw on Adam and Travis.

"What's the necklace for?" I asked. "I noticed you all wear one."

"It reminds us of who we really are."

I knew she would not get any more information than that elusive offering.

"Tell me about your world. The one that is the same as this one but better. "I let the sarcasm flow. "What's it called?"

"Earth, same as yours. Remember we're of another dimension not another planet. Only a doorway separates the two, not a universe."

I had read of portals, wormholes and black holes and was aware of the possibility of other dimensions. But I also read that it would take millions of years for technology to advance to the point of accessing them, if ever. If that was the case then their world must be extremely advanced, yet they spoke of it as a garden state, like the original Eden of the Bible.

"Where's the portal?"

Falcon lit up another and took a quick draw before he answered. "There are many. The closest one to us is the waterfall."

I blinked in surprise. The peculiarity I experienced that night now made sense. "Something happened to me there. Travis said it was altitude sickness, but I know it wasn't."

He expelled a long line of smoke. "You climbed to the top where the veil between the two worlds is very thin. You felt the pull."

"The pull?"

"There's a presence there that will call to your spirit. Some people never feel it, but if you're sensitive to it, you will hear it."

I'd heard a woman singing, three separate times since my arrival, and each time the song had beckoned me, drawing me away from where I was and into the unknown. This must be the presence he was referring to. Was it attempting to call me through the portal? The thought was paralyzing, and I shivered despite the mugginess of the morning. I hoped Falcon wouldn't notice the trembling. He knocked the ashes from his cigarette, and then took a seat on the rock next to me. Again, he spoke as if he was reading my thoughts.

"The presence will speak to your spirit, not your mind so don't waste your time trying to find the logic in everything, and don't waste time being frightened. Listen to it, it will empower you, give you courage, and guide you into the truth." He took another draw and expelled a long slow trail of smoke. His eyes were reminiscing, and I could tell his thoughts were literally worlds away.

"Eden is tropical, set on the snow-white sands of the ocean." He changed the subject, attempting to steer my thinking away, and although the description of his world was intriguing, I couldn't stop thinking of the portal.

"There are many lakes, rivers, streams, oceans... there is a lot of water. All of it is pure and unpolluted. Eden's climate is tropical year around with much vegetation. The rest of our earth is a lot like yours, with different climates in various regions. I'm from a territory called Cold Mountain. It's exceptionally beautiful, a lot like Moonshine."

"But better." We both said simultaneously. He was serious, I was sarcastic.

"Cold Mountain is lush, so green, so many shades of green. The trees in the forest are massive and ancient. They can tell a good story. So much lore hidden within the hills. The earth there has a specific scent. The feel...the music birthed there... There aren't words to describe it. It's something you have to experience yourself. It's... mystical."

My heart raced at the thought and somewhere deep inside I longed to know a place like that instead of living out my life in a rented condo on a crowded beach. The inner urging was so strong a small lump formed in my throat and although it was silly, I felt as if I might cry.

"We eat only the food we get from plants." He continued his oral presentation. "We have many species of animals, none that we have lost to extinction. We live among them with no fear. They are not wild beasts. All are tame, existing among humanity. We communicate with them through our thoughts. We have the same ability as each other if we choose to communicate in that way. We have no need for cell phones; we summon each other with our minds. If I wished to speak with Travis right now, I would simply concentrate and call on him in my thoughts.

Much like this world's attempts at praying except you all are not tuned into the listening part of it."

His words interested me. I had always found praying to be an arduous task and as Falcon described it, as a one ended conversation. "How do you get your mind to tune into the listening?"

He flicked the burning ashes onto the ground, took another small draw and expelled the smoke. "That's the problem. You try to accomplish things with your mind. God will never speak to your brain, Scribe. He only speaks to your heart. Whispers from within. When you learn how to listen, you will hear his answers."

He took another drag of his cigarette, this time expelling the smoke very slowly, letting me contemplate his answer, as he watched a hawk glide overhead. Again, his mind seemed very far away.

We were quiet for some time. Nothing but the sound of trickling water touched our ears. The light lessened as dark gray clouds began to fill the sky, veiling the brightness and warmth of the sun. A sudden gust of wind blew, stirring up a few fallen leaves and bringing the smell of rain. Falcon jumped to his feet and tossed the butt of his cigarette to the ground, crushing it under the heel of his bare foot. "Let's go, Scribe."

"Go where?"

"I'll give you a ride back to the inn before it rains."

"I like walking in the rain."

He climbed on his bike and stared at me through his dark glasses. "I'm going to have a lot of trouble with you, aren't I?"

"That depends on you. You give me trouble; I'll give it right back." I sighed and softened my voice. "Honestly, I'm not ready to head back. There will be so many questions. My friends know I was out all night."

He considered the magnitude of what I said. "Let's go for a ride, then. I won't take you back just yet."

I studied him, perched upon his sleek high-speed motorcycle. Just a few days ago he terrified me, spinning me across the lawn, and all the while he was protecting me from a would-be assassin. His ways were a bit unorthodox and although I wasn't sure I trusted him completely I no longer feared him as I did before.

I climbed on behind him, wrapping my arms around his hard stomach. He swept his hair in a ponytail, to keep it from whipping my face, and then started the engine. He raced down the narrow highway, taking the curves at tremendous speed. At any other time, I would have screamed in fear, protesting, demanding he slow down. However, I felt confident in his ability to maneuver the heavy bike. Besides, if it were his sworn duty to protect me, he wouldn't risk my life by crashing, so I rested in the fact he knew what he was doing, and before long found myself enjoying the intense thrill of the ride. He drove for a while longer before he made a speedy U-turn and stopped on the side of the road. "You alright?"

"It's great," I laughed.

"Rain's coming. You ready to get back, or do you want to go somewhere else?"

I had much rather go somewhere else, but I knew I couldn't delay the inevitable. The longer I was gone, the more intense the questioning would be. I sighed. "I guess I'd better go back."

"To the inn it is." He took off at incredible speed once again and had I not been clutching him so tightly, he would have left me on my ass in the middle of the road.

The rain began to fall just as he whipped the bike into the Inn's driveway. A strange car sat in front, and everyone was crowded on the front porch. Carla Jo was jumping up and down; her hands were covering her mouth. Everyone was gathered around the driver of the car. The sound of our approach drew everyone's attention. All eyes focused on me arriving with Falcon. Pure perplexity stretched across Bethany's face.

Climbing from the motorcycle my eyes suddenly fell upon the driver of the car, my heart raced...

Ryan.

The one person I never expected to see at Sandalwood Inn. I stayed by the bike, my strength escaping, forcing me to remain where I was as the rain fell on my face.

"Look who showed up," Bethany announced sarcastically, breaking the silence.

"I can't believe he's here, on my porch!" Carla Jo squealed as she continued her jumping.

"Hello, Bronwyn."

The sound of his voice knotted my stomach. "What are you doing here?"

"You weren't returning any of my calls, so I came in person."

"How did you know where to find me?" I demanded while remaining planted by the bike.

"Who are you?" Falcon stepped in front of me to block Ryan's view.

"You don't know Ryan Reese?" Carla Jo was shocked.

Ryan bravely descended the porch steps and stood directly in front of Falcon.

"I'm her fiancé," he said, while sizing up the beefy motorcycle rider.

"Ex- fiancé," I corrected.

Falcon stood his ground, unmoving. "What do you want with her?"

"What business is it of yours?" Ryan bit back. "Are you dating her now?"

"And if I am?" He said while lighting up another cigarette. He removed his dark glasses revealing his penetrating eyes and deep scar.

"Look. I don't want any trouble from you mountain people. There's no need to pull out your sawed-off shotguns, I just came to speak with Bronwyn."

Falcon took a long draw, keeping his eyes locked on Ryan in a threatening gaze. "Do you wish to talk to this charlatan?"

"I have nothing to say to him."

Falcon gave Ryan a satisfied grin as he replaced his dark glasses, then blew a cloud of smoke directly into Ryan's face. Ryan backed away, choking on his next words.

"Did your girlfriend tell you she is carrying my baby?"

Collective gasps sounded from the porch. My pulse quickened. My stomach dropped.

"You're pregnant?" Bethany asked.

"No!" my answer collided mid-air with Ryan's "Yes!"

"That bloody well explains the mood swings," Bethany growled.

"And all the fainting," Lillian added.

I couldn't believe what I was hearing. "Come on guys, do I look pregnant to you?"

"Did you abort my child?" Ryan pressed the matter.

"I lost my child," I bit back.

The rain poured down. I looked up at Travis on the porch. He was the only person I'd ever talked to about my pregnancy. Had he betrayed my confidence? What reason could he have for doing that, unless he had told Mavis, and Mavis, in hopes of getting rid of me, had phoned Ryan? But I knew that would be impossible. Almost every woman on the planet wanted to call Ryan Reese. How would Mavis have discovered his private number?

"Who told you about the baby?" I demanded.

"I got a call," his face was smug.

"Who called you?" I was nearly screaming.

"Lillian."

I glanced at her. How could she? Just because she introduced us didn't mean she had the right to interfere. Besides, how did she know about the baby?

"You left a personal file open on your computer. I saw some things and I made the call to Ryan for your own good, love. You are such a martyr, but I couldn't let you have a baby on your own. You need help Bronwyn."

My head began to swim. All eyes were on me. Bethany looked somewhat wounded and insulted. Lillian appeared embarrassed at what she had done but sympathetic, nonetheless. As much as I wanted to be angry with her, I knew she only did what she thought was right.

"I want out of here." I whispered.

"Can we go someplace private?" Ryan asked. "I really need to talk to you."

"You sure pick a fine time and place to talk. There's no place private. It's a small town; everyone will recognize you."

"You can go to my cabin." Travis' offer surprised me. He had descended the porch and was now standing directly behind Ryan. "You can go there. You will have privacy." He directed his words to me only. "It's up to you though. You do not have to go with him if you don't want to."

I looked at everyone watching me from the porch and sighed defeated. "I'll go. I think I need to."

"That's my girl." Ryan said, eyeing Falcon. Falcon took a firm step forward. It was all he needed to do for Ryan to retreat to his rental car.

I remained in the pouring rain, my mind and stomach reeling. I could not fathom this strange turn of events. Everything in my life seemed a bit surreal at the moment. Bethany shook her head in disgust and disappeared inside the inn, slamming the screen door behind her. I wanted to climb on the back of Falcon's bike and ride down the road until he'd taken me far away from everyone and everything. I even contemplated returning to the waterfalls and being sucked through the portal if only to avoid my present situation. Instead, I climbed into the rental car.

∞

Falcon and Travis watched as the car left the driveway and disappeared down the highway towards Moonshine.

"Do you trust him?" Falcon asked.

"I never trust a man who would leave his lady," Travis said. "However, the only threat he possesses at this point is convincing her into taking him back and returning to California. If they reunite, she could leave and soon forget about all she has learned."

Falcon could hear the sorrow in Travis's voice and knew him well enough to know his concern was far deeper than he was showing.

"Then why did you offer your cabin? We could have gotten rid of him pretty easily."

"You can protect her life, Falcon, but you cannot protect her heart. She must work through these matters. There will be many obstacles facing her if she agrees to this quest. This is very small in comparison to what lies ahead. She needs to draw upon her inner strength. Still, I wouldn't be opposed if you kept a close eye. And, if he gets out of hand..."

Falcon replaced his dark glasses and gave Travis his impish grin.

Thirty-Five

The rain tapped hard on the blue tin roof. Ryan walked around the cabin, surveying it. I took a seat on the sofa and curled my feet beneath me while waiting for him to turn his attention to me. He seemed so different from how I remembered him. He had changed. Or something had changed him. On the other hand, maybe Travis was right. Maybe I was finally seeing Ryan for who he really was, not who I had invented him to be.

He stood at the front door looking out over the lake. "This is a really nice place he has here."

"Uh huh. I rode out the storm of a lifetime here."

"Cool." He answered dismissively.

"I'm not so sure it was cool. It was scary to me."

He continued to survey the lake. "Wonder what kind of fish they got in there."

I sighed and waited. "Ryan? Why did you come all the way to Moonshine? I don't think it was to check out the bass and trout in the lake."

Ryan broke his gaze and closed the door behind him, taking a seat on the couch next to me.

"I came because I've been missing you, babe." He paused for a moment, studying my face for impact. "Life's been wow! You know. It's totally insane. I'm constantly surrounded by people. I have my own security guards. It's a wonder I got away to come here. There are so many people advising me, telling me what to do. All of them are trying to control my career and my personal life. It kind of bugs sometimes. I'm not sure I like all this attention. It's great, don't get me wrong, but everywhere I turn, there are cameras and screaming girls, like that kid at the inn. It's so annoying. It gets old, you know. Most guys would love to have girls screaming after them, but not all of them are pretty."

I sat stoically, offering no sympathy.

"I miss you babe. I've been around all these sexy actresses with killer bodies and everything, but man, are they shallow! They are so into themselves. All they want to talk about is how thin they are or how they look. I haven't had one decent conversation. I crave it." He scooted in a bit closer, "Remember, babe, how you and I could talk for hours, planning out stories, and characters and backgrounds? Together we came up with the best scenarios. I miss that."

I smiled. I couldn't help myself. Those were good times. Ryan relaxed, my smile putting him at ease, inspiring him to continue his long-winded rambling. "I miss you. I miss that amazing smile, those deep green eyes, your sexy body. I miss coming home to you and the way you made our place on the beach so nice and comfortable. I miss our relaxing evenings and dinners out on the deck, overlooking the ocean. I miss the way I feel when I am around you. I realize that I am still in love with you...Do you know what Saturday was?"

I knew but offered no answer.

"I was supposed to marry the most amazing woman in the world, and there I was, out at another publicity party, surrounded by flashing cameras and women throwing themselves at me. I was so tired. I wanted you so bad right then. Then I got the call from Lil, telling me about the baby. I thought, wow, how's that for publicity. A baby, just what I need. A great excuse for me to settle down."

"There is no baby, Ryan." I spoke the words quietly. "I miscarried."

He moved in tighter until he practically sat on my lap, "No problem, babe. We can make another one here tonight. I love you. I never wanted to end things, but it was like I had no choice ya know. My agent kinda controls my life. He's always looking for ways to keep me in the spotlight. Gabriella was his idea. He said if we were in a relationship, it would help promote the movie."

The rain continued to tap on the roof overhead. Thunder rolled softly outside.

I sat, silent. Stunned. I'd been waiting for so long to hear all the things that Ryan was saying. For those nights, when I had longed for an opportunity to be with him, wanting him to desire me again, wondering what I did to quell his love for me. Now he was practically begging for me, offering himself and I knew there wasn't a woman in the world that would not give everything they had to be where I was right now.

He surprised me by moving from the couch to the floor. Kneeling before me, he grabbed my hand and slipped an enormous diamond on my finger. It was much bigger than the original one he had purchased.

"I love you babe. Take me back and marry me. This time it will be for real. I won't let anything get in the way again. I promise. You're the best thing that ever happened to me, and I want the best. I need the best. I love you."

It was his way of saying "I love you," that made my mind up on the matter. Suddenly, my decision was right there, final. The last time I'd heard those words, Travis uttered them in the garden. He was not confessing his love to me unfortunately, but offering an example of what true love really was. I remembered his final words that night: "True love is sacrifice."

I fumbled with the enormous diamond.

"You have no idea how many nights I have prayed and dreamed for this moment."

He moved in closer. "Me too, babe. Me too."

"And now that it is actually happening, I realize it's not what I want at all." I turned the ring and pulled until it slipped off my finger.

"What?" He was shocked, taken aback by my rejection.

"You don't love me Ryan, not really."

"Babe!" He protested.

"It's Bronwyn."

He looked confused.

"My name is Bronwyn, not babe, Bronwyn."

"Okay!" his face flushed in frustration. "Bronwyn, Bronwyn, Bronwyn. I do love you. It took me a while, but I realize now that I need you."

I shook my head. "Ryan, I have no desire to be needed by you or anyone. If you're not a whole person without me, you will never be a whole person with me. Everything you said, all your reasons for loving me, were for you, based entirely upon your feelings." My voice rose. "My God, you were even excited about the baby because it was an excuse for you to settle down... not because you loved it."

"I would love a baby once it came. It's just hard to love someone you don't know."

"Exactly. So how can you love me when you don't really know me? Me, not babe. Me."

"God, Bronwyn, how many times do I have to say it? I do love you. I left all that Hollywood stuff to come back to you. My manager will be livid when he finds out what I've done. I've taken a huge risk. How can I prove it to you any more than that?" He practically yelled the words.

I smiled softly. "Then you're willing to stay here with me?"

Pure surprise sprawled across his face. "Here, in this town?"

"Yes. I'm inspired here, I can write here, and I want to write more than anything."

He stood from his kneeling position, agitated, while running his fingers through his blond waves.

"Babe, I can't stay here. I gotta get back. I'm on contract. We can visit here from time to time so you can do some writing, but my career has me there. You know that."

"I thought you were leaving it all behind for me?"

"I would if I could. Contracts, babe."

Silence.

His voice turned whiny. "Awe come on. This isn't fair. I'm not leaving you behind this time. I'm offering to take you with me."

"I don't want to go," I said quietly. "I was unfair to you, Ryan. I loved a man who never existed anywhere but in my own mind. I imagined you to be someone I wanted you to be, instead of seeing you for who you really were. And I'm sorry" I let my voice go softer still. "I can't go with you, because I do not love you."

He stopped his pacing to stare at me. "Is it because of that bad ass on the motorcycle? Are you in love with him?"

I almost laughed at the thought. "No. I am not in love with him."

Ryan didn't say a word. He walked to the front door, and stepped onto the porch, his hands in his pockets, watching the rain. "What do I do now?"

"Find yourself. Know who you are and become a whole person, so when you do find that someone to spend the rest of your life with, it will be two whole people walking side by side, sharing their lives together."

"You see, you're so deep," he said. "I miss that."

I smiled.

The summer rain continued soaking the earth, the sky doing what my soul longed to do. Cry and cleanse. I was sending Ryan away, rejecting his love. Yet, I felt peaceful.

"So, this is what it feels like," he said, pounding his heart with his fist. "Man, it hurts."

"I know," I whispered.

He leaned over and kissed me on the cheek. "I'm sorry. I really am."

I watched as he headed to the car and climbed into the driver's seat. He gave me a slight salute as he pulled away. I watched until the car was out of view, and then sat on the porch swing, pushing off slowly with my feet, hypnotized by the falling rain. Only a few tears escaped my eyes.

I wasn't sure why, but I was not heartbroken. I wasn't in love with Ryan. Spending the past hour with him confirmed that. Spending the past week with Travis had given me a more certain picture of what I desired. A love I not only wanted to experience for myself, but a love I longed to be able to give. Could I ever love someone so selflessly? Could I, as Travis said, send a person away, who I truly wanted and loved, never experiencing them, yet knowing they would experience all they ever dreamed?

I sat there for hours, swinging, and thinking, never moving, just swinging, and thinking. I thought of how trite and superficial Ryan's world appeared in contrast to the men with whom I had communed last night. They lived for a much nobler purpose. I thought of Barak and his final words to me. When he walked me back to my room last night, he talked of the temptation to return to a normal life, a comfortable life. However, he warned me not to settle for good, when my destiny was to be great. True, I could have returned with Ryan and lived an amazing life. But now, I can follow my destiny and be a part of something profound. Barak had also warned me that there was much pain and suffering on the path to greatness.

A warm steam rose from the lake, the golden sun showing its face for the first time in several hours. However, it appeared for only a few minutes before dipping behind the mountains, allowing the moon and stars to take over. I sat in the darkness, watching the fireflies and listened to the crickets and croaking frogs. I inhaled the aroma of the wet earth; remembering my first night in this cabin, and how I was given a second chance at life. There was a life to be lived, a purpose to fulfill, a destiny waiting.

I entered the dark cabin and knew what I must do. I'd made up my mind. I took a seat at the antique desk in the corner of the living room. Turning on a small lamp, I sat at the computer. I opened a new file, typing on the keyboard with speed and accuracy. Bethany would get her rewrite. I didn't care if it was my best work. I wouldn't spend valuable time worrying over it. What would it matter in the whole scheme of things anyway? I would write only one more simple, sappy, love story for the publisher.

I wrote all night, finally finishing my work early the next morning. I stretched, exhausted but invigorated, yawned, and sent the document to the printer. Soon, I held a stack of warm papers in my hand. I laid them aside, picked up a pen and paper and wrote a long letter. I placed it in an envelope, sealed it, and then headed into the bedroom to sleep.

Should I sleep in Travis's bed? I hadn't yet seen the bedroom. I turned on the lamp and looked around. It was simple, yet masculine. Beautiful scenic paintings adorned the walls; no animal heads or antlers hung over the fireplace. I now understood why. In Eden, man, and animals coexisted. They never considered the flesh of an animal as food, so there would be no reason to kill an animal and hang his head. Quite a barbaric act once I thought about it. Furthermore, I had never seen meat on Travis's plate at any of our meals. He ate only fruit, vegetables, and nuts.

Exhausted from yet another emotion-filled day, I crawled on the bed and tugged at the blanket folded neatly at the foot, pulling it over me. As I reached for the lamp, I knocked a small beautifully hand carved box off the table spilling its contents onto the floor. Crawling from the bed, I stooped down to retrieve the items lying scattered on the hardwood. I picked up the first item, a silver chain with a white stone pendant identical to the one I'd seen Travis and the rest of the council wearing. I draped it gently across my fingers, examining it. Turning the stone over, I read the inscription, Kenalycia, carved into the white stone. I gently laid it back onto the velvet lining of the box. The next item was a dark amber vial of some sort. I pried off the lid. An amazing aroma rushed into the room. It was a distinct scent acting as a key, unlocking a deep memory, a feeling lost in the secret places of my mind. The aroma transcended time, trying to remind me of something. I sat on the floor, stunned. Where had I inhaled the opulent scent? What buried memory was it attempting to unlock? I lifted the vial once more, and breathed in, accidentally touching the tip of my nose. A portion of the oily substance clung to my skin, keeping the scent alive. I replaced the lid and put the vial back into the box. The third and final item was a small scroll bound by a ribbon. Should I dare remove the tie and see what was written on the aging parchment? Curiosity getting the best of me, I slid the twine off the scroll and carefully unrolled the aging paper, revealing the face of a Native American Maiden, artistically sketched onto the parchment. A small gasp escaped my lips as if I were looking into a mirror. There was an uncanny resemblance between me and the maiden, seemingly as if we were identical twins. Beneath the portrait at the base of the maiden's neck were the words, Onida of Amadahy. Amadahy! Didn't the prophecy say the scribe would come from Amadahy? Stunned, I stared at the drawing, sketched nearly six-hundred years ago. The mysteriousness of Moonshine deepened with every moment. Onida of Amadahy, I whispered before taking one final look and rolling the sketch and sliding the twine back over it, securing it in place and then carefully placing it back in the box.

Turning off the light, I lay in bed, with the scent of the oil still permeating the room. My eyes grew heavy; and as I drifted off to sleep.

Thirty-Six

DAY EIGHT

Mavis hung up the phone on the kitchen wall.

"Your car is ready!"

If she expected triumphant cheers and cries of relief, to get back on the road she didn't receive any. Her supposed good news was not met by a round of ovations from the girls. Instead, their reactions were more subdued. Each hating to see their week of rest and relaxation come to an end. However remote and quaint, Moonshine had crept its way into their hearts. Mavis returned to the stove and continued her announcements, informing them that Larry would be delivering the car to the inn within a few hours. Bethany sighed and suggested they pack their belongings so they could be on the road before one o'clock. Then she asked Travis to get their bill ready, desiring to take care of their debt immediately. To their shock, Travis informed them that there was no charge, stating that one should never take advantage of someone else's misfortune. Those were the first words he'd spoken all morning.

Stunned, the girls sat in silence.

"Anyone heard from Bronwyn?" Lillian interrupted the sudden quietness. "She never returned to the inn last night."

"She probably stayed out all night making another baby with Ryan," Bethany said bitterly.

Travis shot her a sharp look. She spoke out of turn, but she didn't care. She was angry. Bronwyn had been so different since her break up with Ryan. Bethany had accepted the distance, figuring the pain in Bronwyn's heart was what caused the change in her behavior. Now she understood the distance. When you withhold a secret of that magnitude, it builds an invisible wall. No matter how hard Bethany may have tried, she could not have broken through that barrier. Her anger with Bronwyn stemmed from the fact that she had kept the pregnancy quiet, purposely. She could have been there for her. She had always considered Bronwyn more of a sister than a friend. She would have put her own life on hold to help her through it all. To her, it was a loud proclamation stating that Bronwyn didn't want her help or encouragement and didn't value their relationship as much as she did.

"You have to be happy for her," Lillian said, jumping to Bronwyn's defense. "This is what she has dreamed of for so long. I find it terribly romantic that Ryan would come all this way to find her. She'll have it made now," she bit into her bagel. "Being married to Ryan Reese, she'll never have to work again. Lucky girl."

"She is so lucky," Carla Jo drooled into her cereal.

Travis stood and took his dishes to the sink, exiting the kitchen in silence. Bethany and Lillian exchanged glances; each knew what the other was thinking. Travis appeared angry, not to mention agitated. Bethany was glad Ryan had come. She had not trusted Travis from the beginning. She could not see in him this integrity that Bronwyn insisted he possessed. Furthermore, if Bronwyn had kept something as big as her pregnancy with Ryan a secret, then she'd certainly withhold the truth about herself and Travis. It didn't make sense for two people to be out all night, sneaking back into the inn at ungodly hours, only to insist that nothing was happening. No two people who had just met have that much to talk about.

Bethany made a mental note and recounted how many nights on this short trip Bronwyn had been away. There was the first night during the storms, when she and Travis spent the entire night in his cabin's basement. Then there was the second night, when they both disappeared for some time at the falls. There was the third night, when she and Travis had supposedly sat in the garden until midnight discussing her writing. The night before the festival, Bethany woke to see Bronwyn leave the room. She didn't return until sunrise the next morning. The night of the festival, they were out on the lake watching the fireworks together, not returning to the inn until three that morning. Then there was Sunday night when Bronwyn mysteriously left the porch to take a walk and did not return to the inn until just before sunrise. And what about yesterday afternoon, riding up on a motorcycle with that Falcon guy? What was that all about?

Bronwyn was keeping secrets. Bethany's anger began to rise. Of course, she had been lying. Her best friend, who she thought she knew very well, had turned into someone altogether different. The Bronwyn she knew would never intentionally have an affair with a married man.

Now on the eve of their departure, Ryan shows up. Bethany found herself thinking Bronwyn didn't deserve Ryan, either. She pushed away from the table angrily, stomping up the stairs, to pack her belongings.

Thirty-Seven

I woke with the sun, quite refreshed; despite the fact I had only four hours of sleep. I refolded the blanket, returning it to the foot of the bed, smoothed out the comforter, re-fluffed the pillows and left the room. I washed up cleaning my face with the musky scented soaps, Travis' scent. One whiff and his form materialized in my mind. I shook my head, trying to clear the tempting image of infidelity. He is a married man, ban the thought. I brushed my teeth with my finger and combed my hair with a brush in the wooden cabinet. Realizing I hadn't eaten in almost twenty-four hours, I scooped up the completed manuscript, and headed back to the inn for breakfast. Passing Larry's Garage, I noticed my car parked directly out front. Larry whistled as he finished the final repairs.

I stopped in to compliment him on his skilled work, and as I sat in the passenger seat the familiar smell greeted my nose. I thought back to the fateful night of the breakdown, the storm, riding in the pick-up and seeing the inn for the first time. Running for the front door while dodging hailstones and lightning strikes. I smiled at the recollection. allowing my hand to gently rub across the seat. I hoped Larry's repairs would see the girls all the way back home. I pulled a small envelope from my stack of papers and placed it in the glove box.

With that done, I left. I wasn't sure how I would return home to retrieve my belongings or where I would go to begin writing the story. I wanted to stay in Moonshine. However, there was one problem. Travis. I needed to distance myself from him. He was married and I had no intentions of interfering any further and as much as I hated the thought, I knew it would be best to leave Moonshine altogether.

The Inn was quiet when I entered the kitchen. Only Bethany and Lillian sat at the big wooden table, mulling over a map, trying to decide the quickest route home. I was happy to find the two of them together. I proudly turned the new script over to Bethany who simply raised an eyebrow and scanned a few pages before pushing it aside. I knew she was upset. I would let her stew for now and talk to her before their departure, trying to explain my plan as best I could without relaying the secrets of Moonshine.

I decided to stroll through the gardens. The fragrances were therapeutic as well as inspiring. It would allow me some time to sort through my thoughts and plan out how I would tell the girls I wasn't returning home with them. I was in deep thought, not realizing how far I had walked until I approached the final garden. The door was slightly ajar, the secret garden now accessible. I placed my hand flat against the heavy door and pushed. It moved, bidding me entrance. Thick massive trees, overtaken by moss and hanging vines, guarded the opening, like leafy cobwebs. I swept away the tendrils, each touch of the sprays released a plethora of fragrances. I came upon a wooden bridge crossing over a moderate sized pond, home to Koi and other colorful fish, all swimming gracefully in the waters below.

The bridge led to yet another cobblestone path trailing through more flowering plants and trees. This garden, though seemingly un-kept and extremely wild in nature, proved to be the most beautiful of all. There was a sense of sacredness, a feeling of awe and I wondered why this garden was special. Why did it have a locked door when the others did not? A thought...could this be the place where the legendary tree of life is hidden? My heart pounded at the assumption, and as I looked over the many massive trees growing near the path my eyes fell upon Mavis, on her knees working the soil, planting, and pruning. Gardening tools and a basket filled with plants lay beside her.

I stopped, not sure if I should continue my approach or back away slowly. I wasn't prepared for a one-on-one conversation with her. I could only deny any involvement with Travis should Mavis question me. The fact that I indeed had feelings for him might surface, which I could not refute. So, I decided to back away, retracing my steps quietly.

As if Mavis had eyes in the back of her head, "Leaving so soon?"

Caught! My heart skipped a beat.

"I was looking for Bethany and Lillian. I thought they might be here." I made up an excuse.

"No, it's just me."

I took the information as my opportunity to leave, but Mavis' request stopped me cold. "Can you stay for a minute?" Keeping her back to me, she grabbed a flowering plant from her basket and placed it into a small hole, "Would you like to know how I got my injuries?"

The question surprised me, making my stomach uneasy. I had been curious, wanting to know, yet for some reason I feared the answer. I didn't have a chance to respond, however, because Mavis continued anyway.

"I think you need to know. Why don't you sit there on the nice cool grass? My stories tend to get lengthy."

Despite my inner urge to run, I felt somewhat of an obligation to hear her out. Besides, whatever story may unfold, I was certain it would provide some sort of insight into Travis, his heart, and depth of his faithfulness. So, I sat in a patch of cool green clover, in the shade of a Maple tree, and waited for the tale to unfold.

As though she had eyes in the back of her head, Mavis waited until I settled before beginning her story. "It happened when we came through the portal. The call was swift and unexpected, but we were thrilled to find ourselves here, far from Abaddon's reach, safe at last. What we didn't know was that our enemy was among us. They were desperate and couldn't lose Travis to this world, seeing as he is our Tree of Life. They needed him to remain immortal."

My head grew dizzy with her statement. However, Mavis allowed no time to question, leaving a million inquiries buzzing in my head. "The opening of the portal always causes a horrific storm, like the one that hit the night of your arrival. We all ran for the basement. Once we got down there, I noticed my husband wasn't with us. I waited, but he never came."

My pulse began to race as Mavis continued to dig, plant, and speak. All the while her back was still turned.

"I gave Molly's hand to Carla Jo and told them to stay put. I headed back upstairs. To my surprise, half of the inn was gone. The rain was pouring down, the wind stronger than I had ever seen. I saw my husband lying on the ground. Blood was pouring from a knife buried in his chest. I ran over to help him. I tried to pull the knife out, to help him to safety. The force of the wind working against me made it impossible. He yelled at me to go back underground with the kids. I couldn't leave him there, drowning in his own blood. He was the love of my life. I adored him. I loved more than I loved myself."

I hung my head and closed my burning eyes in shame.

"The next thing I knew, I was hit in the side of the head. It was as if the entire half of the inn blew over on top of me. The last thing I remember hearing was my husband screaming. When I woke a few days later, Travis was there with the kids. As usual, he was doctoring me, seeing to my every need. I could tell by the look on his face that my husband hadn't made it."

My eyes flew open, and I raised her head. What had Mavis said? Her husband hadn't made it? Before I could interrupt with my question, Mavis answered it.

"I lost the love of my life that day." She turned around to face me, sorrow hollowing her face. Pulling herself from the ground, she grasped onto a large, embellished stone for support. A stone that had been blocked from my view was now plainly in sight. I stood from my spot in the grass, slowly, reverently, walking towards the grave marker. Moving my lips, I read almost inaudibly.

"Brennan John Colton

Beloved husband,

Amazing father, brother, and friend.

Prince of Eden

"On this earth, but not of it."

I don't understand," I stammered. "I thought…"

"You thought Travis was my husband." Mavis finished the sentence for me. Speechless, I swallowed and gave an affirmative nod. She smiled.

"Travis is Brennan's brother, my brother-in-law. He and Brennan were extremely close, especially since the death of Ariston. Travis came alongside me during the tragedy, rebuilt the inn, helped me raise the kids, and gave them a father figure."

"You two never married?" I thought I knew what shock felt like, but this revelation brought it to an entirely different level.

Mavis smiled. "No, our hearts both belong to only one person. Mine to Brennan and Travis, well he lost his heart to someone many years ago, and I suppose he'll wait a lifetime for her if it comes to that."

"Who is she?" I asked faster than I should have, prompting my cheeks to fill with color.

Mavis noticed and smiled sweetly, the gaping hole in her mouth not near as unappealing now. "Travis might get upset with me if I share secrets from his personal life. He's a very private man. You'll have to ask him about her yourself."

"Is she from Eden?"

"Yes, she is from Eden, and that is all I am at liberty to tell you."

I wasn't sure how to feel. All the guilt I endured for being attracted to Mavis's husband was suddenly lifted. My heart betrayed no one. Yet all the bliss of that freedom was overshadowed by the new realization that Travis had a lover in Eden. Undoubtedly, she was someone special, a breathtaking, flawless ethereal goddess, with whom I could never compete. Now it was my duty to write the story that would return Travis to Eden, and to the arms of his lover, another world away.

For a fleeting moment, I thought about running to the girls, and heading back to normal life, forgetting I ever set foot in Moonshine. However, there was an ache inside that I couldn't quiet. Not an ache over Travis, I understood that one and recognized it for what it was. This ache was more of a yearning, a calling to step into something bigger than the smallness I was feeling. I had to be honest with myself. The ache began long before I was engaged to Ryan. I thought it was heightened by pre wedding jitters but deep inside I felt it was a warning that I was getting ready to make the mistake of a lifetime. When the wedding plans were called off, I was hurt but deep inside I knew it was for the best. However, that didn't quell the betrayal and abandonment I felt. My loneliness had increased exponentially creating a deep void that needed filling. I could not turn back.

I observed Mavis gazing at the stone marker, her eyes lost in thought. The darkness that took her beloved must have been the same force that came looking for me the first night. The enemy of Eden, riding on the wind, to kill and destroy, devouring whatever lay in its path or posed a threat. A cold chill sent a warning to my soul.

"I'm sorry," I whispered, placing my arm around the innkeeper's shoulder. We stood in silence for some time, staring at the marker, until our solitude was interrupted by a loud honk of a horn announcing the car's arrival.

"Looks like your ride is here," she said.

Thirty-Eight

I left Mavis in the garden and headed to the front of the inn where I found Bethany and Lillian loading their luggage.

"Hey, can I talk to you?" I crossed my arms and leaned against the side of the car.

"I'd rather get going." Bethany rearranged the baggage. "It's a long trip back, there will be plenty of time to chat."

"I'm not going back."

Bethany's head shot out of the trunk. Her eyes were nothing but narrow slits. "You're kidding, right?"

"I pressed my lips into a straight line as I handed her my keys. "No, I'm not kidding. I need solitude, I'm going to stay here and sort some things out."

Bethany shook her head in disgust. "I know what you're staying for."

"No, you don't." I bit. "But I'll leave you with your assumptions, if that is truly what you think of me."

She slammed the trunk shut. "I really don't know what to think anymore. But you're a grown woman. You've made your choices and obviously they don't include me anymore. I hope you're happy here." She glanced at Lillian who was waiting by the car. "Let's go. I want to be off the mountain before sundown." She slid into the driver's seat and started the engine. Lillian gave me a hug. She pulled her head back but kept her arms around my neck. "Are you sure, this is what you want to do?" I nodded. She smiled and gave me a quick kiss on the cheek. "I understand." She whispered. With a wave of her hand, she slid into the passenger seat and before she could shut the door fully, Bethany was pulling out of Sandalwood Inn.

I wanted to talk more with Bethany, but I honored her right to be hurt, although I did regret parting ways with things still unresolved. However, I took comfort in the fact that I'd left a letter in the glove box Bethany was sure to find. I explained some of the events of the week, combined with sincere apologies for never confiding about the miscarriage. I excelled in writing down my thoughts, so a letter might indeed prove to be a better way of resolving hurt feelings.

"Where's Ryan?"

I startled. Travis stepped up beside me and looked more desirable than ever, now that I knew he wasn't a married man.

"I sent him away."

"Why?"

"Because I don't love him."

He swallowed, flexing a muscle flexed in his jaw, like the night we met, and I thought I noticed a hint of a smile in his dark eyes. I hadn't told Travis I was staying behind, and I wondered what he was thinking when he saw the girls leave without me. I longed for him, I couldn't deny it, and even though he wasn't married, according to everyone, he was still completely unavailable. I ignored his gaze and watched the Mercedes disappear down the lonely two-lane highway without me. A wave of loneliness swept past with a slight panic that possibly I'd made an impulsive and irresponsible decision. I quickly reprimanded my thoughts. I would not allow myself to doubt. The decision had been well thought out, hours upon hours on the porch swing last night. Deep inside, I knew I was doing the right thing; still, there was something about watching my friends disappear around the corner that evoked a deep feeling of loneliness.

"Want to go for a ride? There's something I'd like to show you."

Loneliness over. My heart raced at his offer. "Sure," I shrugged my shoulders as if I had nothing else to do and hoped I appeared nonchalant, praying he didn't see the sheer excitement spread across my face.

I climbed in his truck and before I could shut the door, he had it rolling toward the highway, heading back into Moonshine. He drove down the main street, past the church and courtyard, past the lake and road that turned off to his cabin. He drove for some ways before the two-lane road narrowed into a single. I realized now why there was never any passing traffic on the highway. The road dead-ended in Moonshine. It would be impossible for anyone to pass through the town. If one traveled this forgotten highway, it was for one reason only; they had business in Moonshine. Falcon was right, what he said two nights ago, my arrival was no accident, but instead was a prophesied event beyond my control.

We were some distance past the city limits now. Large trees grew close to the road, their foliage making a tunnel over the pavement. Travis drove down the narrow lane for quite a way, offering no conversation. I studied his profile, not sure if he felt my gaze. If he did, he didn't turn to look. His eyes remained straight forward. His thoughts were unreadable.

He turned onto a narrow dirt path. We bumped along over the uneven terrain, the truck making its way across rocks, potholes, and tree roots like skeletal fingers protruding through the ground. He drove until the road nearly vanished, finally stopping near an abandoned cottage, camouflaged within the dense foliage. I opened my door and stepped onto the tall grass. The smell of the earth was even more pungent here, a harmonious blend of the rich dark soil, pine needles, wildflowers, and decaying leaves. Honeysuckles contributed to the aroma, their delicate blooms releasing a sweet fragrance as they gobbled up the trees, twisting and turning over their massive trunks. It was quiet, the only sound was the song of the Cicadas. The gentle rustling of the trees applauded their chorus and an occasional call from a bird asking for an encore. Within seconds the Cicadas started up again and the entire pattern repeated throughout the day. Travis offered me his hand, as we made our way down the narrow footpath leading up to the secluded bungalow.

I looked past the worn fence and surveyed the overgrown dwelling place. Lush vines with blooming flowers covered the roof, cascading down over the large picture windows. Leafy bushes hugged the exterior of the house, wild and unkempt to the point of blocking the steps to the porch. Two weeping willows stood vigil on both sides of a cobblestone path that lay buried by overrun grass and weeds. A tall Elm grew near the cottage, a weathered birdhouse hung from the lowest branch.

"Looks like your real fixer upper. Who lives here...or who lived here?"

Travis picked up a piece of the fallen fence and leaned it against one of the posts.

"No one has ever lived here. It's remained empty ever since its construction."

"Who built it?" I asked. He shrugged. "No one knows. It's a mystery. Legend says, one day its owner will arrive and will have the key to open the door."

The heat rushed in again, weakening my legs and for a moment I thought they might give away. I had a haunting suspicion that Travis believed I was the owner. But I didn't have the key.

"Would I be trespassing if I went in?"

He smiled and with a tilt of his head invited me inside. I grasped the smooth wood of the small gate, my slender fingers fumbling nervously with the rusted latch. The bolt loosened and the handle lifted much easier than I imagined. I pushed it open and stepped inside the much-overgrown yard.

Travis remained silent; his eyes fixed on me as I high stepped through the tall grass feeling much like one of the wildflowers wafting along with the afternoon breeze. I felt a bit on display, under his scrutiny and wondered if this mighty Prince was sizing up my ability to return him to his homeland and the throne. I made my way up the porch steps, pushing aside the hanging vines blocking the entrance. I breathed deeply, placed my hand on the doorknob and turned. It was locked.

"So, is there a magic word I should say?" I asked while placing both hands flat against the door.

The corners of his mouth formed a slight grin, and I wondered if he could tell I wasn't ready to enter the cottage. He nodded to the weathered porch swing, and I immediately took his invitation. He courteously dusted the dirt from the faded cushion before allowing me to sit. I pushed off with my feet, the swing swaying gently releasing a noticeable creak from the eroded chain connecting to the wooden roof overhead. A cool gust of wind stirred the dust and dead leaves on the porch, sending a chill. The smell of coming rain combined with the strong scents of the earth saturated the air. The sun began to withdraw, hiding behind the advancing gray clouds, covering most of the sky. plumb drops pregnant with rain began falling on the tall grass flattening it to the ground.

"It has sat empty for years, a little longer won't matter."

I sighed, "I do want to go in, it's just that...."

"No need to explain. I understand."

I wondered if he could understand. The emotions of the past week were overwhelming. The secrets of this hidden town were unraveling slowly, each revelation taking its toll on me. Now, Travis was expecting me to walk into an abandoned old cottage that supposedly belonged to me, and for some reason I was afraid my mind couldn't handle what lay beyond the door.

"What convinced you to stay behind and write the story?"

There was only one answer to his question. Should I give it? I could play it safe and give sappy reasons, such as I thought it would be a great adventure and my chance to author the epic story I always dreamed of writing. I'm sure he would buy that answer. It seemed plausible. I opened my mouth to allow the trite answer to flow from my lips when I made the mistake of catching his eyes.

"I want to do this for you." The truth was out. At least part of it was anyway. The rest, I would keep to myself. "I want to help you get back what was taken away from you. You saved my life, if I do this, I can save yours."

What I neglected to say was that I believed I was in love with him. Why, I didn't know. It was ridiculous to say the least. How can you love someone you've only known for a week? And aside from that, I didn't really know him. Still, there was something there. Maybe it was his incredible body and gorgeous face. Perhaps it was the sound of his heavy voice or his silence that was just as powerful. But beyond all that, there was still something. It was what I saw in his eyes that night in the cabin basement. In a fraction of a second, I saw a glimpse of what, I couldn't remember just that it was terrifying and comforting all at the same time. I would remember the haunted feeling forever. Maybe it was love and loss. Maybe Travis knew more than I thought. Maybe this is why he explained true love to me in the garden. This was to be a test of my love. Would I be able to write the story that would send him back into the arms of his love in Eden? I could if my love was only for him, and not myself. My heart crashed at the thought.

The rain continued to fall, tip toeing gently across the overgrown yard. A soft rumble of thunder sounded in the distance.

What was done was done. I stood, resolute. "Let's see if the roof leaks."

His dark eyes locked on mine. I nodded to the weather-beaten bird-house hanging from the branch of the large Elm.

"It's always been a habit of mine to keep a spare key in a bird house. If this truly is my cottage, there will be a key in the bottom."

He watched me exit the porch and approached the Elm. The gentle rain kissed my face as I reached my arm into the small birdhouse. I moved my hand about stroking my fingers against an abandoned nest and then a smile pulled at my lips, as I gracefully withdrew my arm from the small wooden abode, waving a tiny brass key in the air.

I passed it to Travis and watched as he turned the lock and pushed open the weathered blue door. I took a deep breath and stepped inside. The peculiar heat sensation once again began at the souls of my feet and permeated upward through my body. My pulse quickened. Was this home? The sights, the design, the furnishings, every part of the cottage was ablaze with my personality. I toured the tiny cottage connecting with every detail. The entrance hall gave way to a small cozy living room. A large three-sided bay window with a soft cushioned seat faced outside on the east side of the property. A soft black couch with colorful, throw pillows faced a beautiful stone fireplace with an oversized hearth. A plush white rug lay in front, taking the chill off the cold hard wood. Beautiful paintings of scenery adorned the walls, and I noticed that each picture was of a night scene and all with a full moon. Twinkling lights were stretched across the beams in the ceiling, creating a starry night indoors. A piano stood in the corner.

The kitchen gave off a warm intimate feeling. Bright gold walls and deep teal cabinetry circled the entire room. Another ample sized picture window, covered with white airy curtains, faced the backyard. A small country table with four chairs sat in the middle of the inviting room. An antique hutch full of beautifully painted dishes rested against the far wall. A comfortable floral loveseat faced yet another fireplace. A smile pulled at the corners of my mouth as I surveyed the colorful yet welcoming room. I strode over to the small antique roll top desk facing the picture window and lifted the cover. On the inside lay a single book. Its leather hide and aged lock gave it the appearance of a secret diary. I scanned the kitchen taking inventory of the window above the sink, the mantle of the fireplace, and the antique hutch and finally noticed the object I was searching for. Cunningly placed amidst the colorfully painted dishes was a miniature birdhouse. I opened the delicate glass cabinet, and retrieved a miniscule key, hanging on a delicate silver chain. Crossing back to the desk I anxiously placed the key into the lock and turned it. The latch clicked as the leather strap fell from its casing. Thunder rumbled in the distance as I opened the book. All the pages were blank, save for the first one. Handwritten beautifully across the front page, in what seemed to be my best penmanship, was the words:

Freedom

A True Story of Love

I sat down hard, the heat rising, competing with my racing heart, and spinning head. Had the keys hidden in the birdhouses not been enough, the book I held in my hands with my handwriting occupying the title page more than confirmed this was indeed my cottage, and I was where I was destined to be.

"I found it." I whispered, cradling the heavy book in my arms.

Travis accepted the book from my hand. His eyes grew troubled as he noticed the key lying on the desk and the open lock on the cover. He glanced at me and then back to the first page. He skimmed through the blank pages as if he were looking for something. His dark eyes closed as he reverently latched the cover. I knew this book meant everything to Him. It was his redemption, his release from the confines of this dimension, the story would place him back in his Eden, and back in the arms of the one his heart belonged to. The thought weighed heavy.

I left him alone with the book and stepped out onto the back porch, inhaling the scents of rain and wet earth, replacing the musty stale air of the cottage. Just like the front, the back was overgrown with vines and plants, dried leaves, dirt, and cobwebs. Two eroded and splintered rocking chairs sat on the porch. A two-tiered cement birdbath full of green mossy water stood near the back porch.

The yard was ample size, resembling more of a meadow blanketed with colorful wildflowers, than a simple backyard. A walnut tree, along with an apple and a couple of Elms, grew tall, giving ample shade on a hot day. I noticed a waterfall cascading down a moss-covered rock wall and emptying into a crystal-clear stream cutting through the back of the property. I gasped with delight at the sigh. I could write here. I was certain any blockage would melt away with the inspiration pulsating from this magical place.

The rain began to increase in intensity, the sound of it so deafening that I didn't hear Travis join me. He removed a knife from his boot and began cutting back the vines growing wildly over the roof and cascading downward.

I leaned across the porch railing, not minding at all that the rain was blowing in my face. My mind was entertaining a thousand thoughts, and now that I discovered the book, I was more than ever eager to begin writing the story. However, there were still things that needed attending to before I could begin. I needed to locate my previous writing of Moonshine, no matter how painful it may be. I hoped my parents had not destroyed the book, but knowing my mother, I was certain she had it packed away and hidden somewhere in the attic. If I could locate the old manuscript, it possibly could shed some light on some of the mysteries still veiled to me.

I also needed to go back to California and retrieve my things. If I was leaving everything behind to pen the story, then there were certainly things that needed to be done before I could settle down and write. I would turn in my notice on the beach condominium Ryan, and I once shared. The place was luxurious, expensive and something I could never afford on my own, but when Ryan left me, he graciously paid for the remainder of the lease which gave me another 10 months. Still, I stayed away as much as possible and the thought of leaving it all together made me feel as if I were moving on.

My eye caught sight of Travis intensely pruning back the overgrown foliage. I watched him for a while. The skill he displayed in using his knife, and the strength in his arms impressed me. Everything about Travis Colton was appealing.

"You're pretty good with that knife."

He threw a handful of cut vines into the yard. "I prefer it. It does the work much more quietly than a gun."

I was taken aback. I'd never sensed a violent side to him, and while watching him hack away at more vines I wondered how futile it would be to shoot them down. It was obvious he didn't carry the knife for pruning and landscaping. I recalled my fourth night in Moonshine when he approached the pre-festival dance, agitated, bloody, and dirty. Later that same night in the gardens, I'd witnessed Falcon slit a man's throat with the same type of knife. During my meeting with the council Falcon had mentioned how he and Travis had taken care of a couple of spies from Eden. I thought back to the grave marker in the secret garden bearing the name of Travis's brother Brennan, and how Mavis confessed that Abaddon's men caused her husband's death. Even though Travis seemed like a peaceful, composed person, I admittedly had only known him for a little over a week, and while some mysteries of this place were revealed to me, there were still multitudes of secrets behind his dark eyes, and what he was capable of, I wasn't sure. However, disturbing this revelation may be, I knew he was carrying the knife for my safety, and the thought sent a chill.

I leaned against the door. "I need to go back to California, to take care of some personal business and get my things. I want to stop in Texas on the way. I'm sure my mother has my old manuscript hidden away somewhere. I want to try and find it. I think it will answer a lot of questions running through my mind right now."

Travis stopped hacking away at the overgrowth. He wiped the rain from his face with his forearm and threw another handful of vines into the yard. "When do you want to leave?"

"The sooner the better. But I have no way to get there, and Moonshine doesn't have car rentals."

He wiped the blade of the knife across his jeans and placed it back into his boot. "You can take my truck."

He walked past me, entering the cottage. I followed him, sensing a change in his behavior. Travis usually appeared calm but now seemed restless and unsettled. I picked up the leather-bound book, along with the key, and headed into the living room.

"What's bothering you?"

He remained silent, staring out of the large picture window facing the front yard. This characteristic of Travis, although somewhat annoying, intrigued me. If he had no desire to answer a question, he never gave a reason as to why, he simply refused to respond. Knowing it would be futile to ask it again, I turned my attention to the piano. I placed the book and key on top of the instrument and took a seat on the small bench. Raising the cover, I gently ran my fingers over the ivory keys while watching him stare out of the picture window and wished I could read his thoughts. I brought my attention back to the piano, walking my fingers down the keys, moving them with ease, gliding effortlessly, playing a melody that struggled to unlock a memory. I fought to remember when I had played the piece before. There had to be an event, a location, maybe a musical I had performed in once. What was the name of the song, where had I heard it, and why did it stir me so? The melody was beautiful, unleashing a flood of emotion. My soul ached and my fingers trembled as I played. The intensity of the piece increased along with the beating of my heart.

The song broke Travis' gaze and brought his attention to me. He watched while I played; my soul was as lost in the music as I was here in Moonshine. He watched as I struggled to remember, to hear the message the melody was trying to tell me.

I finished the piece and sat still, staring at the ivory keys through the tears welling up in my eyes and trickling down my cheeks. I swiped them away, not wanting Travis to see me crying. I collected the book and key from the top of the piano and retreated to the big bay window. Curling up on the soft cushion, I turned my attention to the misty pane, watching the soft rain roll downward. A single tear followed suit as it escaped my eyes and trailed gently down my cheek.

Travis tenderly wiped it away. My heart raced at his touch. And here we were, alone again in a secluded location, while the rain poured down outside. Just as before, I found myself deeply drawn to him. I wanted to ask him about this love of his in Eden, but my heart wouldn't allow it. For now, I didn't want to know. Our eyes locked on each other; neither of us looked away. Bethany said the eyes were the window to the soul; that if you stare into someone's long enough you will connect with them. Yet, I felt at a disadvantage, I knew the longer Travis looked into mine, he could read me, connect with me, know what I was feeling. Maybe that was one of his gifts. However, his eyes still held so many secrets, no matter how long I stared, I doubt I could ever penetrate them. Not wanting to give him an unfair advantage, I looked away, distracting myself with the miniature key I held tightly in my fist. I absentmindedly wound and rewound the delicate chain around my finger; all the while feeling his gaze upon me. I dared not look up again. If his heart truly belonged to another, why did he tempt me so? Why constant observation? Was he oblivious of the effect he had on me when he sat so close? Did he not understand how painful it was to feel the slightest touch of his hand? I wondered about the mysterious woman of Eden who held his heart. Who was she? By what name did he call her? Why had she remained in Eden when so many others were forced to leave? Could I ever compete with her for his love? I imagined some ethereal goddess of perfection locked in a tall watchtower, somewhat like Rapunzel awaiting her rescue by the remarkable Travis. I sighed lost in thought, nervously wrapping the chain in and out of my fingers. His hand suddenly touched mine, as he gently removed the chain. He opened the clasp and placed it around my neck. Feeling my face flushed with color, I turned away and lifted my hair. His calloused hands reached in front as he laid the key on my chest; then I felt his fingers gently touch my neck as he fastened the clasp.

I dropped my hair, my face still colored with heat, and fumbled with the key hanging between my breasts. "Now I feel like Frodo Baggins." I laughed to avert the awkwardness.

Travis smiled though his eyes were serious.

"The rain has stopped. You up for a little walk?"

We left the cottage with the book in tow. Travis led me through the back, past the waterfall, past the trees and up the incline of a steep hill. Soon we stepped into a clearing overlooking the vast mountain range. The view from the ridge was more awe inspiring than any I'd seen the entire week. The rolling hills and mountains became silhouetted against a deep lavender and rose sky, as the sun made its final descent in the cradle of the mountains, giving way to the evening stars glimmering through the violet, burgundy and pink hues of the evening.

I could hear the unseen orchestra once again. The melodious music of an invisible choir sang to my soul, a soothing tranquil song, and I wondered if I was at another doorway, another thin place. Travis led me to a boulder where we both could sit, in front row seats at the most amazing art exhibit I'd ever seen. The fresh painting of the Creator produced an exclusive masterpiece just for us. We sat in silence, watching the fiery sun burn out slowly, as it disappeared from view.

"I'm giving you the opportunity to turn back." His words took me by surprise.

"What? Wait. Why?"

"Because you have no idea of the severity of the quest you are embarking on."

"Well, you picked a fine time to get me off the hook. My ride home left hours ago."

He ignored my sarcasm. "Once you begin to write, there is no turning back. So, before you begin, I am giving you the chance to change your mind." His words angered me. Forget the infatuation. I was livid. "Why would you offer me that? If you are a Prince of a world, and the people of that world are in exile and dying, why would you tell their one hope to turn tail and run? What kind of Prince are you?"

"This is a war Bronwyn, and you could easily lose your life in the process, and then all would be lost anyway." His words softened. "You are not who I imagined the writer to be. And you being who you are, complicates things."

Tears of frustration stung my eyes, and I felt as if my heart would burst. I stormed from the bolder and walked to the edge of the cliff feeling as if I might as well jump.

"Well, I am sorry that I am a huge disappointment. I'm sorry I am not good enough. At least Mila was honest. Condescending but honest. The rest of you lied, acting like I could do it. The story is inside of you..." I mocked. "When in truth you were all probably mind talking, making bets on your demise with me at the helm.

He grabbed my shoulders and forced me to face him. "That's not what I meant."

"Then tell me what you meant. Unlike the rest of you, I can't read your damn thoughts."

He shook his head as if he were having an internal argument with himself and for a moment it seemed as if he might divulge one of the many secrets hidden in his eyes. "There are some things I am not at liberty to tell." Pain framed his statement. "You must discover them on your own."

"Fine!" I bit.

"It's not fine." He clenched his teeth, biting down hard on his jaw. "You're going into this blind but the enemy... the enemy has full sight.

"Too late!" I broke away from his grasp and threw my hands in the air. "Too damn late. I opened the portal, I found the book, I stayed here. I'm committed... unless...unless you don't want me to do this. If my involvement threatens your return..."

He grabbed my arm and pulled me close. "I don't fear your ability. I have faith in you, but I also know who you're up against. You do exhibit a certain amount of stubbornness and if you are adamant about risking your life for this, then you need to let me help. And although I can't answer all your questions, you must always trust me, always."

I calmed down a bit, sensing he was being honest and would tell me more if he could. "Ok, sounds fair." I relented. The setting sun gave me a slight wink before dipping behind the horizon giving way to silver stars applauding against the violet sky.

"I want you to leave tomorrow. You have two weeks to get your affairs in order, and then you must return to Moonshine. You unlocked the book of redemption. The enemy has been informed. It all begins."

THE BEGINNING.

An Excerpt from Book Two, The Secret in the Rubble

I dressed quickly, pulling on a pair of denim shorts and a soft t-shirt and hurried downstairs with my cumbersome suitcase in tow. The aroma of fresh brewed coffee and muffins greeted my nose. Mavis woke early just to prepare food for my departure. I smiled at her kindness. Veering away from the kitchen I decided to load my suitcase first before stopping for a bite to eat. I rolled the heavy bag onto the front porch and stopped abruptly at the sight of Falcon leaning against the front of the truck; a cigarette hanging from his lips despite the early hour. He climbed the porch steps and grabbed my luggage.

"Morning Scribe. Glad to see you're up and ready, I was hoping we'd get an early start." My heart dropped into my stomach. Did he say we?

I followed Falcon off the porch, and watched as he tossed my suitcase in the storage area behind the seat. It fell alongside another piece of luggage that didn't belong to me. My heart sank further. No way! This was not part of my plan! I eyed him suspiciously, "I'm going on this trip alone."

He smirked, "Like hell you are."

"Yes, I am," My mind was resolute as I folded my arms across my chest. "I am capable of making this trip on my own."

Falcon took a draw off his cigarette and blew a long line of smoke, never removing his eyes from mine, "No you're not."

I shifted my feet; uncomfortable at his gaze, "You don't think I can do this by myself?"

He clenched the cigarette between his teeth, "It doesn't matter if you can or can't, which you can't. You're not going alone and that's it."

The two of us engaged in a brief stare down before I ended it by stomping back into the inn.

"Where's Travis?" I demanded of Mavis as I barged into the kitchen.

She gave me a sympathetic smile as she peered over the morning paper. She took a sip of her coffee and then nodded her head toward the screen door. Travis had just left the sheds and was heading to the inn. I stepped outside on the porch and placed my hands on my hips, "Falcon is here, and he says he's coming with me."

Travis mounted the steps, "He is. I asked him to accompany you."

"Well, I don't want him to. I want to take this trip alone."

He walked past me, dismissing my request and headed for the door, "You can't go alone."

Frustration boiled inside of me. Travis wasn't going to fix my problem. He and Falcon were in cahoots, and I realized I had no say in the matter; however, it was not in my nature to give in so quickly. I whirled around blocking the entrance with my body, "Why can't I go alone?"

Travis's eyes smiled at me even though his mouth didn't, "Bronwyn, I know you do not completely comprehend the magnitude of the quest. So, I will remain patient. To sum it up, you opened the book yesterday and now the enemy has been unleashed and will be looking for you as well as the second prophecy. You're not ready for a confrontation with them. Falcon is. He can protect you. That's why you're not going alone. In fact, you're not going anywhere alone anymore. Falcon is your bodyguard. He will be with you all the time."

"And I have no say in this at all?"

He didn't respond and by his silence I knew his answer. His mind was set; his words suffocating, so intrusive of my personal space. I closed my eyes and sighed. My two blissful weeks of solitude were now invaded by the rogue Falcon. My heart plummeted at the thought. Falcon still frightened me. If it was so important for me to have protection, why couldn't Travis do it himself?

"He scares me," I whispered her thoughts.

"He is a bit unorthodox..."

"A bit?" My eyes flew open.

Travis gave way to his smile, "He's eccentric and revolutionary to the core, but he is extremely trustworthy, as well as my best friend. And, since I am not at liberty to accompany you, I believe him to be the best there is. Last night you said you would trust me. This is your first chance to keep that promise." His words seemed to be the final say on the matter. Proceeding to move me aside, he made his way into the kitchen.

Mavis exchanged places with Travis joining me on the back porch. She handed me a thermos of hot coffee and a paper bag full of warm muffins which I gratefully accepted, despite the fact my appetite escaped me the moment I realized Falcon was accompanying me all the way to California and back. I gave Mavis a quick hug goodbye.

"He scares me too," she whispered, "But Travis is right, Falcon is good at what he does. You'll be safe with him, and Travis knows that. He wouldn't trust your care to anyone else."

I sighed defeated, "Let's see if I can squeeze these two weeks into one. The sooner this is over the better." She grinned and gave me a loving hug. "You take care. I'll see you soon." I nodded and headed for the truck only to find Falcon leaning against it gloating as he flashed one of his impish grins, "Let's go scribe. You're wasting time."

Walking past him I yanked the cigarette from his mouth, tossing it to the ground, crushing it beneath my sandal. "You want to protect me? Then don't kill me with secondhand smoke. Besides, it's too early in the day for this."

"I knew she was going to be trouble" Falcon directed his words to Travis as he climbed into the cab of the truck.

Denise Parton is described as one of the purest storytellers of all time, pulling of romance, suspense, and a touch of the supernatural, all in the same piece. Born and raised in Tennessee, Denise Parton sets her stories in the Deep South and her natural southern style charms all her work.

In addition to writing, Denise enjoys directing for the non-profit, Inner Light Family Theatre, that she and her daughter, Brittany founded. She has brought many wonderful stories to life on stage. To Denise, there is nothing more thrilling than bringing characters to life, whether on stage, sitting around a campfire or in the pages of her books.

In her free time, she enjoys spending time with her four daughters, watching fireflies in the evenings, dreaming up her next story and inspiring others.

Denise's books include, *The Secret in the Rubble*, and *The Storyteller's Secret* all a part of her Moonshine series. She is currently writing, *The Final Secret*, the last book in the Moonshine series.

Thirteen For Dinner, a historical time travel romance and *The Haret*, the first book in The Haret series.

Love is the New Pink, a non-fiction book on love and social acceptance.